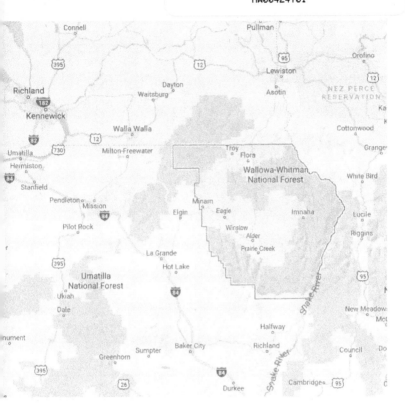

Mouse Trail Ends

A Gabriel Hawke Novel
Book 2

Paty Jager

Windtree Press
Hillsboro, OR

MOUSE TRAIL ENDS

Copyright © 2019 Patricia Jager

Contact Information: info@windtreepress.com

Windtree Press
Hillsboro, Oregon
http://windtreepress.com

Cover Art by Christina Keerins
CoveredbyCLKeerins

Published in the United States of America

ISBN 978-1-947983-96-0

Special Acknowledgements

I'd like to thank the Oregon State Police Fish and Wildlife division for allowing me to ride along with an officer to learn all the ins and outs of the job. Special thanks also go out to Judy Melinek, M.D. for answering my pathology questions, Dr, Lowell Euhus for explaining about the Wallowa County Coroner's job, and my son-in-law for answering my strange questions about law and weapons.

Author Comments

While this book and other books in the series are set in Wallowa County, Oregon, I have changed the town names to old forgotten towns that were in the county at one time. I also took the liberty of changing the towns up and populating the county with my own characters, none of which are in anyway a representation of anyone who is or has ever lived in Wallowa County. Other than the towns, I have tried to use the real names of all the geographical locations.

Prologue

Sunday Morning

"Momma, since we have to leave today, can I go look for more wildflowers to put in my scrapbook? Please?" Kitree knew if she was polite Momma was more likely to say yes.

Her mom looked up from rolling clothes to put in her backpack. "Only if you don't wander far. Stay within sight of the camp, and be back in an hour. I know your dad doesn't want to get home late. He has work tomorrow."

"Thank you!" Kitree dropped the clothing she'd been rolling to put in her backpack and grabbed the wildflower book. She patted her jacket pocket, making sure she had her book, *My Side of the Mountain Pocket Guide.* Darting out of the tent before Momma changed her mind, Kitree headed up the slope behind their camp.

Piles of snow in dips on the mountainside glittered in the sunlight. Where the warm summer sun shone all day long and the snow had melted, she was able to find a small scattering of buttercups. She'd found lots of the small flowers with shiny yellow leaves and many Indian Paintbrush on their hike up the mountain and around the lake. She was hoping for a lily or a bluebell.

Her scrapbook of wildflowers wouldn't be complete without those two flowers.

A boom ricocheted around the bowl of earth that cupped Minam Lake.

Fear froze her feet.

Another boom resounded in the quietness the first had caused.

She'd been on a hunting trip with Daddy just this past fall and knew what she'd heard were gunshots. They'd sounded as if they were around the lake. The only people at the lake this weekend had been her family. They'd hiked around the edge to make sure. Who would be shooting? Daddy hadn't brought a gun on the trip.

Kitree ran down the side of the ravine toward the camp.

Out of breath when she reached the back of the tent, she raised her face to draw in more air and caught sight of motion at the top of the ravine where the trail disappeared over the edge. A man's back and head. Dark longish hair and a plaid shirt.

Lowering her gaze to the area in front of the tent, she spotted Daddy lying on the ground. She ran over to him and dropped to her knees. Her gaze landed on a small red spot on his shirt, where his jacket had flopped open.

"Daddy?"

He didn't look at her. His eyes stared up at the blue

summer sky.

A cold shiver of fear rippled through her body. She leaned closer to try and feel breath on her cheek.

Nothing. Her chest squeezed. How could he be dead? He was Daddy. He held her tight when she was scared.

"Daddy?" she barely whispered.

A clank in the tent drew her attention. Momma! She wasn't alone.

Kitree shoved to her feet and ran to the tent. Throwing back the flap, her gaze landed on Momma lying face up in the middle of the tent. Blood and pink bubbles oozed from her chest. Her eyes were closed.

Kitree knelt beside her. "Momma? Who did this?"

"Run... Kitree," Momma wheezed. "Take... all... can... carry." She sucked in air and more pink bubbles formed on her chest. "Find... Ranger Station. Don't talk... anyone."

"I don't understand. Why can't I talk to anyone?" Kitree wanted to scream and shake her mom. She wasn't going anywhere. She'd stay here and help Momma. They would both leave together. All they had were each other with Daddy dead.

Her mom's eyes fluttered open. Slowly her gaze focused on Kitree. "The man...this." She sucked in air. Her chest bubbled out more pink. "Kill you...don't let... him... see you... Go! Take food... Go!"

"I can't leave you and Daddy." Kitree cupped her mom's cheek. Her heart and mind raced trying to figure out what to do. Her mother needed her, but to get help she had to leave. They had no way to contact anyone. And then she had to stay away from a man. Fear for her and Momma made it hard to make a decision. Thoughts

9

and fears banged into one another in her head. Finally, she knew of no other way than to find help. "I'll get help. I'll come back with –"

"No... Too late... Save... Self... Take map... Stay... off... Trails... Ranger Station..." Her mother sucked in air and coughed. Blood trickled at the corner of her mouth.

"I'm not leaving you," Kitree said, dabbing at the blood drizzling out of her mom's lips with her bandana and trying to hold back tears. She had to be strong for Momma. To get her help.

"No... I'm leaving you. Remember...we love you," her mom barely whispered the words. Her body shivered and went still.

"No Momma! Don't leave me alone!" Kitree fell on her mother, crying. Grief tore at her heart, making her chest ache. Daddy and Momma were gone. She was alone. They had no other relatives. Her thoughts stuttered to a stop and her mind shouted, "You are an orphan!"

A bird screeched.

Kitree jolted at the sound. There was more to worry about than being alone. She had to protect her parents. She'd heard birds pecked at the eyes of dead animals. That couldn't happen to Daddy.

She raised off Momma. Her shirt felt cold and wet on her chest.

A glance down caused a nasty taste in her mouth. She shoved her jacket off and ripped her bloody shirt over her head, throwing it away from her.

Kitree grabbed a sweatshirt out of her pack and pulled that and her jacket back on. Without looking at Momma, she hauled a sleeping bag out to Daddy. She covered him with the unzipped bag, kissing his forehead before hiding his face. His face was so still, so calm. If not for the unseeing eyes and still chest, she'd think he was watching the clouds for shapes. A game they'd played many times. Anguish sucked the air from her lungs. She'd never hear his voice again or play any games with him. Tears burned, but she held them back.

She scrambled to her feet and returned to the tent to cover Momma with another sleeping bag. Kissing Momma's forehead, Kitree vowed to find the person who took her family away.

There was only one thing she could do. Find a ranger station without being seen, and find justice for her parents.

Kitree rolled up her sleeping bag without looking at the one that covered Momma. She didn't want to think about leaving her parents. But leaving was the only way to find the person who'd killed them.

She dumped everything out of Momma's backpack and shoved the sleeping bag and as much food as she could carry, along with her pocket guide and wildflower book, into the pack. Momma's sky-blue rain slicker lay on the floor beside the clothing Kitree had dumped out. She added that to the pack and found all three of their water bottles. Filling the bottles with the water Momma had boiled that morning for their hike out of here, tears trickled down her cheeks.

They should all be going home. Daddy to his job, her to see her friends, and Momma to her computer. Kitree blinked hard. That life was gone now.

She swiped at the tears to look for the water purifying drops. She found it and slid the small bottle into a side pocket on the pack.

Kitree shouldered the pack. The straps were out wider than her shoulders. She dug through Momma's belongings and used one of her bandanas to tie the straps together in front of her chest. The map sat open on the floor. They'd all three checked the course they had planned to take that morning. Daddy's bold line going along the east fork trail wouldn't work. She glanced at the trails and decided the best way to avoid the killer was to go west from the lake and over the mountain.

She walked out of the tent without looking down at Momma under the sleeping bag. Tears weren't going to get her to a ranger station and help.

A quick glance at Daddy's body under his sleeping bag blurred her vison.

She hoped someone found them before the wild animals did. "I love you Momma and Daddy, and I'm going to make sure someone pays for this."

With a grieving heart and a determination to find the man who killed her parents, she set out to carry out her mom's wishes.

No trail.

Tell a ranger.

Chapter One

Two Days Later

Crackling on the radio caught Hawke's attention.

"We have a missing family. The man's employer and a neighbor both called State Police concerned that the family haven't returned from hiking this weekend. Their car is at Two Pan Campground, but we didn't find a trail registration form," the dispatcher said.

Hawke was traveling down the west fork trail after checking out suspicious activity reported by a helicopter on Sturgill Peak. On his way up the mountain, he'd encountered two families backpacking and had stopped and visited with them. "Do you have names?"

"Ronald and Sylvia Poulson and their daughter, Kitree."

He pulled out his log book. Yes. It was the family of three he'd passed on Friday afternoon as they ate a snack at the side of the trail. The father had said they were headed to Mirror Lake. Hawke had warned them about the cold temperatures in June in the mountains. Their equipment had all looked recently purchased. Shiny, colorful and hardly any dirt. People hiking for the first time in these mountains and high lakes didn't always realize the weather conditions at 7500 feet.

"I talked with them on Friday. They were headed to Mirror Lake. I'm about two hours from there."

"Report in when you find them."

"Copy." Hawke turned his radio off to save the battery and shoved it back into the packsaddle. Grabbing his mule's lead rope, he swung up onto his gelding, Jack, and whistled for Dog. "Come. We have to look for a family."

This was the part he disliked about being an Oregon Fish and Wildlife State Trooper. When there was someone missing up here, in the Eagle Cap Wilderness, it almost always meant sorrow for someone.

He turned the animals back the way they'd come. They passed the Copper Trail and continued south to Minam Lake to take the less than four-mile trail from there over to Mirror Lake. His gut said something was wrong, but his mind kept going over his visit with the family.

The girl had been nine or ten, and smart. She'd shown him her *My Side of the Mountain Pocket Guide* and a wildflower book, then began to tell him what the plants were and if they could be used to live on. She'd reminded him of himself at that age. He'd soaked up everything he could from his grandfather. The older family member had taught him tracking and how their people, the Nez Perce, had survived on these same mountains.

14

The two hours it took to get to the trail to Mirror Lake felt like ten. He reined Jack to the left at the fork. After three-and-a-half miles, he became alert, scanning the area into and around the lake for a new-looking tent.

His gaze darted everywhere as he followed the trail into the green flat area on the north side of Mirror Lake. This time of year it was hard to find enough flat area around the water to camp. He checked the usual places where backpackers camped. There was no sign of the family. Had they changed their mind?

It was Tuesday. If they'd headed out on Sunday to get back home and had complications, they could be on any trail headed to the base of the mountains. If he didn't find them by this evening, he should call in Search and Rescue.

After checking all the places around the lake, he continued on the trail. The path split, one way went to Sunshine Lake and the other to Moccasin Lake. He opted to try Moccasin first. It was larger with more flat ground for camping.

Wandering along the banks, he encountered a group of backpackers setting up tents.

He showed his badge. "I'm Trooper Hawke with Fish and Wildlife. I'm looking for a family of three. Mother, father, and daughter, about ten. They said they were camping at Mirror Lake, but they aren't there."

A man of about thirty stepped forward. "We saw a family like that setting up camp at Minam Lake on Saturday."

"Minam?" Hawke didn't understand. They had a map and had told him Mirror Lake. "You're sure it was a girl of about ten? She had short brown hair. Maybe carrying a book?"

"The father had grayish hair, tall, thin. The mother dark hair like the girl, pulled into a ponytail," the man said. "And I noticed they had all brand new packs and gear."

Hawke nodded. That sounded like the Poulson family. He sighed. It was almost dark. He knew his animals were getting tired, but they'd have to make it to Minam Lake. If nothing else he could, hopefully, pick up their tracks and be able to tell Search and Rescue where to look.

He pulled out his log book. "Can I get your name?"

"Ted Stanhope."

"Thanks."

He scribbled the name in his log book and what he'd learned, before turning his horse and mule around and heading back the way he'd come. It was nearly four miles by trail back to the other lake. If he'd known they were at Minam, he would have been talking with them or maybe have found tracks by now. With darkness falling, there was a good chance he'd have to abort the search until morning.

June nights in the mountains were cold. He'd pulled out his heavy coat and was glad that morning he'd thought to pour the extra coffee in his thermos. He sipped the warm liquid as his horse plodded along the trail, using the minimal moonlight to see the dirt path.

Horse slowed their progress every thirty minutes by being a stubborn mule and refusing to walk.

The lead rope jerked for a fifth time. Horse pulled them to a stop, again.

Hawke dismounted, tossed the remainder of his coffee into the bushes, and walked back to the mule and his packsaddle to stash the cup he'd been drinking from.

"Horse, this is no time to act like a mule. If you'd quit stopping, we'd be at the lake and you'd be relieved of your pack." He patted the mule on the neck and made the decision to camp in the flat area where they were. They were only about thirty minutes from the lake, and he couldn't look for the Poulsons in the dark anyway.

"You win." He led the mule off the trail and used a weighted tether to tie him.

Dog had grabbed Jack's reins, leading him over. The two had come into Hawke's life at the same time and had become friends. Hawke had taught the dog to lead the horse. It came in handy when Horse was being his natural self, a mule.

"Good boy." Hawke patted Dog on the head and started taking the pack off of Horse and unsaddling Jack.

When the animals had been tethered out to eat grass, Hawke pulled a bag of jerky, dried apricots, and water from his pack. He sat on his rolled out sleeping bag, leaning against the pack. Dog sat beside him.

He shared the jerky with Dog, wondering why the family had told him one thing and went another direction. And they hadn't left a registration form to aid the Forest Service in knowing how many people were in the mountains and where.

It was Tuesday. If the adults were to be back to work on Monday, it made sense people had started calling and wondering where they were. But why hadn't they gone back to their lives?

"So many questions, Dog." Hawke patted his friend's smooth head and watched the sparkling stars in the cold crisp sky.

He eventually crawled into his sleeping bag with Dog lying just inside the open zipper.

《》《》《》

Kitree sat wrapped up in her sleeping bag at the base of a big pine, trying to ignore the sounds in the darkness for the third night. Her stomach growled, and she took a swallow of water. She'd eaten a granola bar and a packet of gummy snacks for her dinner and then using cording that had been in a pocket on her mom's pack, she'd hung the backpack from a limb in a pine tree a good thirty feet from where she would sleep.

Her *My Side of the Mountain Pocket Guide* had suggested doing that to keep bears away from camp. She was carrying two empty tuna packets and didn't know how well bears could smell. She had all of her trash as well as her food in the pack. Not only did she want to be a good custodian to the wilderness, she didn't want anyone, especially the man who'd killed her parents, to be able to follow her.

As she had every night since becoming an orphan, she cried, wishing her parents were with her. During the day she had to think about what direction to go, how the straps of the pack bit into her shoulders and the weight turned her legs wobbly. She didn't have time to think about missing her parents. She was too busy moving. Going for help.

But at night, when her muscles and heart ached, she fell asleep with tears streaming down her cheeks.

Without a fire and darkness all around, she pretended she was a warrior scouting for a place to keep her family safe. That was the only way she could go on. She had to survive to make sure the man who'd killed her parents received his punishment.

《》《》《》

Icy air blowing against his side woke Hawke. His limbs were stiff and his back ached from the cold ground. Dog had wandered off, leaving the zipper opening for the frigid morning air to enter the sleeping bag.

The golden glow of sunshine barely lightened the area. Hawke crawled out of the bag, moved his legs and arms to warm them up, and cursed his aging body. At fifty-three, he was the oldest member of the Wallowa County Fish and Wildlife State Troopers. Being single and able to do more of the backcountry work, he stayed as fit and able as the youngest member. But cold mornings like this, his body took longer to get moving.

He picked up sticks and rotten chunks of tree as he wandered about. Back at his camp, he dug a small indention, ringing it with rocks. He put moss on the bottom, small twigs, and steepled larger pieces of wood. He pulled out a waterproof match and lit the moss. The small wisps of smoke gave him hope there would be warmth soon.

The flames crackled and popped as the wood caught fire. The scent of pitch heating and wood charring reminded him of home as a child. He'd loved sitting in front of the wood cookstove in the mornings watching his mother get breakfast ready. That was a long time ago. Before his father left them and before his drunken stepfather.

Hawke gathered his coffee pot, coffee, and cup along with a packet of freeze-dried eggs. He poured water from his canteen into the pot. While the water hissed and heated, he wondered what he would find at

19

Minam Lake.

When the water boiled, he added it to his eggs before putting coffee into the pot.

The horse and mule stood with their hips cocked. He knew they were able to get some water from the grass they ate during the night, but they'd need to be watered when he got to the lake.

He'd taken time at Mirror Lake for them to get a drink as he'd scanned the shoreline but hadn't come across water deep enough for them to drink from since then.

He finished his meal, drank the coffee, and put everything away. The sun was up, warming the earth and the creatures.

Hawke had everyone ready to go in ten minutes. He'd been doing this for so long, he and the animals had a pattern to their lives on the mountain.

He swung up into the saddle and headed toward Minam Lake. If he couldn't find where the family had camped, he hoped to find another camper there who could tell him.

As he walked Jack down the trail closer to the lake, he noticed birds circling in the air to his right. He followed the path that direction. Reining Jack off the trail, he used the circling birds as navigation.

Two hundred yards up from the water in a small clearing, sat a new tent. Between the firepit and the tent was a torn up sleeping bag with a hand sticking out that had been ravaged by wildlife.

His gut twisted. What happened here?

Hawke dismounted, tied his horse and mule to the trees, and told Dog to heel.

As he walked closer, he had a hunch this person had

been dead at least four to five days from the animal tracks around the area and the state of the body.

He raised the tattered sleeping bag from the face of the person and shook his head. It was Mr. Poulson. A small hole in the man's shirt was the only sign of anything wrong, other than the animal markings. He did a quick scan of the area and didn't see any other bodies. Had the mother killed the husband and taken the child? Or had the mother and daughter run away in fear?

Standing, he walked to the tent. The stench of body gases wafted out when he unzipped the flap. He steeled himself to see the mother and daughter inside. He only found the mother under a sleeping bag. Animals hadn't destroyed the reason she lay dead. Blood and a pinkish substance had dried on her shirt in the middle of her chest. Whoever shot her, hit the lungs. She hadn't died the instant death of her husband. Why? If one shot had been dead on, why hadn't the other? He studied the area inside the tent. Someone had covered her up. The daughter?

Had the girl killed her parents?

He didn't think so. If she had killed them, it would have been with a poisonous plant, not a gun. The shots were too precise to have been from a ten-year-old. There was no apparent gunpowder on the woman's clothing around the wound. It ruled out someone she knew who was close to her at the time of the fatal shot.

Was the girl taken or had she managed to get away before the killer knew she was here? There wasn't a third sleeping bag in the tent. He'd also seen a pack by the fire, yet it appeared as if the mother's clothing and some cooking utensils had been dumped on the floor of the tent. Had someone been looking for something?

Without disturbing the contents, he looked for the book the girl had shown him. He found her pack with her clothing but not the book. There wasn't a child-sized coat in the tent either. A child-sized shirt was in a ball by the side of the tent.

He walked over, and using a cooking utensil, held it up. It had dried blood on the front of it. Had the girl been wounded and managed to get away? This upped the ante on finding her if she were wounded. She could be able to name who did this to her parents. Unless the blood was from her leaning over her mother to make sure she was dead... He didn't like that thought but knew he had to keep an open mind, or as his sister called it, a cynical mind to do his job. He'd learned the hard way, you never truly knew a person. After arresting his brother-in-law for selling drugs, his wife of five years left him. Saying he'd always hated her brother and family, and she should have known better than to marry him. It still hurt that she felt that way. He'd loved her family nearly as much as he'd loved her. With women, and people in general, he'd learned to not get close.

He stepped out of the tent and studied the ground. It had been days since the shooting happened, but he had to find which way the girl had traveled in order to find her. Not only was she considered a lost person and possibly a wounded child, she was also a person of interest in this shooting.

Walking around the tent slowly, he peered at the ground, studying the dirt, grass, and twigs. He noticed a cracked, displaced twig. Ten inches or so farther along there was an indention in the ground. He picked out the imprint of a boot sole. Moving along with his head down, Hawke studied the ground and found another disturbance in the dirt larger than an animal's paw would make. It was old, but it was a boot impression, and from the size of the indention, showed him this was the girl's print as she left the area. The uneven edges revealed she carried weight she wasn't used to, making the pressure points in her print different than ones he'd witnessed around the camp.

Knowing the direction she was headed, which was away from any trails, he had to believe she'd either seen the shooter and was hiding or had killed her parents and was hiding. Either way, he had to find her.

Hawke led his animals down to the lake to drink and pulled out his radio. He turned it on and contacted dispatch.

"Hawke. I found the Poulson camp at Minam Lake. You'll need to copter in a retrieval team for two Caucasian adult bodies. One male. One female. It looks like they were shot. The girl either witnessed or did the shooting. She gathered supplies and is headed off the mountain away from the trails. I haven't seen anyone else camped at the lake at this time. I'm going to head after the girl. That is more important than me keeping the wildlife away from the bodies."

"Where is the camp?" dispatch asked.

"Northeast side. You can't miss it with the birds circling." Hawke shifted the radio to his other hand. "I'll call when I know more about which direction this kid is going."

"Should we send out Search and Rescue?"

"I'll let you know tonight. You might want to give them a head's up they may be headed up here soon."

"Copy."

Hawke turned the radio off, shoved it back in his packsaddle, and led the horse and mule back toward the camp.

Dog chased a raven away from the dead man.

Hawke pulled a tarp out of his packsaddle and covered the body, tapping stakes through the grommet holes to hold the tarp in place. It might keep the birds from pecking at the body, but the heat from the tarp could bring out more gases and the smell was sure to bring in predators.

He stored the mallet in the packsaddle and headed to where he'd found the girl's tracks headed away from camp. Even though her footprints were several days old, as long as he followed them, he was sure to catch up with the girl.

She was carrying weight she wasn't used to, and he had the aid of a horse.

Chapter Two

Kitree was tired, but she'd watched the clouds gather all afternoon and knew she had to make a shelter in case it rained. She pulled out the guide book and used the information in it to make a lean-to out of branches from the fir trees.

She found a large enough rock to give her room to sit up and to lie down without her feet or head sticking out in the rain. The book called for a tarp to help keep the rain out. All she had that was waterproof was Momma's raincoat. She used that under the top layer of branches.

Not wanting to worry about her pack getting wet, she propped it up on one end of her lean-to, allowing her access to food and water all she wanted. Wrapped up in her sleeping bag, she drank a bottle of water and then set the bottle outside with a wrapper from a granola bar folded into a funnel in the hole on top. The wrapper would make more area for rain water to be caught.

She ate another granola bar and knew she'd have to start watching for edible plants as she walked. The easy to eat and carry food she'd brought with her was running low. If she had a flashlight, she could have checked the map while she sat in the dark wondering where she was and how much further she had to go. But she hadn't thought to find one before she'd left.

The bottle of water had worked its way through just as she thought about sliding down to the ground and sleeping. She slithered out of the bag. The cold damp air quickly made her wish she didn't have to pee.

She walked a short distance from her lean-to and squatted. As she stood, she noticed a light beam moving on the outside of the trees. Her heart stopped and panic squeezed her throat making it hard to breathe. Had the man who killed her parents been following her?

The rain would help hide her tracks, but tomorrow, she would need to work harder at hiding her footprints.

She hurried back into her lean-to. Shoved off her boots, slipped into her sleeping bag, and prayed for sleep.

《》《》《》

It was nearing dark when Hawke started seeing fresher and fresher tracks. The girl was headed to the west. She'd climbed the mountain west of the lake and traveled just below the snowline, avoiding trails. She was either running scared or didn't want to be seen. Or both.

She'd removed the pack about every quarter mile. Since following her, he'd also noted the three times, during the three nights she'd been running, he presumed, that she'd spread out a sleeping bag and slept. She'd not built a fire any night and had been careful to clean up after herself. She was a good naturalist.

Clouds had moved in during the afternoon. They now covered the moon, making it hard for him to follow signs without a flashlight. He was tired and should quit, but he didn't like the idea of the girl out here alone any longer than was necessary. He was close and hoped to catch her before she headed out again in the morning.

He dismounted, found water for the animals, and sat on a downed log, eating jerky and dried fruit. A cup of coffee would be good to keep him going, but he didn't have time to make a fire or brew the coffee.

The two equines finished drinking and started eating the grass as Hawke and Dog shared the jerky. The stop wasn't more than the ten minutes it took him to eat and take care of business.

Back on the trail, Hawke walked, leading the animals and keeping his high beam flashlight on the trail the girl made. The sign was fresher, easier to spot.

About midnight thunder rumbled and rain started. The signs were going to be compromised by the weather. He was tired, but he didn't want to lose her because of rain. Hawke continued, staring at the ground, seeking the overturned foliage, broken twigs, and displaced rocks.

His eyes started to blur and the rain continued to fall from the dark sky. He didn't like it, but he found refuge for himself and the animals under a rock outcropping at the edge of the trees. He'd get some sleep and start on the trail again as soon as the rain let up. He unsaddled the horse and mule, stacked the saddles against the bluff, and leaned against them.

Dog laid down beside him, making his leg wet. Hawke shivered and threw his rain duster over the two of them.

《》《》《》

The rain stopped right before dawn. The clouds moved off to the south and the birds started chirping. Hawke had lain awake the last half hour trying to imagine where the girl could be headed. If she was going for help, she'd taken a long way to get there. If she was running from the killer, he wasn't following.

After drying off the horse and mule and saddling them up, he pulled out his radio and turned it on to see if he had any reception.

"Hawke to dispatch." He released the button and listened. Crackling and static. He dialed in another channel. The position he was on the mountain, he might be able to reach a local dispatch rather than the state police.

"This is Trooper Hawke on the south side of Brown Mountain, do you read me?"

"Trooper Hawke this is the Union County dispatch," a female voice said.

"I'm tracking a young girl. Her parents were killed at Minam Lake on Sunday."

"We're aware of the situation."

"I was getting close last night when the rain started. Contact Wallowa County Sheriff and State Police. Tell them I'm headed around the southside of Sturgill Peak. And to send up a helicopter and see if they can locate the girl. I'll keep going." He hoped the girl was headed to the Standley Guard Station. If so, she'd pass by Charlie's Hunting Lodge, and hopefully,

Dani Singer, the owner, would have heard about the homicides and keep the girl there and call officials.

"Copy."

The static disappeared. The sounds of the birds and wind whispering through the rocks brought him back to his situation.

He led the animals back down to where he'd left the girl's trail. The only thing he could do would be to continue along, keeping to the trees at the edge of the snow pack, and hope he caught up to the tracks she'd made this morning. Or overtake her wherever she'd weathered the rain.

A half an hour later, Dog tipped his nose in the air and ran to the right. He started sniffing and whimpering at a boulder and pile of tree limbs.

Hawke investigated. Damn! He'd been close to the girl last night. If it hadn't rained, he would have caught her.

She couldn't be that far ahead of him now.

A smile curved his lips. The girl was clever. She'd made a lean-to out of fir limbs, crisscrossing them. It appeared she had something waterproof as well because the dirt was dry under the lean-to. There was a trench dug along the edge and away from the area where she'd lain dry, and hopefully, warm in her sleeping bag.

"Good job, Dog." He patted the animal on the head and wished he'd been able to keep going last night. She would have been found and with him this morning.

He studied the ground for her tracks.

If she continued at the pace she had been, they'd catch up to her by noon.

He found the boot print he'd now know out of thousands. Grabbing Jack's lead rope, he followed the tracks. A mile passed where he could easily see the trail.

Then it disappeared.

Hawke stopped and glanced around the area. The terrain wasn't any different from the last mile, but the track had disappeared. Just when he'd thought he'd catch up to her.

Perplexed, he walked back twenty feet and tied the horse and mule to eat grass while he studied the area.

Following the tracks, back to where they'd disappeared, Hawke crouched and examined the area. It looked like wind had blown the grass and debris around in a specific area. He brushed aside the debris and discovered a boot imprint. Why did she decide to cover her tracks? What was she using?

Now that he knew what to look for, ground debris that appeared swept or swirled by wind in a two-foot-wide path, the trail was more visible than following the boot imprints and displaced leaves and twigs.

He gathered his animals and continued.

An hour later the swept trail ended at the edge of a rocky landslide. The end of the slide could be seen from here. Why hadn't she gone around rather than over?

He wasn't chancing Jack or Horse getting hurt walking through the rocks when it would only take fifteen minutes more to walk around. Hawke swung up onto Jack's back and led Horse down the side of the canyon and around the slide.

Riding up the other side of the slide, he found the girl's tracks. He grinned. She no longer tried to hide them. She'd believed by walking over the rocks, she'd lost him.

The more he followed the child, the more he

respected her intellect and maturity for a girl her age. She had to be scared navigating the wilderness alone, knowing she'd never see her parents again.

If she didn't do any more tricks to avoid him, he should catch up with her any time.

She was once again moving just inside the trees below the snow line. If she'd drop down lower in the canyon, her hiking would be easier. But it was apparent she didn't want to meet up with anyone.

It was getting late afternoon when the tracks disappeared again, this time it was after she'd crossed a small stream of snow melt and he'd heard a helicopter coming up the canyon. To be seen by the helicopter, he'd have had to move out of the trees. He hoped the girl was in a spot that the aircraft could see her when it flew over. The pilot could pinpoint her location and relay it back to Search and Rescue.

Knowing he couldn't rely on the helicopter seeing them, he crossed the small stream and dismounted, searching upstream for tracks that she'd exited the stream on the opposite side. The edge of the snow was only fifty yards up from where she'd crossed. Hawke headed downstream and downhill, scanning the edge of the water for boot imprints, misplaced rocks, and bent grass. He went a hundred yards not finding any tracks. The sun was going down, and he'd spent another day tracking a child who had been cagey at losing a master tracker.

He doubted she'd be able to stand the icy water on her feet for more than the hundred yards, but went down another hundred just to be sure. When he still didn't find any tracks, he retraced his path, stopping at every small detail that looked out of place. He found several places where animals had come to the stream to get a drink, but no sign of the girl.

The sun was setting, casting the area around the stream in shadows and making it harder for him to find clues to where she'd exited the stream.

Cursing under his breath, Hawke led Horse and Jack over to a grassy spot and took off their saddles. It would be another night alone for the girl, and he'd get little sleep trying to figure out how she'd bested him, again.

Chapter Three

Kitree giggled, watching the man with longish hair and a plaid shirt lead his horse and mule downhill along the opposite side of the stream.

She stood up on the snow bank watching him disappear into the trees.

When brushing her trail with a stick and the rock slide hadn't worked to get away from this man, she'd remembered watching a movie where an Indian had walked in a stream and walked back out the same side he went in. The people following him had looked all up and down the side he should have come out. Like this man was doing.

She picked her pack up and continued across the snow until almost dark. Then she walked downhill and back into the comfort and seclusion of the trees.

She'd hardly slept the night before, between the rain and wondering how she would get away from the person following her. There was no need for a lean-to tonight. She pulled out food and wished she'd had a chance to refill her bottles. But she hadn't wanted the man to catch up to her. She'd known he wasn't far behind.

He was good, but then a killer would probably have to learn how to follow the people he killed. A shudder sent a cold chill through her body. There wasn't a night went by she didn't remember her dad's unseeing eyes or hear her mother's last breath. Tears burned.

She knew that if she kept going north and west, she should come to a hunting lodge. That's what the map had said. There she should be able to contact the officials.

For the first time since leaving her parents, Kitree fell asleep without crying.

《》《》《》

Hawke rolled out of his sleeping bag before the sun touched the trees. The only explanation he could come up with as he fell asleep the night before, was the girl had exited the same side she'd gone in. It was an old trick and one he should have thought of. But he'd let his fascination with her skill ruin his focus.

Sure enough, he found her tracks on the same side she'd walked in and they led him to the bank of snow. He even found the spot where she'd stopped and set her pack down. Her toes pointed to the stream. When he looked back toward the stream, he had a notion she'd watched him looking for her.

Hawke couldn't stop the grin. She was one intelligent little girl.

He followed the tracks back down to the grass and then returned to saddle up his animals. Before following the tracks, he pulled out his radio. He hoped to get better reception to the county or state police.

"Trooper Hawke requesting information on the helicopter that flew over the Eagle Cap Wilderness yesterday."

"Hawke, this is Dani Singer."

His body came to life hearing the woman's voice. Since their first initial meeting where he'd thought her a suspect in a murder and an interloper taking over the hunting lodge, he'd grown fond of the woman.

"Have you been apprised of the situation up here?" he asked.

"Yes. What do you need relayed?"

"I should catch up with the girl today. She's been avoiding me."

"I don't blame her," the woman quipped.

He laughed. "Good one. We're headed toward the lodge, if she keeps going the direction she is. Could get there tomorrow at the earliest. See if the troopers can give you any information on her family. It would be nice to know why her parents were killed."

"I'll see what I can do. We'll be ready for you when you get here."

"Appreciate that." He knew the conversation was finished, but like a smitten teenager, he didn't want it to end.

"Hawke?"

"Yeah?"

"Be careful."

Her soft-spoken words nearly knocked the air out of him. His feelings for the woman had been growing, but he hadn't thought she gave a rat's ass about him. Her barely whispered comment made him think differently.

"I will. It's just a little girl."

"Copy."

The radio fell silent. He wondered if he should have said something else. He couldn't think of anything else, so he shrugged, put the radio in the pack, and returned to the spot where the tracks went into the trees.

He found the area where she'd spread out her sleeping bag. Her tracks went to a spot where something had been tied around a tree. He studied the area and realized she'd hung something in the branches. There was a spot where bark had been worn off a limb.

Picking up her tracks, he led the horse and mule forward quickly. He would catch up to her today.

The sun was directly overhead when he spotted the bright green pack in the trees ahead of him.

Hawke tied the horse and mule and continued on foot until he was only twenty feet behind her.

"Kitree, stop!" he called out.

The pack stopped, dropped to the ground, and the girl took off running through the trees.

"Dog, Go!" he said, running behind her as Dog shot by him and after the girl.

Hawke ran through the brush and over the trees the girl jumped. Dog caught up to her, grabbing the bottom of her coat in his teeth.

She was quick, slipping her arms from the sleeves and running on.

"Dog, leap!" He huffed as loudly as he could. Hawke hated to have Dog take her to the ground, but she wasn't going to be stopped any other way.

Dog hit her in the back with his feet, knocking her to the ground. Then he sat on her.

"No! No! Don't kill me!" the girl shrieked.

Hawke arrived by the girl's side. He grasped an arm before telling Dog to get up. As he'd figured, as soon as the dog's weight left the girl, she shot to her feet.

"Stop! I'm not going to kill you."

She stared at him, taking in his collar-length hair and checkered shirt. "You're the man! You killed Momma and Daddy!" She pummeled him with her fisted hands.

"No. I'm not the man who killed your parents." He pulled her arms behind her back to keep her from flailing them.

"I saw you leaving. You had dark long hair and a plaid shirt. You're lying!" She continued to struggle.

"Kitree, if I had wanted to kill you, I could have just shot you when I first spotted you." He didn't dare let go of her, but he hated that having to hold her this way made him appear to want to harm her.

"You're hard to track. All those tricks you did." He raised a hand and pulled the chain around his neck, drawing his trooper badge out from under his shirt. "I'm State Trooper Hawke. Remember I talked with your family on Friday. You showed me your wildflower book. I was sent to find you and your family. I found your parents. I'm sorry for your loss."

Tears glistened in her eyes.

"I'm not here to hurt you. I'm here to help you." He released her wrists.

She swiped at her eyes with her fists. "Are, are my parents taken care of?"

"They should be headed to where ever you live."

"Walla Walla. Daddy teaches at the college." She

sniffed.

"What does he teach?" He didn't want to make it any more difficult for the child by mentioning it in past tense.

"Mathematics. But Momma's better with numbers than Daddy."

Dog sniffed her, and she started to pull away.

"He won't hurt you. He was only following my orders to knock you down." Hawke grinned down at the girl. "You're a fast runner."

She didn't smile back but put a hand on Dog's head.

"Come on. I have a mule you can ride. I bet you're tired from all that hiking you've done." Hawke led her back to her pack. He picked it up and continued. Her footsteps rustled leaves, following behind him.

"I saw your horses," she said when they walked up to the animals.

"I know you did. You stood up on a snow bank and watched us looking for you."

"You saw me?" She stared at him in awe.

"No. I could tell by the tracks you left in the snow. You put down the pack and stood peering down at the stream."

"Wow! How did you get so good at tracking?" she asked as he moved things around on the packsaddle to make it comfortable for her to ride.

"My grandfather taught me how to track when I was younger than you. It's a tradition in our family." He tied her pack to the back of the packsaddle and held out his hands. "I'll help you up."

When she was seated on Horse, he asked, "Why did you leave your parents and avoid me and all the trails?"

Her eyes glistened again. "Momma told me to go to a ranger station but stay away from trails and men."

"Your mother was still alive?"

Tears trickled down the child's face. "She could hardly breathe when I found her. She told me to go. To get help. When I told her I would stay with her, she said to go. And then she...she...died."

He patted the girl's knee. "And your father?"

She shook her head. "He was dead when I got back to camp."

"Where were you?"

"Looking for stupid flowers." She spat the words out. "I should have been there helping them take down the camp. If I'd have been there, we could have been done and gone before that man came."

He shook his head. "Looking for flowers saved you so you can help us catch the man who killed your parents."

She wiped at her tears but didn't say anything.

Hawke swung up onto Jack and started downhill. Now that he was no longer following the girl who was staying up high, he could get down to ground that was easier to navigate.

There were lots of questions he had for the girl, but he decided to wait until they camped for the night.

Once they were down low. Kitree spoke up. "Don't go on the trail."

He stopped and looked back at her. "Why not?"

"Momma told me to stay off the trails." She peered at him with the steely nerve he'd seen in people much older when they were determined about something.

"You are with a State Trooper. I'm not going to let

39

anyone hurt you."

"Do you know who the man is that shot them?" She crossed her arms.

"No, but—"

"Then wouldn't it be best to stay hidden?" She cocked her head sideways.

Hawke tried hard to not grin at the girl. He understood her fear of the man. To keep her from running from him, he turned back up the mountain a hundred yards.

The sound of a helicopter had him shifting in his saddle to get a glimpse of the aircraft as it flew overhead. The blue belly and white on the sides didn't look familiar. Either the Oregon Department of Fish and Wildlife or the State Police must have commissioned a new pilot to fly for them.

Now that he had Kitree, he didn't see any sense in having the copters flying around. It was taxpayer's money being spent. The next opening, he stopped and dismounted.

"You can get down and stretch your legs while I let dispatch know I have you." He walked back to the mule and helped the girl down before digging in his packsaddle for the radio.

"Why don't you carry the radio on you?" she asked.

He handed her a bottle of water and a granola bar. "Because it's too big and bulky, it would let people know I'm a game warden, and I keep it off unless I'm using it, to conserve the battery."

She nodded. "That makes sense. Except why don't you want people to know you are a game warden?"

He waved his arm. "I'm up here to help find lost

people and catch people who are illegally hunting.
What do you think someone who was illegally hunting
would do if they saw me walking or riding up to them
in a uniform?"

She closed her eyes. "Hurt you."

"Yes. That's why I don't wear a uniform when I'm
up here. It would make me a target."

"Like Momma and Daddy."

Hawke peered at the girl. "What do you mean?
Were they in law enforcement?"

"No. We had to move to Walla Walla because of
Momma going to court against someone. Daddy said if
we stayed where we were and used our real names,
we'd always have a target on us."

The shooting now made sense. And the man's
actions. Not filling out a permit, telling Hawke they
were going to one lake and going to another. All the
things they did to be safe and it didn't help.

The sadness in the girl had him reaching out and
drawing her into a one-armed hug. "We'll get the man
who did this. Do you have family where you came
from?"

She shook her head. "The U.S. Marshal told us it
was good we didn't have any relatives."

Hawke held the girl tighter. She had no one to go
to. His heart ached for the child. He'd always had
family. Many times he'd wished he didn't, but they
were better than nothing.

Words wouldn't come. There was nothing he knew
that could console the child. He released her. "Eat the
granola bar while I talk to my friend at the hunting
lodge."

He walked ten yards away from the animals and

the girl. Dog sat at her feet. Apparently, he'd judged her to be an easy mark to get a treat.

"Charlie's Lodge, this is Hawke."

"This is Charlie's Lodge," Dani replied.

"I have the girl. We're headed your way. Should be there about noon tomorrow. Tell State Police to call in the FBI. It sounds like the family was in witness protection."

"Oh, that's sad. Does that mean she has no one to take her in?" The sorrow in Dani's voice echoed his feelings.

"It sounds like it. Do you know if there is a helicopter still flying around looking for us?"

The radio crackled. "...know of."

"Repeat," he said.

"Not that I know of. I told them this morning you should make contact." Dani's voice came in through the crackling.

"Ok. See you tomorrow."

"I'll get a room ready for her."

The connection went quiet. Hawke glanced over at the child. She was putting bits of the granola bar on the dog's nose and watching him flip it up and eat it.

At least Dog knew how to put a smile on the girl's face.

"Come on, we can go a few more miles before dark." He walked over and lifted the girl up onto Horse.

"Thank you for finding me. I was getting lonely." She put a hand on his shoulder.

"You're welcome." He swung up into his saddle, dreading what was in this child's future.

Chapter Four

Hawke decided the small flat area would work for a place to spend the night. He stopped his horse and dismounted. Dog growled and backtracked the way they'd come.

Something was following them.

He raised his hands up to Kitree. "Come on. I know you're tired, but we need to get away from here."

Her eyes widened, and she looked the direction Dog had disappeared.

He untied her pack, shoved his radio, flashlight, and food in it. Then he pulled his shotgun out of the scabbard on Jack. He led Kitree over to a large pine.

"Stay behind this with the pack and my rifle. I'm going to send the horses on," he whispered.

At Jack, he unclipped the reins from the bit and shoved them into the saddlebag. He swatted the horse on the butt, sending Jack off with Horse being pulled along.

Hawke quickly scuffed his boots through all of

their tracks and over to the tree. "Come on." He shouldered the small pack, picked up his shotgun, and led the girl up the mountain away from the direction Jack would go. The horse knew the mountains as well as Hawke. The gelding would go straight to Charlie's Hunting Lodge. It would alert Dani that there had been trouble.

"What about Dog?" Kitree asked in a low voice.

"He'll find us." Hawke hoped what or whoever Dog had noticed didn't harm him. If it was the man who wanted Kitree dead, there was no telling how trigger happy he'd be.

They continued up the side of the mountain without stopping until dark. He'd hoped to give the girl a hot meal, but knowing there could be a man looking for them, a fire wasn't a good idea.

"We'll stop here." He placed the pack on the ground at the base of a large boulder.

They made a small campsite, Kitree sitting on her sleeping bag and Hawke leaning against the tree, his shotgun beside him.

Hawke handed Kitree one of the water bottles and a bag of jerky. He would have given his left arm for a pot of coffee to help him stay awake and keep guard.

"Why did you let the horses go? Couldn't we have just kept going in the dark?" she asked, opening the bag of meat.

"If it's the man who killed your parents following us, and if he continues following the horses, he will have a harder time finding us. We should be able to get to help before he realizes he lost us." But Hawke also worried if the man followed the animals to the hunting lodge, he may have put Dani and her employees in danger.

"You look worried. Do you think he'll find us?" Kitree held the bag of jerky out to him.

"I'm worried for my friend at the hunting lodge. I'm sure that's where Jack will go and could lead the man to my friend and cause trouble there."

A scowl wrinkled the child's forehead. "Maybe we should go there to make sure they are okay."

He liked the way the girl thought, but didn't want to bring her to the man who wanted to kill her. "We'll see. Dog needs to catch up to us, and we have to avoid everyone."

Kitree patted the pack sitting between them. "You could call your friend."

He shook his head. "There are two ways that the person could have come upon us so fast. One—they heard the radio conversation between my friend and I and two—they were the helicopter that flew over."

"They?" The child's eyes widened in fear.

"One man can't get around or hear things if he is out in the forest following tracks." Hawke took a piece of jerky from the bag now dangling from the girl's lax hand. "We'll be fine. Between your intelligence and my knowledge of this area, we'll outwit them."

She gave a half smile.

Rustling in the direction they'd hiked from had Hawke picking up his shotgun. "Get behind the boulder," he said quietly.

Kitree stood and hurried behind the large rock.

Hawke cocked the shotgun and waited.

A blur of brown shot out of the brush and landed in his lap.

Dog!

Paty Jager

He licked Hawke and whined.

"Good boy. I knew you'd find us." Hawke ruffled the dog's ears. "It's just Dog," he said to Kitree.

Hawke felt the weight of something in his lap. Dog's feet were on the ground beside him. He looked down. The object in his lap was something he'd only seen once. The weapon had been on a suspect in a killing in 2005. The suspect had been an ex-special ops marine gone mercenary. The Strider SMF was a knife made for the fight on terrorism. He reached for the folded knife and drew his hand back, remembering it could be evidence.

He reached in his pocket and pulled on a leather glove. Picking the knife up, he studied the worn handle and ease in which it flipped open. The person who owned the weapon had used the Strider a lot. A niggling in his gut told him they were being followed by a professional. He wasn't sure sending the horses in a different direction would deter the man.

"What's that?" Kitree asked, walking around from behind the boulder.

"Dog brought us a present." Hawke held the knife on the palm of his hand.

She stared at the knife, her brow wrinkling into a frown. "Where did he find it?"

"My guess would be the person following us. Dog has the habit of bringing me presents from people he wants me to know about." Hawke patted Dog on the head and slipped the knife into a side pocket on the pack. Having let the horse and mule go, he no longer had his evidence kit, latex gloves, or any of his usual equipment. "We'll hang on to this. When we get to a guard station and get you safe, I'll take it and have the fingerprints lifted."

The girl peered at him. "You mean that could be the knife from the person who killed my parents?"

"Yes. And if his prints are on the knife, we'll know who it is."

The girl stared at the pocket where he'd placed the weapon. "Do you think he's still following us?"

"I'm hoping he's following the horses." He knew better than to lie to the girl. She'd figure out he was worried about the man following them when she saw the path he planned to take them on tomorrow. "Lie down in your sleeping bag and get a few hours of sleep before we take off again."

Kitree walked over to her sleeping bag and slid in. Hawke had been glad to see her parents had been wise enough to buy good camping equipment. The sleeping bag would keep her warm at thirty below zero.

Dog walked over and laid down beside her. With his dog keeping guard and keeping the girl warm, Hawke figured he could have a couple hours of sleep before they needed to head down this side of the canyon.

He wished he knew whether or not the person following them was able to intercept his radio conversation. He would have liked to call Dani and give her a heads up about Jack and Horse and the man possibly following the two. He cursed under his breath. "I should have put a message in the saddlebags." It was too late to do anything now. His main task was to keep the girl alive and hope the man following them would get caught by Search and Rescue.

《》《》《》

The sun barely peeked over the mountain top and

roused Hawke from a deep sleep. His body was
cold. He forced his eyes open and peered at the
sleeping bag. His worry erased at the sight of the
lump in the bag and Dog still by her side. If the girl
had left, the dog would have followed.

Hawke decided to get up and stretch, warm up
his muscles, and see if he could find something
close by that they could add to their granola bar for
breakfast. It was early June, but sometimes in this
slightly lower elevation on the mountainside a few
ripe strawberries could be found. He wandered
away from the boulder, found a spot to relieve
himself, and meandered through the spots more apt
to have ripe strawberries.

He came up empty and hurried back to the
campsite.

Dog must have roused the girl. She had her
boots on and her sleeping bag rolled up beside the
backpack. She peered into the forest, a hint of fear
widening her eyes.

He stepped out of the trees at the same time
she spotted him. Relief erased the wrinkles that had
formed on her forehead.

"Good morning. I went for a walk, trying to
find some wild strawberries but all I could find
were green ones."

"I haven't seen a single ripe strawberry this
whole trip." Kitree opened the backpack and held
out a granola bar for him and one for her.

"I know it's early but I was hoping. These
granola bars and jerky get old after a while."

"Is that all you eat when you're up here on the
mountain?" Kitree opened her granola bar and took

a bite.

Hawke nodded his head and ripped open his granola bar. "Yeah, it seems like I eat more of this dried food than I do regular food all year long."

"Are you the only game warden here?"

"I come up here more than the others because I'm not married and don't have a family. They like to be home every night. I don't have anyone who worries about me other than Jack, Horse, and Dog." Hawke took a bite of his granola bar and chewed.

Kitree stared at the interesting man. The first few minutes she was in his presence, she'd realized that he wouldn't hurt her and hadn't killed her parents. He had a quietness about him that reminded her of her father. And he treated her like she was an adult. She always liked the adults who didn't talk down to her or treat her as if she didn't know anything.

There was one question that had been bothering her ever since she'd met him. "Why do you call your mule Horse?"

Hawke's mouth tipped up at the corners and his eyes lit up. "Everyone asks me that. I call him Horse because I want him to believe he is a horse. Have you been around mules much?"

She shook her head.

"Mules can be stubborn. Make up their mind to not do what you want them to. I named him Horse, so he will think he's a horse and not act like a stubborn mule."

Kitree thought that was funny. "And how's that going?" she asked and giggled.

The man studied her and laughed out loud. "Some days better than others."

49

Another thought struck her. "Why do you call dog, Dog? That's what he is."

Hawke glanced down at Dog. "He is good at being a dog."

Kitree shook her head. "For someone who spends so much time alone out here in the forest, I would think you could come up with a better name than Dog."

The game warden chuckled. "I imagine so."

Kitree finished off her granola bar. She guzzled water from Momma's water bottle. Holding it up, she noticed there was only about a quarter of the bottle left. "What are we going to do for more water?"

The game warden studied the side of the mountain above them. He tipped his head toward the trees and said, "There is a spring up there. We'll go there, fill the bottles, and spend the night. Might even be able to catch something to eat."

She tipped her head to one side and stared at the man. "Like what?"

He studied her for a few minutes before asking, "Are you one of those people that doesn't eat meat?"

She giggled. "I ate jerky yesterday."

"That's right you did. We'll see what kind of trail we find, and what we can catch." He picked up the backpack. "Are you ready to go?"

Even though they were hiding from a man who wanted to kill her, Kitree was ready for an adventure with this even-tempered man.

She patted Dog on the head. "Let's go."

Chapter Five

The area around the spring was bursting with
wildflowers and tracks from rabbit, deer, bear, and
grouse. Hawke wished he could get a grouse. It would
be tastier than a cottontail, but the spruce grouse in this
area couldn't be hunted. As a Nez Perce, he could hunt
a deer or any other game animal out of season and not
be breaking any laws. His ancestors had hunted in these
mountains and were still allowed the privilege though
many recreational hunters disagreed. But he knew the
rules and laws that pertained to hunting in this area and
didn't think playing his heritage card was needed at this
point. If they were both starving and a deer walked in
front of them, he'd take it down. But that wasn't the
situation.

They'd reached the area shortly after noon. He'd
stopped several times to let Kitree rest. He could tell
though she was athletic, her lack of good food since
heading out on her own was making her weak. Which

led him to wonder if a rabbit would be enough food.

"What are you doing?" she asked, as he cut a length of the cording he'd found in the pack.

"I'm making a snare to catch a cottontail." He made a loop with a slip knot.

"Can we make a fire to cook it?" She glanced around the area.

"While we wait for the snare to do its job, we'll gather the driest wood we can find. The less moisture in the wood the less smoke it will put out." Hawke told Dog to stay and wandered into the trees looking for a well-traveled rabbit path. He found what he was looking for only thirty feet into the trees. Scanning the length of the trail, he found the perfect opening in the underbrush to attach the snare.

Returning to the spring, he found Kitree filling the water bottles. She spun around at his approach. He liked that she had a keen sense of her surroundings. That would keep her safe when he wasn't near.

"Save the purification drops. This is a safe spring. While we're here you can drink all you want." Hawke knew the water came out of the ground and the only source above it was snow.

"Are all the springs and streams on the mountain safe?" Kitree asked, before guzzling from a bottle.

"No. Don't drink any other water straight without asking me first." He pointed back the way he'd placed the snare. "Don't go that way when we look for wood. I don't want you tripping the snare."

She nodded.

"And we're moving all of our belongings into the trees, so if anyone flies over, they can't see us."

Kitree stopped walking. "Don't we want to be

found?"

"We want to be found, but by the people we trust. I'm sure the helicopter that flew over the other day had the man who is following us. I don't want them to see us." He stared up into the blue sky. "If I hear a helicopter, I'll check to see if it's one I know. If it is, then I'll make sure they see us."

"Good plan. Show me what kind of wood to get." Kitree walked into the trees.

Hawke followed, carrying the pack.

He showed her how to tell if the wood was dry and sent her off collecting while he dug an indention in the ground and made a ring of rocks to contain the embers and ash from the fire.

Kitree brought her first armload. Hawke inspected the gray dry branches and told her to keep it up.

He found green limbs to use to roast the rabbit and then also hunted for dry wood.

Kitree wandered about the forest with Dog at her heels. She'd always wanted a dog but her parents had said they were too much trouble. From what she'd seen of Dog, he was a help and not trouble. But maybe not all dogs were as smart as he was. She knew not all people were smart. A crack to her left shot her gaze that direction.

The game warden was walking along picking up sticks too. She liked that he didn't act as if she were a burden. He told her what was happening and what they were going to do. He would have made a good teacher. Better than the one she had in Walla Walla. The woman treated all the fifth graders as if they were babies. She rolled her eyes, glad she was here and not sitting in class.

She bent to pick up a stick and noticed a round white puffball. Excitement bubbled in her chest. She'd read that these could be eaten. Grasping the mushroom, the size of a softball, she plucked it from the ground and looked around for another one. She found three.

Back at the area where Hawke had made a fire ring, she placed the three mushrooms on the rock ring and went back for another armload of fire wood. Hawke might provide the rabbit for their dinner, but she'd provided the side dish.

Picking up the wood, she wondered how they would cook the puffballs. She'd dumped all the cooking utensils out of her mom's backpack. That was a small thing to think about. She hoped the fire didn't help the man find them.

《》《》《》

Hawke returned to the firepit and spotted three five-inch round puffballs sitting on the ring of rocks. He smiled. The girl had recognized an edible mushroom. He set his sticks down and placed the moss he'd brought back with him in the middle of the fire ring. Next, he steepled smaller twigs over the moss, adding another layer of a little bit bigger sticks.

Dog arrived by his side. Hawke glanced the direction the animal had come and spotted Kitree carrying a stack of limbs.

She dropped the wood with the rest on the ground. "Do we need more?"

"You can take a break." He nodded toward the puffballs. "I see you found food if the rabbits outsmart me."

She studied him and must have realized he was joking. She smiled and said, "You know rabbits are

54

pretty smart. They know how to multiply."

Hawke laughed and shook his head. He usually enjoyed his solitude on the mountain, but he found this girl companionable. If only they didn't have to worry about someone trying to kill her.

He was fairly certain that they had slipped the man. His thoughts last night as he tried to sleep were on Dani and the others at the hunting lodge. If his actions had put them in danger, he'd never forgive himself. His first thought had been to get the man off their trail. Keeping others out of danger was usually his first instinct before he acted.

Dani would understand. He'd reacted to keep the girl safe. But he'd not forgive himself if anyone at the lodge were hurt because of his actions.

"Why do you look so serious?" Kitree asked.

Hawke sat back on his haunches and studied the girl. She'd proved she was strong enough to hear the truth. "I'm worried for the people at the hunting lodge."

She placed a hand on his shoulder. "We should go there instead of running the other way. You could leave me and Dog somewhere not far from the lodge and then go in and check on things. The man doesn't know who you are. He hasn't seen you. He's looking for me. A girl."

He'd been thinking the same thing. "You're one smart kid, you know that?"

She grinned. "Daddy said that all the time." Her voice fell off as if realizing she wouldn't hear him say that again.

Hawke put an arm around her small shoulders. "I know he's thinking that as he watches over you."

She sniffed and pushed away from him. "I

promised myself I won't cry. I have to make sure the man who killed them is caught."

He liked her attitude. "We'll make sure that happens." He had an idea. "Tell me about your parents and your life in Walla Walla."

Kitree sat down cross-legged on the ground and picked at the young plants in the circle of her legs. "Daddy taught at the college. Momma stayed at home, but she was always on the computer. Daddy joked, saying she was writing the great American novel." The girl glanced up. "She wasn't writing a book. She was working formulas on the computer. I saw them one day when I went into the office to ask her a question. She didn't get the screen turned off before I saw it."

Hawke wondered what the woman had been doing that required formulas. "Have you lived in Walla Walla your whole life?"

She shook her head. "We were in Washington D.C. before a man came to our house in the middle of the night. He took us onto a plane, then by car, and we started living in the house in Walla Walla with a different last name."

Now he was getting an idea about why the father had been so secretive and the mother had urged her daughter to run. They had been in witness protection. But from who? The U.S. Marshals would know. They should have been brought in on this by now and know their witnesses were dead. Would they give a rat's ass about the daughter?

"They told me it was Daddy's job that moved us. But I figured it out. For some reason the Marshals moved us and made us change our names." Kitree tossed the unopened head of a dandelion into the firepit.

"Where did your mom work before you moved?" he asked nonchalantly.

"I don't know. Momma and Daddy never talked about her job. I just knew she left the same time Daddy did and sometimes didn't get home until late at night. And there were some nights she'd get a call and would leave."

He had a feeling her mom had something to do with national security. But who would want to kill her?

The squeal of a rabbit ripped his attention to his growling stomach. He'd caught dinner. "I'll be right back." Hawke told Dog to stay and walked out to where he'd placed the snare. A large doe was caught. He made sure she was dead before he returned to the camp.

Kitree studied the animal but didn't appear to be squeamish.

Hawke started the fire. "Tend to this while I clean our dinner."

She nodded.

He walked over where she couldn't see and dressed out the animal. At the spring, he cleaned his knife and rinsed off the carcass before returning to the fire.

Kitree had kept the fire stoked. There was a good bed of embers and flames licking at the wood she'd added.

Hawke skewered the rabbit with the green limb he'd stripped of bark and placed it in the Ys of two sticks on either side of the firepit. "Want to get your contribution to dinner ready?"

"Yes. What do I do?" she asked.

"Take this flat rock over to the spring and scrub it with water and another rock." He handed her a flat rock about eight inches by eight inches. It would make a good surface for her to peel and then slice the puffballs on.

She grabbed the rock and hurried over to the spring.

While she was gone, Hawke pulled out his radio and tried all the different frequencies to see if anyone was talking. He caught a few garbled words on the emergency frequency, but he didn't dare try to communicate. He'd thought about Morse Code, but there was a strong chance with this man being military, he or someone he worked with, would intercept and decode the message.

Kitree returned with the wet, shiny stone.

"Take my knife and peel off the outer layer. Then slice it a good two inches thick. I'll get some sticks to use to cook it over the fire."

She took the knife and began peeling the thin outer layer off the mushroom. When Hawke felt she knew how to use a knife, he walked ten feet away and broke off green shoots of an Aspen tree to use to roast the mushrooms.

Back at the fire, he retrieved his knife from Kitree. Stripping the bark from the aspen shoots, he handed them over to the girl. "Stick two of these through each slice you made, from side to side."

Kitree did as he told her while he turned the rabbit. The carcass was beginning to brown and emit the scent of roasting meat. He hoped they were able to eat the food and burn it in the fire before any large predators caught a whiff.

"Lean the sticks up against the side of the rocks on the outside," He took one of the skewered slabs of mushroom from the girl and leaned it over the fire using the rock ring to lean the sticks against. "And place a rock on the end to hold it there." He grabbed one of the extra rocks in the area and held the sticks in place.

She did the same with the other six pieces of puffball.

The mushrooms began cooking.

"Eeeww! Do they taste as bad as they smell?" Kitree asked, covering her nose with the neck of her shirt.

"No. They actually taste good, but for some reason they smell awful when cooking. But that's a good thing. It will help hide the scent of the roasting rabbit." He glanced into the shadows growing under the canopy of pine and fir trees.

"You mean cooking may bring the cougars and bears?" Kitree's eyes widened, and she scooted closer to Dog.

"It could but you don't have to worry. Dog and I won't let anything happen to you." Hawke smiled and placed his hand on his holstered handgun.

Chapter Six

Hawke sat leaning against a tree, listening to the
birds settling in for the night and the hushed
movements of the night creatures coming alive. Kitree
had finally drifted off to sleep after eating and watching
the rabbit carcass burn in the fire.

He'd decided that tomorrow they would make their
way toward the hunting lodge. It was eating him up that
he'd put people in danger. Kitree had agreed to be left
with Dog in a safe place while he checked out the
hunting lodge. He didn't need her to decide to wander
off looking for help after he left her. So far, she'd
proven trustworthy and willing to listen and obey when
given an order.

"Stay. Guard," he ordered Dog in a quiet voice and
headed back the way they had traveled earlier in the
day. He wanted to make sure there wasn't anyone
following them. He'd doused the fire before dark to
keep the glow of flames from being detected. They'd

gathered good dry wood that had made barely any smoke. But he wasn't taking any chances. If someone was following them, he wanted to get a jump on them, rather than the other way around.

Hiking by himself, he covered the miles they'd hiked that day in a couple hours, taking a more northerly course, but close enough to the original trail he'd notice anyone tracking them. He found the spot where they'd spent the previous night without seeing anyone. He checked for any sign of extra tracks and spotted none. It appeared the man had followed the horses. All the more reason for him to get to the hunting lodge as quickly as he could.

Taking a southerly route back to where the girl and Dog slept, he made up his mind they would take the most direct path to Charlie's Hunting Lodge. He hoped the meal he'd given the girl would help her with the grueling hike they were going to embark on tomorrow.

《》《》《》

Kitree wiped at the sweat dripping into her face. Hawke had told her that morning that they were headed straight to the lodge and the traveling would be hard and fast. But she hadn't thought he'd take her on a trip like this. She swatted at the brush as it slapped back at her after Hawke pushed through. It was becoming evident to her that there wasn't a direct trail to the lodge. They had crawled over logs and shoved aside brush a half hour into the start of the day.

"I need a drink," she said to the bush swishing back in place in front of her.

Dog stuck his head through a gap between the bushes and licked his lips.

"You, too?" She drank from her water bottle that

was quickly going down, then cupped her hand and gently poured water into her palm for Dog to lick up.

"What are you two doing?" Hawke asked, pushing the bush to the side.

"We're thirsty." She glanced up at the man. He was sweating as much as she was. "Are you drinking water?"

"You shouldn't waste your water on Dog. He can drink any water he finds." Hawke raised his canteen and drank.

"He looked thirsty to me." She put the lid on her water bottle and asked, "Are we getting close?"

"It's going to be after dark when I leave you and Dog under a rock outcropping about a mile from the lodge." Hawke capped his canteen and watched her. "You still promise you'll stay where I leave you until I get back?"

She nodded. "As long as Dog stays with me, I'll be okay." She patted the animal on the head.

"Good. I'll do reconnaissance and decide if it's safe or not. If it's safe, I'll be back in the morning to get you. If it's not, I could be back sooner, or possibly later, depending on what I find."

"We'll stay there until you come get us." She had a thought. "What if you can't come and you send someone for me?"

He pulled his badge on a chain out of his shirt. He held it down for her to read the numbers. "If I send someone, they'll have this with them. Besides, Dog, Horse, and Jack, this is my most prized possession."

She peered into his eyes. He had the look she'd seen in her daddy's eyes when he looked at her and Momma. The badge meant a great deal to him. That was why she'd trusted him. He took his job seriously. And why they were headed to the lodge to make sure no one had been hurt.

Kitree brushed her finger tips over the warm metal of the badge and memorized the numbers. "If they don't show me this, I'll sic Dog after them and run straight up the mountain so you can find me."

"It's a deal." He slipped the badge back inside his shirt, and they started hiking again.

《》《》《》

Mid-June was one of the prettiest months to be wandering about in the Eagle Cap Wilderness. The wildflowers were blooming and the early summer grasses were bright green and lush. It also helped that the sun stayed up longer, giving them more daylight to navigate the terrain.

Hawke knew he'd pushed Kitree to near exhaustion. He was ready to collapse himself, but he'd leave her to snuggle in her sleeping bag with Dog and make his way stealthily down to the lodge.

"This is where you'll hang out until I come get you," he said as they walked up to a granite outcropping with a small cave dug into the earth under the outcropping.

"Dog, go," he ordered Dog to go into the cave and see if anything chased out.

"Do I have to stay in the cave?" Kitree asked, staring at the gaping hole.

"Only if you see or hear someone coming." He set the pack down beside the opening as Dog wandered out. "Keep the pack and your sleeping bag near the opening so you can pull it all in with you if you hide."

He glanced down the mountainside wishing there

was a view of the lodge. The tall pine and fir trees along with the leafy alder hid this spot well from anyone using binoculars from the lodge.

"If you hear aircraft, plane or helicopter, stay under the rock. We don't know if it's help or the people out to hurt you."

Her stomach growled.

"Get something to eat, but same rules as always. Make sure all empty wrappers are put in a sealed bag and all food is sealed. There are animals out here, that if they smell food, could come looking for it."

Kitree's eyes widened. "Dog will protect me."

"Yes, but help him stay safe by not leaving anything unsealed." This was the first time Hawke had given her orders. Now wasn't the time for her to not follow his directions.

"I'll make sure everything is sealed. I don't want anything to happen to Dog." She patted the animal's head.

Hawke nodded. "Good." He put a hand on her shoulder. "I'll get back here as soon as I can. I wish I had more provisions to leave you with, but we didn't expect all the circumstances to have happened." He tapped the pack with the toe of his boot. "I'm leaving the radio with you. If for some reason, I, or no one else, comes to get you in three days, you use that to contact authorities. Hopefully there should be someone close by to get you before the bad guys."

"Where do I say I'm at?"

He grinned down at her. Luckily, he'd been up here a couple of times with both his counterparts at the Fish and Wildlife. "Tell them at Hawke's perch. My co-workers know where this is."

She smiled. "You and Dog come here a lot?"

"It's one of our places we like to stand watch from." While the lodge couldn't be seen from here, he used binoculars on many occasions to watch the hunters going to the lodge on the north rim trail. He could see if they had been successful or if it looked like they packed more kills than there were people in the party.

"Stay quiet. Don't build a fire. There is a spring up the mountain a short distance. Tomorrow at first light, go up there and fill your water bottles. Don't go out any later, someone in the sky could see you."

"Okay."

Hawke patted Dog on the head. "Stay with Kitree. Guard." He turned and headed down the mountainside.

"Hawke?"

He looked back up at the outcropping and girl and dog. "Yes?"

"Be careful."

"I will." He waved and smiled, but his gut was squeezing with apprehension. He didn't dare take her into the lodge without knowing what the circumstances were. Her best bet at staying alive was to stay here, alone with Dog. But that didn't mean Hawke liked the situation.

《》《》《》

It had been years since Hawke had second-guessed himself as much as he did hiking the mile down the mountainside to the hunting lodge. His first five years as a State Trooper he'd been on patrol and wished he could have made different judgement calls several times, but since working as a game warden, he'd never doubted his actions, until today.

He eased out of the trees at the back of the barn

and scanned the area beyond to the landing strip. There it was. The blue helicopter he'd watched fly overhead the day before they had someone following them. His instinct had been correct. As much as he hated to admit it, leaving Kitree up on the mountain had been the right call.

Now to see what was going on without being seen. The maximum people the helicopter could carry was four. That meant there was the possibility of five people here that wanted the girl dead. And could be holding Dani and her employees captive.

He used the tool room door to enter the barn. He hadn't seen Horse or Jack in the corral. If they weren't in stalls in the barn, there was a good chance someone had taken them on down the trail to the guard station before the man following them arrived. There was a narrow door that couldn't be seen from the inside of the barn that led into the tool room. It had been Charlie's secret door, he liked to use it to disappear and awe the greenhorn hikers.

Using that door, he barely moved the board and peered into the dark interior of the barn. If someone were in the barn, they'd have a lantern or flashlight on. It didn't make sense to be sitting in the dark.

He pushed the door aside and stepped out of the tool room. Using his memory, he walked over to the stalls and was greeted by two soft noses and a nicker from Jack.

"Hey boys. Quiet. We don't want anyone to know I'm here," he whispered, running a hand down their long faces. Knowing his animals were safe, Hawke retraced his steps to the opening. He entered the tool room, crossed, and peeked out the door before leaving the barn.

He stayed hidden behind the barn and moved along to the side closest to the shower house and lodge. It made sense that if the people who worked here were being held captive, they would all be in the lodge. Unfortunately, the only windows in the back of the lodge looked into the two guest rooms, Dani's room, and the dining room. If they were all in the great room, it was going to be harder to determine what was happening.

Chapter Seven

Kitree rolled her sleeping bag out close to the cave entrance, but not in front of it. Even though Dog had been in and out of the opening several times, she didn't want to be in the way of any animal coming home or leaving.

Right after Hawke left, she'd shared two granola bars with Dog. She'd offered him a piece of the fruit leather, but he'd refused. Kitree finished off her water, knowing there was a spring to refill all the bottles in the morning.

She walked behind a bush and peed. A giggle escaped. It was silly to go behind a bush when it was only her and Dog, but she couldn't just squat in the open. Back at the sleeping bag, she unzipped the bag, folded it back, and sat down. She unlaced her boots and placed them at the top of her bag where she could grab them if there was a need to hide or run.

Slipping into the bag, her eyes quickly lowered.

The day had been long and tiring trying to keep up with Hawke. All the other days they'd hiked together, he'd gone slow and made sure she was rested. Today, she'd realized how responsible he'd felt for the people at the hunting lodge. He'd taken her over rough rocky areas and through thick brush all the while keeping up a fast pace. She was so tired, she hoped to fall asleep without memories forcing her eyes open.

Dog came over and laid down on the bag right next to her, keeping her warm. She hugged his neck, kissed his head, and fell asleep.

《》《》《》

Hawke eased up to the shower house. Splashing sounds came from inside the building. He doubted he'd get lucky enough to catch Dani or an employee in there. He'd wait and see who came out. If he didn't know them, he'd apprehend them and see if they were a guest or someone from the helicopter.

He stood in the shadow of the building listening for anyone approaching and for the water to stop. He didn't have long to wait.

The water stopped. Humming that sounded low, like a male, came from inside the small rough-hewn timber building. The plank door opened.

Hawke leaned his shotgun up against the structure and stepped behind the door. He noted the man was taller and broader shouldered than anyone who worked at the lodge. Dani could have hired someone to help with the summer months, but he'd been here only three weeks ago and she hadn't mentioned hiring anyone else.

He grabbed the man's arm, yanking it behind his back.

"Hey!"

Hawke shoved his wadded-up bandana in the man's mouth and quickly cuffed him. He shoved and wrestled the man straight into the trees in case anyone had heard the man's shout. Thirty feet into the forest, he shoved the man's back against the tree and stared into his face the best he could at night under the canopy of pine boughs. The tang of pine scented the air. He must have shoved the man onto a pitchy spot on the tree.

The man ducked his head as if to ram him. Hawke sidestepped and the man went down. He'd shoved the cording from the rabbit snare in his pocket. Grabbing one of the man's legs, he dragged him to a smaller tree, looped the cording around the man's ankle and grabbed his other leg, hobbling his feet on the opposite side of the tree as his body. He regretted the man was face down, which meant he could rub the bandanna out of his mouth and call for help but his size had made getting him apprehended a matter of the quickest, easiest way.

Hawke grabbed the man by his ponytail and raised his head up. "Who are you?"

The man glared at him. "Screw you!"

"From your reply, I guess you aren't going to tell me how many people are in the lodge."

The man opened his mouth. But he didn't speak, he yelled.

Hawke unlatched his sidearm and knocked the man in the head. That would hopefully keep him quiet long enough the situation could be assessed. He took the time to rip the bottom of the man's shirt and put a gag in his mouth. Without knowing what he was up against, the more people he could keep out of the equation the better.

Hawke returned to the edge of the trees.

Another man walked out of the lodge. "Jake? Jake, you drowning in there?" The man opened the shower door and then closed it slowly.

Hawke stepped behind a tree as soon as the man ducked his head in the shower house. Not finding his friend, he'd start searching.

"Jake!"

Peering around the tree, Hawke saw the man open one outhouse and then the other.

"This isn't funny. You know we're all supposed to stay in the lodge." The man glanced toward the barn and then across to the bunkhouse. He scanned the trees again and headed toward the bunkhouse.

Watching the man walking away, Hawke was torn between finding some rope and tying the man up and checking on the occupants in the lodge. He decided it was best to make the odds more even.

He hurried through the door to the tool room and fumbled around feeling for zip ties. His hand landed on a pile of the plastic ties. He shoved a handful inside of his shirt and used the hidden door into the barn.

Footsteps crunched on the gravel in front of the bunkhouse. Hawke opened the barn door slightly. "Over here!" he whispered loudly and backed away from the door.

Footsteps grew louder as he neared the building. The door opened. "Jake, this isn't funny."

Hawke put the barrel of his pistol in the man's back. "Put your hands behind you."

The man whirled around, swinging. Hawke was ready and hit him in the side of the head with his firearm. The man crumpled to the floor in front of him.

Hawke quickly zip tied the man's hands behind him and his feet together. Then he used a rope to tie the man to a barn beam. He shoved a clean rag in the man's mouth and tied it there with another rag.

Two down. If the helicopter was full there were three left. If he was lucky, only two flew in with the helicopter and the only person left was the man who'd followed the horses here. This man had short hair and the other had a ponytail. Kitree told him the man had looked like him from the back. Shoulder length dark hair and a checkered shirt. Though Hawke's only touched his collar. He didn't get a haircut as often as his patrol sergeant would like. This time of year he spent most of his time, here, in the mountains, and wanted to blend in.

He left the barn the way he'd entered, hurrying by the back door and the shower house. He wanted a glimpse at who was inside the lodge. The lights were out in the two guest rooms. It would have been too easy to have found Dani and her employees left alone in one of those rooms.

The only room left to see into was the great room. The only way to do that would be to sneak in the back door or look through the windows at the front of the lodge. Peeking through the windows gave him more chance to get away if he were seen.

Walking quietly along the back of the house and the end, he peered around the corner to see if anyone stood guard on the porch. The light from the great room illuminated the area enough to see no one lurked there.

Putting his hands on the porch railing, he tugged to see if it would support his weight. Dani had made many repairs to the lodge since inheriting it. He hoped the railing was one of them. When the railing held, he was glad her military background made her more particular about the place than her Uncle Charlie had been.

He stepped up onto the edge of the porch and swung a leg over the railing. With both feet settled on the inside of the railing, he brushed up against the log wall of the lodge and shuffled his feet toward the first window. Grasping his cowboy hat off his head, he leaned toward the window enough to get an eye on the people inside.

Dani sat in a chair by the fireplace. The scowl and pursed lips proved she wasn't happy. A couple in their sixties, possibly seventies, sat together on the couch. The top wrangler and cook, husband and wife, sat with the wife in a chair and the man on the arm of the chair. The younger wrangler, he was happy to see, was Dani's cousin. He'd met the young man on one of his other trips. Thankfully, there was only the one couple who were guests. But that still made things difficult.

A man holding an automatic rifle stood between the people and the door. His shoulder length dark hair brushed the collar of his plaid shirt. This had to be the man who killed Kitree's parents and wanted her dead as well. He would kill without any provocation.

Hawke eased his back against the side of the house. How did he keep these people alive? It was his fault the killers were here in the first place. He should have just stayed on the horse and mule and headed straight down the canyon to help. But that would have made them sitting ducks to anyone in the helicopter looking for them.

Another voice.

He peeked in the window.

A man stood in the opening to the hallway. "The radio chatter has a search and rescue group on the mountain looking for the girl and a guy named Hawke." His gaze was on the man holding the rifle.

Without taking his gaze from the people in the room the man with the weapon said, "I guess we need to get rid of these witnesses and get after them ourselves. He's not coming here, and they aren't talking."

Hawke shot his gaze to Dani. He studied her in the lantern light. What he thought was a shadow before, he now recognized as bruises. He peered at her employees. They had all been beaten to try and get answers. His gut clenched. *That was my doing.*

"You can't shoot all of them. That would cause an investigation." The man walked away from the hallway and up to the other one.

"Easy, this old place caught fire, with everyone asleep in their beds." The man with the rifle handed it over to the other guy. Keep watch while I tie them up in beds."

"You won't get away with this!" Dani said, starting to stand.

"Thank you for volunteering. Which one is your bed?"

When Dani refused to say, the man slapped her. "Bruises don't show up on a charcoal body." He laughed.

Hawke willed Dani to go to her room peacefully. It was near the back door. He could slip in and get her loose and have an extra body to help him get the others out before the place went up in flames.

He also had a thought about how to make the two men think their friends had left them. Hawke hurried to the back of the house, and staying in the shadows, returned to the barn. He caught two of the lodge's oldest horses and led them to the back of the barn.

Inside the barn, the man had come to. He glared at Hawke and shook his body as if to try and intimidate him.

Hawke untied him from the post, picked up a couple more lead ropes, and dragged him out to the horses. It took a bit of energy to get the struggling man flopped, belly first, over the back of the horse, but he made it and tied the man's hands and feet together under the belly of the animal.

Leading the two horses toward where he'd left the man in the forest, he heard the man shouting as he drew closer. Nasty words he'd heard from drunks and people he'd separated in fights spilled out of the man's mouth.

Hawke dropped the lead ropes on the horses and walked over to the man.

He was still on his belly but his face was to the side, allowing him to cry out for help.

Kneeling beside the man's head, he picked up the wad of shirt that lay on the ground, shoved it in the man's mouth and pulled the tied piece up over his lips to keep the cloth in place.

With a tug on the cording, the knot he'd made came loose. He quickly grasped the man under the arms and pulled him away from the tree keeping him on his belly. Before the man could try to raise up with his arms handcuffed behind him, Hawke tied his feet and dragged him over to the riderless horse.

This man was smaller and easier to shove up onto

the back of the horse. He tied the man's feet and hands together under the animal's belly as he had the other man.

He led the two horses to the trail head leading down to the Standley Guard Station. Before letting them loose, he pulled out his log book and wrote a note.

Get to Charlie's Hunting Lodge. People in need of medical care. I have the girl but the killer is after her. Hope to be at the station in two days. Hawke.

He placed that in the back pocket of the first guy with a bit of it sticking out.

"You might want to keep your balance or you'll end up under the horses' bellies." He led the two animals to the head of the trail, released the lead ropes, and swatted them on their rumps. They trotted down the dirt path.

Now to get back to the lodge and prevent six people from dying senselessly.

Chapter Eight

Returning to the lodge, Hawke noticed the lanterns were on in the bedrooms. Unsure if one of the men could be out looking for accelerant for the fire, he cautiously approached the old log structure. Once the logs caught on fire, the building would go up like striking a match. Poof!

He had to get the people out and then worry about saving the building. His conscience nagged that this was his fault. Charlie and all his ancestors and Hawke's would be disappointed in him if he didn't save this icon of Nez Perce freedom. The hunting lodge and property had been in Charlie Singer's family even when Nez Perce were not allowed to own land or set foot in this area. Charlie's great-grandfather had befriended a white man who pretended the land belonged to him. As long as the white man lived here, no one ever looked at the deed, or if they did, they didn't think about the last name Singer as being Indian.

His job was to protect the wildlife in Wallowa County. He did it not only for the government, but also his people, who once roamed this land. Hawke knew if he let this lodge go up in smoke, he would have failed on two levels.

He peeked in Dani's bedroom window. The man had tied her to the bed with strips of sheets. Clever. There would be no sign of rope or any restraints when everything burned.

To be sure the two men weren't near the back door, he peeked in the other two rooms. The two men were in the farthest room, tying up the husband and wife who worked for Dani. He wondered what they had done with Tyson. The young man had shown the same grit and determination as his older cousin. He hoped the boy hadn't fought the man.

He returned to the back door and eased it open. The door to Dani's room was closed. Good. He could close it, and hopefully, keep the two from knowing he was in there.

Three steps and he grasped the knob, slipping inside the room. Dani's gaze went from defiant to relief in a flash as she recognized him.

"What are you doing here?" she whispered.

He sat on the bed next to her and pulled his knife out of his boot sheath. A quick swipe of the blade across the taut sheet and her hands were free. "My conscience got the better of me after I released Jack and Horse. I knew they'd lead the man following us here."

She narrowed her eyes. "I thought they'd killed you and the girl when your animals showed up here." She slugged his arm. "You could have put a note on them. I would have transported everyone out of here if you had."

He nodded his head. "I thought of that after I let them loose. Sorry." He reached down to cut her feet loose.

She grabbed at his arm. "Get the others, I can finish in here."

He shook his head and cut the sheet binding her feet to the end of the bed. "We have to wait for the men to leave the house. I'm not getting in a shootout with them. I'm the only one who knows where Kitree is hiding."

Dani grasped his shoulders. "You left her alone out there?"

"She's not alone. Dog is with her." Hawke nodded to the door. "As soon as they leave the building, get on the radio and call for help. I'll get the others loose. You can all hide in the shower house until they leave. Then get everyone off the mountain. I'll go get Kitree."

"I'm not leaving here until I know the place isn't going up in flames," Dani whispered and crossed her arms.

Hawke slipped to the door and opened it slightly. The two men opened the front door and left. "Now!" he whispered and headed down the hall and into the first guest room.

The older couple's eyes widened at the sight of him. He pulled his badge out from under his shirt and walked up to the bed. "I'm State Trooper Hawke. Dani and I are going to get you out of here, but you have to be quiet and follow orders." They both nodded.

He quickly cut them loose. "Wait here for Dani to come get you."

"Why do we have to wait here?" the man asked.

"If the men see you moving about, they'll know someone is around and won't leave. We need them to leave so Dani can fly you to safety." Hawke inched the door open and peered out. They hadn't returned.

He swiftly moved to the next room.

Tuck and Sage Kimbal had been whispering when he opened the door and entered.

"Man, am I glad to see you," Tuck whispered.

"We have to be quiet." Hawke pulled out his knife and cut them loose. "Stay in here until Dani comes for you."

The couple were in their forties. From his previous visits, he'd learned Tuck had to quit the rodeo circuit due to injuries, and Sage had helped in her family's restaurant most of her life. They both knew horses and had been the perfect fit for Dani's needs of cook and head wrangler.

"We could take them," Tuck said, taking a step toward the door.

"No, you can't," Sage said, grabbing his arm.

"Stay here. If they think they have you all tied down, they're going to be careless. I'm hoping to prevent them from burning the place down." He peeked out the door and then glanced back. "Do you have any idea what they did with Tyson?"

"You might check the room off the kitchen. They took him that direction," Sage offered.

He nodded, checked for the men and headed to the dining room and kitchen beyond.

Dani stood in the hallway. "I radioed. Now, I'm getting everyone out."

He nodded. "I'm getting Tyson. Be careful. They could come back at any time."

She didn't even acknowledge him as he continued through the dining room and into the dark kitchen. They hadn't left any lanterns burning in these rooms.

Hawke fumbled along the wall until he hit the back wall of the room. Moving along it, he stopped. The sound of someone rustling cloth came from the corner. It had to be Tyson trying to get free of his bonds.

At the door, Hawke whispered, "Tyson, it's Hawke."

"We have to get Dani and the others free," he replied.

"I already have. I wasn't sure where you were." Hawke followed the sound of the young man's voice and bumped his shin on the bed. He found the sheet tying Tyson's hand to the bed and slit it with his knife.

"Hold still, I'm using my knife and don't want to cut you." He moved his hand across the young man's chest and found the other strip of cloth. He cut that then moved his hand down Tyson's leg to first one and then the other binding.

Hawke placed his knife in his boot. "There. Come on, Dani is getting everyone out into the shower house."

"We can't let them burn the lodge down." Tyson started to push by him.

"Stop. Use your head. We can't prevent anything if we get caught." He found the kitchen door and they entered the dining room. The two men were talking in the entryway on the other side of the dining room door.

"Someone used the radio."

"Damn! Check the beds. Make sure no one—"

Hawke didn't wait for anything else to be said. He ripped his badge off his neck and handed it to Tyson.

81

"The girl is at my nest up the mountain. Show her this and get her to the Standley Guard Station. Go out the window. Tell Dani and the others to get in the helicopter and take off."

He shoved the young man toward the dining room window and pushed the door open, revealing himself to the two men.

He had to give the others enough time to get away.

Chapter Nine

Kitree rose the moment the sun gave enough light for her to walk up the mountain and fill the water bottles. "Come," she said to Dog, and they headed up the mountain in search of the spring Hawke had told her about.

She'd walked about fifteen minutes when she spotted the greener, lusher bushes and grass. Dog trotted over and began lapping up the water in a small puddle where the spring splashed down over a rock.

"This is a pretty place." She crouched by the water spilling over the rock and filled the three bottles and Hawke's canteen.

The sound of a helicopter shot her to her feet.

"Come!" she called to Dog and stood beside the largest pine tree she could find, hoping its many branches would shield her from whoever was in the air.

"We left my sleeping bag and pack sitting out." The fear of being discovered made her hands shake. To stop the shaking, she patted the dog's head. "Well, not completely out. They are under the rock roof. They shouldn't see them there, should they?" Kitree gazed into Dog's eyes. He didn't seem the least bit bothered about the helicopter. Since he was all she had at the moment, she took comfort in his not being upset. He was only a dog, but thinking he wasn't worried helped her feel less frightened.

The sound of the propeller vanished. She moved away from the tree and finished filling the bottles. This time as she returned to her hiding spot, she stayed under the trees and hurried across any opening.

Back at the cave, she put the water bottles in the pack and rolled up her sleeping bag, shoving it into the pack. She hoped Hawke arrived this morning. The food was getting low. Only two granola bars and one fruit leather.

Dog's hair stood up as he stared at the trees down the mountain from the cave.

"Come on," She tugged on his collar and shoved her belongings into the cave. Kitree backed into the area she had been avoiding and pulled Dog in with her. "Shhh. Quiet," she whispered, hoping they were in far enough no one could see her. The sun was up but this side of the mountain was shaded. She hoped the shade would keep her and the dog hidden from anyone's view.

A man, much younger than Hawke, stepped out of the trees and continued up the side of the mountain toward the cave.

Dog quivered under her arm that held him.

Would he kill the man to save her? She didn't like to think about Dog doing such a thing, but she also didn't want to die before the police caught the man who had killed her parents.

The man walked up to within twenty feet of the opening. "Dog? Little girl? Hawke sent me." He held out what looked like Hawke's badge.

Her chest squeezed. What had happened to Hawke? Dog had stopped quivering. Did he recognize the voice? The person?

"What are the numbers on the badge?" she called out.

The man read them off.

It was Hawke's badge.

She released Dog.

He ran out and greeted the man. "Hey boy. Are you doing a good job?"

Kitree crawled out. "Where's Hawke?"

"He stayed to keep the men from following us."

"Us? You and me?" She peered into the trees.

"Mainly the others who were at the lodge. The bas— bad guys were going to burn the lodge down."

Her throat tightened. Had they set the fire with Hawke in the lodge? "Did they?"

"I haven't seen or smelled any smoke, so I don't think so." He looked at the cave. "You have any belongings we need to take?"

"A pack. But I'm running out of food." She crawled in and pulled out the pack. The badge still dangled in the man's hand. Kitree grabbed the warm metal and hung it around her neck, dropping the badge inside her shirt like Hawke had worn it.

"If we hike and keep hiking until dark and then start out as soon as we can see in the morning, we'll be at the guard station by late tomorrow." The man picked up her backpack.

As he started along the mountainside, her gaze traveled downhill. She didn't want to go to a guard station, she wanted to see if Hawke needed help.

《》《》《》

Hawke regained consciousness and wished he'd had his Kevlar vest on. Lucky for him the man without a weapon had yanked on the killer's arm when he shot. Something about "I'm not killing a cop." The bullet had hit Hawke in the shoulder. He'd banged his head into the door behind him as he went down. Both his head and shoulder hurt like hell. He wasn't sure if his wooziness was from hitting his head or loss of blood. He wouldn't die from either one. At least not if he didn't get an infection or lose more blood.

The sound of a helicopter taking off gave him hope Dani had loaded everyone up and gotten away. He used the door he'd fallen backwards into, to help pull himself to his feet. His arm needed stabilized to lessen the pain. And he needed something to stop the bleeding. Flickering of light drew him into the great room. They'd started a fire in the fireplace and from the kerosene smell, had splashed it around to make the place burn. Most likely with him in it.

He hurried across the room to assess the situation. There was a broken kerosene lamp on the hearth. He'd pull the rug it was on away and get a bucket of water to douse the fire.

Bending to grab the rug, his eyesight blurred and blackness tried to descend. He dropped to his knees. When his head cleared, he grasped the corner of the rug with the hand on his good arm and started crawling backwards on his knees. He'd made it about ten feet from the fireplace when he heard banging and voices.

Tuck hurried by him with a bucket of water, followed by his wife and Dani. They all threw water in the fireplace, sputtering out the flames.

"Hawke, are you okay?" Dani asked, dropping to her knees beside him. "You're bleeding!" She and Tuck helped him to his feet. "Sage, go get the first aid kit. Mr. and Mrs. Harvell sit down and relax."

Dani maneuvered him into a chair.

"I thought I heard you leave," Hawke said, putting a hand on her arm.

"It wasn't us. They tampered with my aircraft. The plane and the helicopter wouldn't start. I was getting ready to try theirs when I heard a gunshot." She eased his arm out of his long-sleeved shirt and used his knife to cut his t-shirt away from the hole the bullet made just under his collar bone.

"Ouch!" He ground his teeth together as she dabbed at the wound with a piece of his t-shirt.

"I ducked behind a tree when they ran out to their helicopter." She turned her attention to Tuck. "I'll need alcohol." He nodded and disappeared from Hawke's sight.

"They took off, so I rounded up everyone to make sure they hadn't been shot. Tuck spotted the smoke in the chimney. I had a pretty good idea what they'd done. We grabbed buckets of water and came in here."

He nodded, taking in all she was saying. "Tyson. Did he get off to get Kitree?"

"Yes. He told me what you said to him."

"Good." His eyes popped open. "Do you think he'll have enough sense to stay off trails and out of sight?"

Dani shrugged. "Some days he's mature, others…"

He hoped the young man listened to Kitree. She had good survival instincts. But as soon as Dani had him doctored, he was grabbing Jack and Horse and heading out after them.

《》《》《》

Kitree headed straight down the mountainside.

"Hey! Get back here. I'm supposed to take you to the guard station." The man, who hadn't even told her his name, came bounding down the mountain behind her. He grabbed her by the arm. "You can't run off like that. Hawke told me to get you to the guard station. That's where I'm going."

"Who are you? I don't know your name and how do I know you didn't hurt Hawke and take this from him?" She put her hand on her chest over the badge.

"I'm Tyson Singer. Dani's cousin. She's the lady who owns the hunting lodge." He released her arm. "What's your name?"

She narrowed her eyes. "You don't know my name? You're supposed to help me but you don't know who I am?"

She spun away from him. "Dog, come!" she called and took off through the trees and brush, hoping to get away from the man. Something had happened to Hawke. This man could have been the one to do it. She wasn't going anywhere with him. The only people she trusted on this mountain were Hawke and Dog.

When she didn't hear anyone crashing through the brush behind her anymore, Kitree slowed her pace and followed Dog, who seemed to know where he was going. His tail was wagging as he kept a steady pace straight down the mountain.

《》《》《》

Hawke lifted the saddle onto his horse with one arm. The good news about his wound, it wasn't in his dominant side. He could still do most anything he wanted to do. That was if he hadn't lost so much blood.

"This is asinine. Tyson will get the girl to the guard station."

"What if that's what those two in the copter think? She and Tyson will be sitting ducks as they walk up to the guard shack." He shook his head. "I promised that little girl we'd catch the person responsible for her parent's deaths. And I'd keep her safe."

"Let me go with you?" Dani said, putting a hand on his arm.

He gazed down into her concerned eyes. There would come a day when he'd lean over and kiss her, but this wasn't it. The more he was around the woman, the more he respected her. Thoughts like he'd just had would get him in trouble and deplete his brain. He didn't like working with people who were so smitten with their love interest that they made stupid mistakes. His days of being stupid were over.

"You need to figure out what they did to your aircraft and get these people out of here. I hope the rangers have stopped people from coming up the trails. The two men out there—"

"Just heard from the Standley Guard Station." Tuck interrupted. "They have the two men in custody that you sent down on the horses. Two more game wardens are coming up on horses and the search and rescue are spread out coming up the canyon."

"See. There is no reason for you to go off looking for the girl and Tyson." Dani grabbed his saddle to pull it off his horse.

"The two men in the helicopter can find her and land before any game warden or search and rescue members find her. And Search and Rescue aren't trained to confront the type of man that is after Kitree." Hawke retrieved his saddle from Dani and flung it up on Jack's back.

She threw her hands in the air. "You're impossible. If you need to play cat and mouse with these people, I'm going to fix the plane and fly these people out of here. I'll come back for the helicopter to pick you and the girl up. And you damn well better be on the top of Jim White Ridge between Jerry and Jungle Creek with that girl when I get there."

He watched her straight back and head held high as she marched out of the barn.

Tuck whistled under his breath. "That sounded like an order to me."

Hawke grinned. "Yeah, to me, too."

The wrangler scratched his head. "She does know that Jim White Ridge is the opposite of where everyone thinks you're headed?"

That was what told him that Dani would be waiting for them. She had figured out everyone would be looking for them between the lodge and the trailhead. Not going the opposite direction. "That's why she said it."

Hawke grimaced as he tightened the cinch.

"You want a saddle on Horse instead of the packsaddle?" Tuck grabbed one of the youth saddles off the rack. "Wouldn't take but a minute to loosen the cinch and make if fit him."

"That's a good idea. Thanks." Hawke finished

bridling Jack as Tuck saddled up Horse. The mule laid his ears back but put up with the change of tack.

Hawke led the two animals out of the barn.

Dog came running up to him whining.

"Where's Kitree?" he asked, patting the dog's head and staring the direction the animal had come from.

He spotted movement in the trees. It was the girl and twenty feet behind her was Tyson.

When she spotted him, she burst forward at a run. She flung her arms around his waist. "I thought you were…" She didn't finish the sentence.

"I told Tyson to take you to the guard station." He narrowed his eyes at the young man loping toward them.

Tyson bent at the waist and put his hands on his knees. He gulped in air.

"Why are you chasing her?" Hawke asked.

"I'm not." Tyson drew in two long breaths. "She didn't believe you sent me and took off. I was just trying to keep up with her."

Hawke knelt.

Kitree's eyes widened as her gaze landed on the bandage holding his arm in one place. "You were hurt."

"Why didn't you listen to Tyson?" he asked, drawing her gaze from his shoulder.

"He didn't know my name. He didn't know anything about me."

"Did he show you my badge?" Hawke glanced up at Tyson, who nodded.

Kitree pulled on the chain around her neck and drew his badge up over her small head. "He did. But he should have known more about me if you sent him."

"I'm sorry. I didn't have time to tell him much. He

had to leave before he was caught." Hawke took the badge from the child's outstretched hand, pulled his hat off, and placed the chain around his neck. "This works out better anyway. I don't have to find you. We're getting some food and heading to the top of a mountain where Dani, Ms. Singer, will come get you and take you to the authorities."

"You're not coming with me?" Her eyes glistened as if tears were going to begin.

"I have to bring Jack and Horse down off the mountain. They are getting lonely for their friend, Boy, back at the stables."

Her tearful eyes dried up. She glared at him. "Don't talk to me like I'm a child."

Tyson grinned at him.

"I'm not. I'm telling you the truth. Jack and Horse miss my other horse when they are gone too long. I don't want to leave them up here for who knows how long." He stood and grasped her hand. "Tyson, tie these two to the hitching post. Kitree and I are going to raid your cousin's pantry."

He led the girl over to where Dani was decked out in overalls and checking out the plane. "Dani, Ms. Singer, I'd like you to meet someone." He knew he was being overly polite but he wanted the child to meet and remember Dani. Just in case he wasn't able to make it all the way to the top of the mountain with her.

Dani turned from the aircraft with a wrench in her hand. "Hello, you can call me Dani. What's your name?"

"Kitree. Wow, you work on planes?"

"And helicopters, and I fly them, too. Did Hawke tell you I'll pick you two up on the ridge later, when I get the aircraft running?"

The child shook her head. "He said, you'd pick me up. He has to bring Horse and Jack home."

Dani narrowed her gaze on him, but returned it back to the girl. "Well then, I can give you a lesson on flying without any interruptions from him."

Kitree giggled.

"We were going to raid your pantry for food to last us until we get to the top of the mountain and you show up." Hawke tipped his head toward the aircraft. "How much damage did they do?"

Dani's lips turned up in a smug grin. "They probably thought I'd be grounded until someone could bring a part from down below. Surprise is on them. I have two of every part this thing needs in my tool room." She closed the cover on the helicopter. "But they ripped things out. It will take time to dismantle the part they sabotaged and then put the new one in. We'll be headed out of here as soon as I get this fixed. I'd say in two or three hours. You better get going in case those guys come back. We'll be ready for them this time."

"We better go. We'll wait for you to show up down in the tree line." Hawke turned Kitree toward the lodge. "Did you get any sleep last night?" he asked, noticing her steps weren't as springy as when he'd met her. He was glad they would have horses to carry them to the top of the mountain.

"Yeah, some. But I'm more hungry than tired."

He led her into the lodge.

Sage jumped up from her seat in the great room. "Where did you come from?" Her eyes lit up as if she'd found a diamond ring.

"This is the person those men were looking for,"

Hawke said. "We need food to keep us full until tonight."

"Come on." Sage put her arm around Kitree's shoulders and led her into the dining room. Hawke followed, wondering at how motherly Sage seemed. He hadn't asked Dani or the couple about their family.

In the kitchen, Sage handed Kitree two sugar cookies and began digging through the cupboard. "I can make up some peanut butter and jam sandwiches."

"That will work," Hawke said, stealing a cookie from the jar in the middle of the prep table.

"I have some granola bars...and here," she handed Kitree a plastic bag. "Put as many of the cookies in there as you think you'll need."

Kitree took the bag and filled it, leaving only six cookies in the jar.

Hawke winked at her. "You don't happen to have any dog food around here for Dog, do you?"

Sage spun from making the sandwiches. "Actually, there were four cans left behind by someone with a dog. I think they're in the barn. Tyson should know where they are."

Hawke grabbed another cookie. "You wait here for the food. I'll go make sure Dog gets something to eat."

Kitree nodded and pulled a cookie out of the bag she'd filled.

Hawke walked into the great room and found Tyson hauling the older couple's bags out of their room. "Sage said there should be some cans of dog food in the barn?"

"Yeah, in the tack room. A guest left it." Tyson hauled the bags off toward the plane.

Hawke wandered to the barn. Dog appeared from

the shadow of the barn near the horse and mule. "Come on, I've got something good for you."

The dog followed him into the barn. Hawke found the cans easily and was happy to see they had tabs to open them. He opened one and dumped the contents into a grain pan. Dog gobbled it up in seconds. "We'll take the others with us. You've missed too many feedings. I bet you caught some rodents though, didn't you?" He scratched the dog's head and walked out to the horses.

He put the cans in his saddlebag and turned in time to find Kitree and Sage carrying out their food.

"Here you go. I gave you more than you asked for. It sounds like Kitree hasn't had enough to eat since taking out on her own." Sage put a hand on the girl's shoulder. "Now don't forget, you should come back and see us when things are settled down."

Kitree handed the cookies to Hawke and hugged the woman around the waist. "Thank you."

Hawke took the food from the cook and put it in the saddlebag as Sage hugged the girl.

"Take care of Hawke. As you can see by his sling, he gets into trouble." Sage grinned at him and helped Kitree up onto the mule as if she'd helped children mount up before.

"I will. Thank you for the food," Kitree said, as Hawke kneed Jack forward and led Horse. They had several miles to cover and mostly uphill to be at the ridge when Dani landed to pick Kitree up.

Chapter Ten

Storm clouds started building as the day wore on. Hawke made sure they stopped every mile to give the animals a rest. The straight up switchback wildlife trails they followed were hard work even for Jack and Horse who climbed mountainsides often.

The mountain hemlock, lodgepole pine, and fir trees hid them well until they came to a grassy meadow not yet bursting with wildflower colors. At the meadows, Hawke circumvented the open areas by staying inside the tree line, which meant more distance to cover, but it was worth it to keep hidden.

At one point, he heard a helicopter fly over. If Dani had hustled, she could already be waiting on the ridge for them to arrive. He hoped if the people out to get Kitree were still flying around themselves, they hadn't noticed her.

He figured they had about two more hours to get to the meeting spot. The wind had started blowing with a vengeance. Thunder rumbled and lightning crackled overhead. Hawke stopped Jack and tugged Horse's lead rope to make him come up alongside Jack.

The girl was hunched in the saddle as if cold.

"The thunder and lightning are just the Creators way of telling the creatures to find cover," he said, noticing lines of fear on the child's face. Hawke leaned over and unbuckled the saddlebags behind her saddle and pulled out her sleeping bag. "Wrap this around you."

Kitree huddled into the sleeping bag with only her head poking out.

"We can't stop. If this weather keeps up, and Dani is waiting for us, she won't be able to stay with the helicopter not tied down."

She nodded.

Hawke urged Jack forward.

Rain poured from the sky. The only good thing about the weather, it should keep the men looking for Kitree on the ground and not in the air. If Dani could keep her aircraft from blowing away, he hoped Kitree would be off the mountain without difficulties. He didn't want either female in danger.

As he worked his way through the trees, using them like a leaky umbrella, he worried more about Dani sitting up on the top of a ridge with the wind, rain, and occasional lighting strike.

Unfortunately for them, this wasn't a short summer shower. The deluge of rain continued and even though they were avoiding the worst of the downpour riding under the trees, Hawke was soaking wet and beginning to wish he had his rain slicker. All of his outer gear was back in the packsaddle at the hunting lodge.

He glanced back at Kitree. She had the sleeping bag over her head, but it was becoming so wet, it hung lower on the mule's sides than before. He didn't need her getting sick from all of this.

Stopping Jack under a heavily branched large pine, he pulled Horse up beside him and dug in his saddlebag.

"I think we both need some food to warm us up." He handed her a sandwich and the bag of remaining cookies. "Wish I had some hot chocolate to give to you."

She took the offered sandwich. "This is good."

Kitree knew Hawke was trying to ease her fears and help her warm up the best he could. What she feared the most was getting to the place they were to meet Dani and finding it empty. She was tired of the hiding, little to eat, and fear they wouldn't catch the people responsible for her parents' deaths.

The lady, Sage, at the hunting lodge had been nice. She'd liked how the woman gave her hugs like Momma. It had been hard to hold in the tears knowing she'd never have a hug like that from her mother again. Thinking about it now, warm tears filled her eyes, blurring the sandwich in her hand.

"Need a drink?" Hawke asked, holding a water bottle in her sight.

She took the bottle knowing she wouldn't be able to swallow a drop. A large lump had settled in her throat. It wanted out, but she feared if she allowed it, she'd start bawling like a baby. She didn't want water or food, or warmth. She wanted her parents.

After sitting there for several minutes, holding the water bottle in one hand and the sandwich in another,

Hawke gently took the bottle from her hand. "Eat. You need your strength."

His voice sounded different. Soft, almost as if he were sorry for something.

Kitree batted the tears back, swallowed the lump that landed hard and cold in her chest, and glanced over at Hawke. He was studying her. Had he known she was holding back her tears?

"I guess I'm not that hungry." She held up the sandwich.

"I'm not moving until you eat that." This time he sounded like a father.

"I'm not hungry." She stared at him defiantly.

"You may not think you're hungry. Grief is a powerful thing. It can knock a person down just as swift and vicious as a disease. Keeping your body strong helps you keep your heart and mind strong." He glanced up at the tree above them. "My ancestors wailed when a loved one died. It was a way of letting all that grief out into the universe and helping to heal."

He returned his gaze to her. "You might want to wail a bit. Get that grief out, so we can catch the person responsible for taking away your mother and father."

She wasn't sure she knew how to wail and wondered how it could help.

"Dog, show Kitree how to wail," Hawke's gaze dropped to where Dog sat next to Jack's front legs. The man held out half of his sandwich. "How bad do you want this?"

Dog pointed his nose in the air and opened his mouth. A loud, mournful howl echoed under the big tree. He started in again when Hawke shook the sandwich.

The sound, while being sad, pulled at her feelings. She raised her face to the sky and opened her mouth. The sound that erupted came from down deep in her belly, gaining power and sorrow as it moved up and out of her mouth. As the sound came out, she saw Momma and Daddy as they'd been when she'd rushed back to the camp. Her heart hurt. She released another howl and this time she saw her parents as they'd been before— laughing, teasing, and loving her. That was the image she would remember. The one she'd keep in her heart.

Dog stopped howling.

Hawke tossed him the sandwich. He'd hoped to get Kitree to admit her grief and get it out. There was nothing more cleansing than a good wail. She'd started out shaky, but he could tell toward the end, she'd understood the process.

"Get that sandwich eaten. We need to get to the helicopter."

《》《》《》

Hawke's arm and shoulder throbbed by the time they started up the last climb to the top of the ridge. It was also getting dark. He hoped Dani had survived the wait and weather.

Kitree had seemed energized after eating and wailing.

Of course, his choice of words had her asking him what he meant by his ancestors. He told her how the Nez Perce had once hunted these mountains and lived down in the Wallowa Valley and Imnaha areas part of the year. Since he had her attention, he also told her how after the army chased them to Montana and they were taken prisoners, that all the Nez Perce, including the treaty ones, were not allowed to hold land or be in the Wallowa Valley for many years.

"That's not right. It was their land," Kitree said.

"No, it wasn't their land. They didn't believe in owning land. They believed it was there to sustain them, and they took care of it for the bounty it provided."

"Like the deer and rabbits and birds?" she asked.

"Yes. And the edible plants and fish. The American Indian only took the meat and resources they needed to survive, nothing more. It is a good lesson for everyone. Only take what you can use, nothing more." And that was how he led his life. He rented an apartment over the stable where he kept his horse and mule. He owned a pickup and only the necessary clothing. He had small needs and yet felt he lived well.

"I wish I would have lived back then. I would have known how to shoot a gun and could have gone after the man…" She didn't finish the sentence.

"You are best to live now. With your help, we will get the person responsible." Hawke felt rather than saw the top of the ridge as Jack no longer surged forward, pulling himself uphill with his front legs and pushing with his back legs.

The rain had let up, but the clouds still remained, making it dark and gray and hard to see since dusk had settled moments before.

"I don't see anything," Kitree said in a hushed voice.

Chapter Eleven

Hawke's stomach clenched. Had the weather made Dani leave their rendezvous point?

"Maybe she's down the other side to avoid the wind and lightning." He led the mule across the top of the ridge and down to the southeast side. The other explanation was the weather had kept her from meeting them.

"Let's find a place to build a fire and dry out. She may have had to turn back due to the weather. We'll hangout here until noon tomorrow. If she doesn't show, we'll head for Moss Springs." He continued down the side of the ridge until they were back in larger trees. A small flat area looked good and there was an old pile of downfall where he hoped to find dry wood for a fire.

"This looks like a good spot." He swung down off his horse and grimaced as his cold feet landed on the ground.

Before he could help Kitree off Horse, she was on

the ground, draping her sleeping bag over a bush.

"If you want to dig down in that pile of slash and see if you can find some dry pieces of wood, I'll get these two unsaddled and comfortable." He pointed to the pile of limbs and pieces of tree.

Kitree nodded and walked over to the pile.

Movement would help to warm her up. Hawke was thankful for the sling that kept his arm immobile. After the jarring ride, he was ready to lean against a tree and rest. However, the animals needed tended as well as the child.

Once Jack and Horse were eating the wet grass, he built a fire ring and went in search of some dry moss to get the fire started. When he returned, Kitree had piled an impressive amount of dry wood by the rock circle.

He fluffed up the moss, steepled the smaller limbs over it and added a few larger ones. Digging in the depths of his shirt pocket, he came up with his waterproof match case. He held the case in the hand of his injured arm and struck the match. After the flame flared, he lit the fire. Early on, he'd learned to always carry his matches on his person. It was too easy to lose them if they weren't in a pocket. A fire to warm up or cook with was a must.

The flames grew and crackled.

"Add this," Kitree said, walking over with a blob of pitch on a small limb.

"That will heat things up. Wish I had something to heat water in. That would warm us from the inside." Hawke found a couple of rocks that would work for low seating. He rolled them, one armed, up beside the fire.

Kitree disappeared and returned with a metal cup. "This was in my pack." She handed him the cup and his canteen.

He studied the girl. She surprised him all the time with her ingenuity and unflappable determination. "Thanks. I'll take the metal flask out of the sling and heat the water that way. You can have some in your cup and I'll drink from the flask."

Slipping the metal canteen out of the canvas sling, he unscrewed the top and placed the vessel up against the rocks on the inside of the pit. Not in the flames but close enough to warm the liquid in the flask.

"Want something to eat while we wait for the water to warm?" he asked, picking up the saddlebag he'd leaned against the base of a tree along with the saddles and other tack.

"I'm just going to sit here and warm up first." Kitree sat on one of the rocks and held her hands out to the fire. That's when he noticed she was trembling.

"Come here." He knelt on the ground behind her rock, drew her wet jacket off her and pulled her up against him with his good arm, wrapping his coat around her. He hoped their combined body heat would warm her.

She snuggled back against him.

He picked her up, shoved the two rocks together and sat her on the one closest to the fire.

"I've read about people not freezing to death by killing an animal and climbing inside its warm belly." Her voice was eerily soft.

"We aren't going to have to do that. Once the fire gets to blazing and your clothes dry, you'll be feeling warm again. There won't be any hypothermia on this ridge tonight." He rubbed up and down her arm with his right hand, hoping to get her circulation going.

A wisp of steam trailed out of the canteen. Hawke pulled a glove out of his pocket. Kitree helped him pull it on his hand then set her cup on a rock near the flask.

He picked up the canteen and filled the cup, before quickly setting the vessel on the ground on the outside of the fire ring. "You might want to let that cool off a bit before you try to pick it up or drink it."

Steam swirled off the cup of water. Kitree held her hands out to the fire.

Hawke slipped out of his coat and stood, placing it around her shoulders. "I'll throw some more wood on here and see if I can figure out a way to dry your sleeping bag."

She snuggled into his coat. The wool lining, even wet, made it warmer than the jacket she'd been wearing.

Using his knife, he cut four poles about six feet long. Kitree held onto the poles as he used a rock to pound the sticks into the ground at a slant over the fire. He made sure their sitting rocks were on the inside of the poles.

Hawke walked over to where the sleeping bag was draped over a bush. He wrung it out the best he could one handed and then draped one side about six inches over the ends of the poles and stretched the rest down the poles. It not only brought heat to the sleeping bag but also made a warm area to sit in. Dog lay down between the rocks and the sleeping bag.

Kitree's stomach grumbled.

"Ready to eat?" he asked.

"Yes. Do you want your coat back?" She started to shrug out of it.

"No. I'm good."

"There's blood on your sling." She pointed to his injured shoulder.

"I'm fine. The rain probably soaked through." He grabbed the saddlebag with the food and handed the girl a bag of carrots and a sandwich. Sage had thought of everything a child might like.

Hawke pulled out a sandwich for himself and sat down to eat. His canteen was cool enough he could hold it but the warm liquid trickling down his throat felt wonderful. He glanced down at the cup and noticed Kitree had drank some as well.

"Do you really think it was the weather that kept Dani from picking us up?" Kitree held the sandwich in front of her mouth, watching him.

"I can't think of any other reason. She was determined to get us off this mountain. It had to be the storm that prevented her from being here." As he said the words, he remembered her order. *Be here*. She'd pick them up. It had to have been the weather that kept her away. Even a military pilot had to know when conditions should be avoided. He had a feeling she hadn't told anyone that she was coming back for them. She'd been angry with the people who'd come to her hunting lodge and harmed her employees. She'd want to make sure that Kitree didn't fall into the hands of the violent men.

He pointed up at the few stars that twinkled through the tree limbs. "See those stars? The weather has changed already. I bet she lands at that spot shortly after daylight."

Kitree peered up into the tree. "I bet she does, too."

They ate their sandwiches listening to the crackling fire, an owl calling, and the far-off howl of a wolf.

"Have you ever had to shoot a wolf or a bear?" Kitree asked as she drew a carrot out of the bag.

"I carry a shotgun up here. It makes a much louder noise than a rifle. When I encounter a hungry bear, wolf, or cougar, I shoot up in the air. The sound usually scares them away."

She nodded. "Have you ever shot a person?"

He had on only three occasions as a State Trooper. One he wasn't proud of. He'd been a rookie in a position where he'd discharged his weapon out of anger rather than fear for his life. The other two, it had been to incapacitate the suspects to keep bystanders from getting hurt. Those were justified in his mind and the eyes of the judicial system.

"I have shot three people in my career as a State Trooper. None of the shots killed anyone. They were done to save other innocent lives." He didn't feel the girl would understand his first shooting. Best to not go into it.

"Why would someone shoot someone else to kill them?" She still held the one carrot stick in her hand and the bag of carrots dangled forgotten in her other hand.

"There are some people who learn how to kill others for their job and then realize they are good at it and hire out to make money. Then there are the others who have mental issues that just randomly go into a school, church, or place of business and start shooting. They don't aim, they don't care who they kill. They want their few minutes of fame or have issues that no one may ever know about. It could also be someone doing something wrong and when they get caught, they kill to escape. And then there are the people who drink and drive or do drugs and hurt others while under the influence. Or it could be a family member who kills another member out of jealousy or greed." He shook his head. "No one has or will ever figure out what makes a person feel the need to take another's life." He hadn't planned to give her the whole textbook on why people kill, but he didn't want her to think her parents were the only ones. Though he bet her loneliness made her think that way.

"My parents were the first kind, huh?" She didn't look at him. Her gaze was on the dancing flames.

"From what you've told me and your father's actions, I'm pretty sure their deaths were done by someone hired to kill them."

"And me," she said quietly.

"Not if I have anything to say about it." He put a hand on her shoulder. "You are going to live. We are going to catch the man who killed them and the person who paid him." He gave her shoulder a squeeze. "I promise."

Chapter Twelve

Hawke opened his eyes after only a few hours of sleep. The sun shone on the ridge between them and Moss Spring. He'd slept with his back propped against a tree to keep his injured shoulder elevated. He stretched his good arm and rubbed his back. His legs felt numb. He hoped it was from his position and not from cold.

Last night, after the part of the sleeping bag over the fire had dried, he'd switched it and placed the dry half on the ground and settled Kitree down to sleep. He'd kept the fire going until his eyes wouldn't stay open any longer and he'd wrangled his coat from the girl and placed the other dried half of the sleeping bag over her.

He stood and Dog appeared at his side. "Did you clean up that food I gave you last night?" He ruffled the dog's ears and reached into his saddlebag for another can of dog food. A tug on the tab and the scent of meat and gravy filled the air, making his stomach rumble.

If Dani didn't pick the girl up this morning, they'd be out of food before they made it to Moss Springs.

"Is she here?" Kitree asked from her sleeping bag.

"Not yet." He walked over to the fire, picked up a limb, and dug up coals before tossing on a few smaller sticks. They had enough water to heat up some more this morning. "I'll make some more warm water. How about a granola bar and cookies for breakfast?"

Kitree sat up and reached for the saddlebag. She handed him a water bottle.

He filled his canteen and set it in the coals and flickers of flames trying to catch fire.

"Which kind of granola bar do you want?" she asked, holding up two different ones.

"Doesn't matter to me. Food is food. You pick the one you like."

She wrinkled up her nose. "You eat stuff you don't like?"

He grinned. "I've tracked people for days and ran out of food. You eat what won't kill you to keep your stomach from gnawing at its self."

Her eyes grew rounder. "Really? What's the grossest thing you've eaten?"

"I didn't think it was gross. I found a nest of duck eggs. I poked a hole in the shells and sucked the uncooked egg out."

"Ewww! That is gross!" She shuddered and shoved a granola bar at him. "Don't do it while I'm with you."

He laughed. Even though he was keeping the girl alive, this was one of his better trips in the mountains. It was her company that made what should have been a boring journey, pleasant.

"I'll try not to." He took the offered granola bar and was pleased to see she'd given him the dry, hard one. He actually preferred them over the fruity soft kind.

The water started to steam. He pulled on his glove with his teeth and picked up the canteen. He poured the tin cup full and set the canteen down to cool.

The faint sound of helicopter blades slicing through the air caught his attention. "Stay here." He rose, taking his granola bar with him. They didn't need to rush up to the ridge. Dani would have to land and slow the blades before they could approach the aircraft.

"Where are you going?" Kitree stood.

"To make sure it's Dani. You stay here." He glanced around for Dog. He was licking his chops over where Hawke had dumped out the dog food. "Stay. Guard," Hawke ordered.

He left the two and headed up the small incline. Before he arrived at the top, the thump of the blades sounded close. He remained under a tree and scanned the sky.

There was a helicopter, but it wasn't Dani. He studied it. It was the one he'd seen fly over when they were headed to the hunting lodge. He spun around and descended the ridge. Something was up. Dani should have been here. He didn't like this. Didn't like it one bit.

"Was it Dani?" Kitree asked, when he was in sight of their camp.

"No. We're getting out of here." He went straight to Jack, saddling him as quickly as he could with one arm.

Kitree stuffed everything into the saddlebags.

He tied his on behind his saddle, using his teeth and the one hand. After Horse was saddled, Kitree handed him her saddlebag and pack. He tied those on behind her saddle and helped her up onto the mule.

He'd planned on riding out to Moss Spring on the trails after putting Kitree on the helicopter. No one would be looking for just him. But, now that someone knew to find them at the ridge, they could be flying around looking for them. That meant they would have to take a more direct path to Moss Spring and avoid the trail.

First thing, he had to find a stream for the animals to drink.

《》《》《》

Kitree sat atop Horse as he drank in long slurps from the stream they were about to cross. She could tell Hawke was either worried or thinking real hard. He'd said very little since coming back and telling her the helicopter hadn't been Dani.

She decided to ask what she wanted to know. It was better than wondering. "What are we going to do when we get to Moss Springs?"

"The same thing I was going to do after putting you on the helicopter. Call my landlord and have him come pick up the animals and us." Hawke sat on his horse as if he and the animal were one.

She was still in awe of the fact he was an Indian. Nez Perce and Cayuse was his heritage and Umatilla was the name several tribes living on the same reservation called themselves. She'd heard all the names before, but planned to read more about them when she had the chance.

"Why him and not other policemen?" She wanted

to tell other lawmen what she'd seen. She wanted them out looking for the man.

"Because someone had to tell the people who showed up this morning about our rendezvous with Dani. That means either someone in the police is giving out information or they have a way of hearing what goes on. I prefer to drive you to the state police myself." He swiveled his head and studied her. "You do trust me, don't you?"

She nodded. He'd saved her and only did what was best for her. "I trust you, Dog, and Dani." She thought a moment. "And Sage."

He nodded. "And when you meet Herb, you'll trust him, too."

Hawke moved his horse forward across the stream and Horse followed. He had no choice. Hawke led him as he had the whole trip. She wondered if the mule had ever had a bridle or if he was just always dragged along behind Jack.

"Do you ever ride Horse?" she asked.

"Once in a while. Why?" Hawke glanced back at her.

"Because you always lead him around. Maybe he'd like to go his own way once in a while." She'd get tired of always having to do something the same way all the time.

"The thing is, Horse behaves better when he's led than when you ride him. That freedom you think he needs is what gets him in trouble." Hawke glanced forward, scanning the trees and area ahead of them. "Some people are the same way. They behave better when they have rules to follow."

She didn't mind following the rules if they made

sense. But some teachers had silly rules that didn't make sense. "Even if the rule is silly?"

"What's a silly rule you have to follow?" Hawke didn't look back at her, he just talked louder.

"My teacher says we can't have anything unhealthy in our lunch unless we bring something to share with the whole class." She'd thought on this rule a lot. "Why would she want us to share something unhealthy with everyone? If Momma and Daddy don't care that I have a candy bar in my lunch, why do I have to bring one for everyone? Especially, Ginny Jones? She can't eat anything anyone else brings anyway because she has allergies."

Hawke's laugh filled the space between them and made her feel normal until the sound faded and she remembered why he was escorting her through the forest.

"I think your teacher made up the silly rule because most parents wouldn't want to purchase enough candy bars to feed the class. That makes sure all of you eat right and aren't hyped up on sugar for the afternoon." Hawke stopped his horse and pulled the mule up beside him. "Your teacher made her silly rule to make her life easier. You'll find people who can make rules will sometimes do that."

She nodded her head. It made sense. Mrs. Jones liked everything running smoothly. "Do you have to follow silly rules?"

He stared forward for so long she thought he had forgotten she rode beside him.

"I've had to deal with lots of silly rules my whole life. I thought being in law enforcement would give me clear rules and that others would have to follow them, too." He shook his head and glanced at her. "But not everyone follows rules and those that don't tend to break other laws as well."

"Which gives you job security."

Hawke chuckled and stared down at the girl. Her intelligence amazed him. "What do you know about job security?"

"My daddy talks about it all the time. He told me job security is when there is a need for your job. His job, teaching people math, is something everyone needs, so he has job security, no matter where he goes." She patted Horse's neck. "That's why he said it didn't matter how many times or where we had to move to keep Momma safe, he would always be able to take care of us."

Tears glistened in her eyes. "His job security didn't keep them safe."

Hawke reached out, placing a hand on her small shoulder. "The person who killed your parents took everything away from your family. It's not right. The man broke the number one rule. You don't kill."

"What about in wars? People kill then." Her eyes which should have held innocence while asking this question shone with maturity and the harshness of life.

He sighed. He'd been one of those who killed others in war. "Both sides know that they must kill or be killed. What happened to your parents was one person making a decision your parents had no control over. They didn't know what would happen that day. They wanted to get back to their regular life. The killer ended it."

Tears trickled down Kitree's cheeks.

Now he felt like the villain having made the girl

cry. "I'm sorry. I didn't mean
to make you cry."

"You didn't. I miss Momma and Daddy and wish
we hadn't gone camping. They did it for me. I wanted
to collect as many wildflowers and edible plants as I
could. You know, for my fifth grade science project
next year." She wiped at her cheeks.

"They took you because they loved you. You will
always have that with you. Even though they were
taken from you, their love wasn't." Hawke remembered
his mother telling him this when his grandfather died.
He'd been a heartbroken fourteen-year-old. But he'd
thought he was too old to show others how badly he
missed his grandfather. When he finally let the grief
overcome him and wailed as well as spoke to others
about his mentor, he'd found relief in the knowledge
everything his grandfather had taught him would
always be with him. He would carry a piece of the man
he loved with him the rest of his life.

Kitree sniffed and nodded. "They always told me
they didn't have more children so they could give me
all of their love." Her face tipped up to him. "I could
feel their love every time they looked at me."

"Hold that memory. You will always be loved no
matter where you are." Hawke released the lead rope,
letting Horse fall behind Jack. He hoped the child was
put into a loving foster or adoptive home.

Chapter Thirteen

As soon as Hawke had cell service, he called Herb.

"Hawke, where are you? All kinds of rumors have been going around," Herb Trembley, his landlord, answered.

"I'll tell you when you pick us up at Moss Springs. Bring a horse trailer, sandwiches, cookies, and milk."

"When do I need to be there?"

He knew he could count on Herb. "We should be at the trailhead in an hour and a half."

"I'll be waiting for you."

"Is he coming?" Kitree asked.

"Yes. Let's keep moving." They'd managed to get down the last ridge staying under the cover of trees and battling less and less brush. He'd heard the thump of a helicopter at one point but it had sounded far off.

They crossed Little Minam River. The trees were thick the rest of the way to the trailhead. He didn't know when he'd been so relieved to leave the mountains. He usually didn't want to go back to civilization. But this trip had turned from a routine into a mystery and a life or death adventure.

Another forty minutes and the horse and mule walked out into the wide-open parking lot. Hawke scanned the half a dozen trucks and trailers. Herb hadn't arrived yet.

He spun the horse and mule back to the trees and pulled out his phone. Scrolling through his contacts, he found Herb's number.

"Herb," the man answered.

"Hawke. What's your location?" He glanced over at Kitree. He didn't want to alarm her, but he didn't like the fact Herb hadn't been here when they arrived.

"Just about there. I had to evade the FBI. After I talked to you, an SUV full of them rolled up to the stable." Herb cursed under his breath. "This road is full of potholes, I'm going as fast as I dare without shaking the trailer apart."

"Take your time. We'll hang out inside the tree line until you get here." Hawke disconnected. Why had the Feds been at the Trembley's looking for him?

"What's wrong? You're scowling." Kitree's young voice pulled him from his reveries.

"Herb was held up. He'll be here soon." Hawke dismounted, grimacing at his stiff and swollen shoulder. He didn't like that it was swollen. He didn't have time for an infection of any kind.

Kitree slid off Horse and patted Dog on the head. "I hope it's soon. I'm starting to itch."

Hawke grinned. She'd gone nearly two weeks without a shower. A boy wouldn't care, but she was showing her feminine side by wanting to be clean.

"You can get a shower as soon as we get you to the state police. Someone can run to a store and get you clean clothes."

"Can't I stay with you?" she asked, sitting on a downed log.

"I'm sorry, but you can't." He glanced at her. He didn't like the idea of her being in foster care with people who wouldn't know how to deal with someone who might be out to harm her. He wished he could hide her someplace. But the law was the law. She had to be turned over to child services.

He pulled out his phone and dialed Lt. Titus, his superior, in the State Police at La Grande.

"Titus."

"Sir, I'll be bringing the Poulson girl to headquarters within the hour. Could you make sure there is a woman to help her get a shower and send someone to purchase a set of clothes for your average sized ten-year-old girl?" He smiled at Kitree. She gave him a half-hearted smile back.

"I'll have everything ready." The lieutenant closed the connection.

"Why can't I stay with you?" Kitree asked again.

"I'm single and live in a two-room apartment over a stable." He shrugged. It was pretty plain he didn't have a need for family by the way he lived. But this little girl and all her charms were making him wonder if he might be missing out on something by not having a wife and children.

"An apartment over a stable?" She plucked a stem of grass and placed one end in her mouth. "Isn't that kind of smelly?"

He laughed. "Some days in the summer it can be.

But Darlene cleans out the stalls every day. And I take care of the paddock I rent for Jack, Horse, and Boy." He studied the girl. "Darlene gives riding lessons. She has an indoor arena. That's where my apartment is. At one end of the arena."

"Fun! Do you get to ride…" Her excitement dwindled. "I guess you ride so much for work, you don't really want to ride in the arena."

"The kind of trail riding I do, I don't need to practice in an arena. But it's a good place because I can live close to my animals."

Her eyes lit up. "I've always wanted animals."

He hoped she got her wish with whomever she lived with.

They were only far enough in the trees to not be seen. He watched the road that Herb would be coming in on. The front end of the Trembley's truck appeared at the end of the parking lot.

"Here he comes." Hawke led Jack and Horse out into the parking lot with Kitree beside him. Dog walked ahead of them.

Herb pulled up beside them and parked.

The sound of helicopter blades thumped in the air.

"Jump in the pickup," Hawke told Kitree.

She did as she was told. Hawke casually walked the animals to the back of the trailer where Herb held the door open.

"From the looks of you, I should drive you to the Grand Ronde Hospital." Herb nodded toward Hawke's bandaged shoulder.

"It can wait. We need to get Kitree to the State Police." Hawke tied the horse and mule in the trailer and walked out.

The helicopter hovered over the parking lot. Shit! He didn't need the killer finding them now.

"Don't think we're going to make it to the State Police with that little girl. That's the FBI. They've been flying in and out of the county ever since they brought the man and woman's bodies off the mountain." Herb shook his head and closed the trailer door as the helicopter landed across the parking lot from them.

FBI. All this time he'd been hiding from people who could have saved them all the backcountry travel. Hawke mentally slugged himself and walked toward the two men climbing out of the aircraft.

They both had on dark glasses and suits. "Trooper Hawke," the first to meet him held out a hand.

Hawke shook hands.

"Special Agent McKinney. This is Special Agent Dolan."

Hawke held out his hand to shake with the other agent and realized it was a woman. She was tall, thin, and the suit didn't show off any curves. Her hair was cut pretty much like Agent McKinney's.

"Ma'am." Hawke glanced at the helicopter. "You the ones that have been flying all over the mountain today?"

"We are. Once we persuaded Ms. Singer to tell us where to find you, we've been in the air looking for you." The agent nodded toward the pickup and trailer. "You're a hard man to find."

"Just protecting a witness."

The dark glasses hid the man's eyes but his brown eyebrows rose above the black rims. "Ms. Singer didn't say the girl saw the man who shot her parents."

He couldn't tell by the agent's tone if he found that

a good thing or a bad thing. The hair on the back of Hawke's neck tingled. He didn't like this guy, FBI or not.

"If you hand over the girl, we can be on our way." As McKinney said this, Agent Dolan took two steps toward the pickup and trailer.

"I'm taking her to the Oregon State Police headquarters in La Grande. You're welcome to join us there." Hawke pivoted and headed to Herb's vehicle. He wasn't going to let these two take Kitree anywhere until he'd cleared them both.

"We have seniority on this case," McKinney said, walking beside him.

"How?"

"The parents were in the federal witness protection program."

"And see where that got them?" Hawke stopped, put his good hand out, and stopped the agent twenty feet from the pickup. "I'm taking my witness to State Police Headquarters. When, and if, my superior says to hand her over to you, I will. After I've made enquiries into your trustworthiness and the statutes."

The pickup engine started. Hawke hurried over to the vehicle, hopped in, and Herb headed back the way he'd come.

"What was that pissing match about?" Herb asked.

"Tell you later." Hawke stared in the side mirror, watching to see if the agents followed them. They looked to be in a heated conversation as the trees blocked his view.

"Did they want me?" Kitree asked softly from the back seat.

Hawke turned the best he could with his sore

shoulder, trying to look her in the eyes. "They did. But I'm not turning you over to anyone I don't know."

The relief that smoothed the child's etched brow, had him vowing to keep that promise.

«»«»«»

By the time Herb pulled the pickup and trailer into the State Police headquarters in La Grande, Hawke and Kitree had eaten three sandwiches, all the cookies and drank two of the small cartons of milk.

His brain worked better on a full stomach, but he'd noticed Kitree was getting sleepy. He pulled out his cell phone and called his superior in the building.

"Titus," the lieutenant answered.

"Lieutenant, this is Hawke. I'm sitting in a pickup outside headquarters with Kitree Poulson. I need to see a doctor, and she needs sleep before she talks to you. Any chance I can take her to the county, let her sleep and get some food before I bring her back here for you to interview?"

"Hawke, you can't haul a possible suspect in a shooting all over." The lieutenant's voice reprimanded.

"She isn't a suspect. I took a bullet to the shoulder to keep the man I'm pretty sure killed her parents from killing more people along with Kitree." Hawke pinched the bridge of his nose. His shoulder throbbed, and he wanted to sleep for a week.

"Hawke, bring her in here. I promise she will get cared for and be safe. You need to get to a hospital."

He closed the conversation and opened his door. His shoulder was beginning to throb and ache, making it harder to think. He trusted every officer in the State Police and if Titus said they would keep the girl safe, they would.

"Want me to help you?" Herb asked, from behind the wheel of the truck.

"I'm fine."

"You don't look fine. Your face gets paler and paler." Herb got out of the driver's side and came around, opening the back door of the truck. "Come on, sweetheart, you need to come with us."

Hawke stepped back as Herb navigated the child inside the building. He followed not wanting to get too much distance between them. Once inside, they were met by Lt. Titus, a female trooper, and someone who said she was with Child Services.

"Hawke you look like hell," Lt. Titus said, pointing to his shoulder. "Get that fixed up, some sleep, and get your report filed. We need to know what we are dealing with."

The female trooper and Child Services' woman started to lead Kitree away. She whirled around and ran back, flinging her arms around Hawke's waist. "I don't want to go with anyone else."

He knelt on one knee. "You'll be safe here and I'm sure," he glared over her shoulder at the Child Services worker, "that this woman will make sure you are in a place that will keep you safe." He reached in his pocket, pulled out his business card case, and held it out to her. "Take one of these and my pen."

Kitree did as she was told.

"Write my cell number on the back of the card." He recited the number and she wrote it down.

"You can call me any time, I don't care if it's day or night, if you need to talk or you're feeling scared." He took his pen and gave her a one-armed hug. "You won't be alone if you remember your parents and call me when you need to talk."

She sniffed, kissed his cheek, pulled her wildflower book out of her coat pocket and tucked the card in the book. Staring at the floor, she walked slowly back to the two women.

He watched her disappear through a door.

"Looks like you became attached to our witness," Lt. Titus said.

Hawke slowly stood and faced his boss. He wasn't going to admit to his superior how attached he'd become. "Two FBI agents met us at the trailhead. I told them I wasn't handing over the girl until they were checked out. They were McKinney and Dolan." He went on giving their descriptions. "I told them I was bringing her here, and they could come here. If they show up make sure they are legit. There were four men who tried to get Kitree. Whatever the reason the parents were killed, it's bigger than the witness protection."

"We're already digging into the deaths. I'll make sure the FBI doesn't get their hands on the girl. She's our witness. I'll do my best to find out what they want."

"Thanks. Herb will take me to the doctor and then I'm going home to sleep." Hawke slid a glance at the door where Kitree had disappeared and walked out of the building. He had to get healed to help with the investigation.

Herb followed him out the door and to the pickup. "The hospital here?"

"Yes. Then home." Hawke tipped his head back and closed his eyes.

Chapter Fourteen

Kitree's body shook. "Leave me alone. I want to sleep," she muttered.

A female voice, not her mother's, spoke. "Kitree, we're at the home where you'll stay until something permanent can be done."

Her eyes popped open. She'd fallen asleep as soon as the case worker put her in the car. She stared out the window in the late afternoon light at a house surrounded by fenced pastures with animals.

This place might not be so bad. She sat up and realized, all she had from her life with Momma and Daddy were her two books that she'd tucked into the pockets of her pants. Her *My Side of the Mountain* guide and the wildflower book.

And Hawke's phone number. She sighed and slid out of the back seat of the car.

"Kitree, this is Mr. and Mrs. Dahlren. Mr. Dahlren is a retired State Trooper. He will make sure you are safe." Mrs. Trainer, the case worker, patted her head like she was a dog.

"Kitree, we're happy to have you staying with us." Mrs. Dahlren walked forward, holding out her hand.

Kitree shook hands with the woman and studied the man. He was retired alright. She wasn't sure he could keep anyone from harming her. His white hair, small body, and pursed lips reminded her of a grumpy character in a movie.

"Here are a few changes of clothes. I'm afraid she comes with very little in the way of possessions," Mrs. Trainer said, in an apologetic tone.

Kitree watched as the two women spoke quietly together.

"Come along. Mother had dinner about ready to go on the table." Mr. Dahlren waved for her to walk into the house with him.

She glanced over her shoulder and wished Hawke had followed them and said he'd take her off their hands. She missed his calm assurance that everything would be fine, and Dog.

《》《》《》

Because he'd refused to stay overnight in the hospital, the emergency room doctor filled Hawke full of antibiotics after cleaning out the wound and bandaging it. Herb drove him home, where Darlene had a pot roast dinner waiting for the two of them. He excused himself to shower before sitting down at Darlene's table. Feeling clean and his arm hurting less from the ibuprofen the doctor told him to take, he dressed and headed to the main house for a substantial meal.

"It's terrible that poor child is all alone," Darlene

said after Hawke and her husband had eaten their fill. "I wish you could have brought her here. Taking her to people she doesn't know… I feel awful."

Hawke peered at his landlord. "She wouldn't have known you."

"But she would have had you, who she does know, close by." She glared at him as if he were some halfwit.

"I gave her my phone number and told her to call me anytime to talk." He knew loneliness. He also knew she feared for her life. He had wanted her to know he was available no matter what.

"From the bond I saw between you two, I'm sure you'll be hearing from her soon." Herb raised a cup of coffee to his mouth.

"I doubt I'll be hearing from her tonight. She'll sleep for two days. I hauled her a lot of miles over the mountains keeping her safe. Thank you for dinner. I'm as beat as Kitree." Hawke excused himself and wandered back to his apartment over the arena.

He and Dog climbed the stairs. He fell onto the bed, without turning out the light or undressing.

《》《》《》

Pounding on the door and Dog barking pulled Hawke out of the deepest sleep he'd had in years.

He tried to call out, but his mouth and throat felt as if he'd chewed up and swallowed a ball of cotton. The pounding and barking continued.

Hawke grabbed a bottle of water from the refrigerator and crossed to the door. He took a big swig to moisten his mouth, and opened the door.

"Stop pounding."

Agent McKinney. Two steps down behind him stood Agent Dolan.

"Where is the girl?" McKinney asked, pushing into the room.

"Take a look around. She's not here." Hawke guzzled half the bottle of water as the two looked into the only other room, the bathroom. He smiled to himself. Lt. Titus must not have told the two where the girl was taken. Why they thought he had her, he'd never know.

"You're going to lose your job over this," McKinney said, standing in front of him.

Hawke shrugged. He didn't know where the child had been taken. After his hospital visit, he was put on medical leave. He wasn't on the case, officially.

His only objective was to keep Kitree safe. It appeared that had been the same objective of his Lieutenant.

"Where is the girl?" Dolan asked, getting in his face.

He took a step back. She'd had something with onions for dinner. "I told you I was taking her to the State Police Headquarters in La Grande. That's what I did."

"She's not there. They said they didn't know where she was. Yet here you are in your own comfy bed, and it appears you've been to see a doctor." McKinney pointed to Hawke's arm in a sling.

"I'm on medical leave. Can't do anything with this arm tied up." He tossed the empty water bottle in the trash can. "She's not here. I need sleep." He walked over to the still open door and waited.

"We're going to tear this place apart and find that girl," McKinney said, stepping out onto the stairs.

"Go right ahead but know there are a couple horses

down there that don't like strangers in their stalls." He didn't wait to see their reaction. He had more hours of sleep calling his name. He shut the door and didn't think about them again.

《》《》《》

Hawke rose at nine. It was Horse's high-pitched bray that woke him. Which made him wonder why Darlene hadn't fed his horses, knowing he had only one working arm. Being already dressed was an asset. He pulled a ball cap on his head and headed down to the stalls.

From the shambles of buckets, feed bags, halters, and ropes, the agents had taken their frustration with him out on the stable. Darlene was probably working her way through the mess, cleaning it up. It was his fault. He'd feed his animals and get busy setting things right.

He found trying to haul hay to the run in the wheelbarrow hard to do with one arm. He tossed several pitchforkfuls over inside the barn and went to work cleaning things up. He had the inside all put right when Herb arrived.

"What are you doing?" he asked.

"Putting everything up that the FBI agents left on the ground."

Herb laughed and said, "They were mad when they didn't find that little girl in our house. Asked about the clothing in the guest room. We told them it belonged to our grandchildren. Showed them the photo of the kids hanging on the wall."

"I bet Darlene's mad about the mess they made out here at the barn and stables."

"She is fuming, but she's mad at the people who

did it, not you."

"Good." Hawke thought about asking the lieutenant when he could see Kitree, but in case the FBI was watching him, he needed to stay away. He didn't understand their need to find the girl. She would tell the State Police everything she knew. They were the ones solving the murder case.

His stomach grumbled and his phone rang. It was a number he didn't know.

"Come on in. Darlene made extra breakfast for you." Herb patted Dog on the head and pivoted, walking out of the barn.

"I'll take this call and be in." He tapped his phone with his thumb.

"Hawke."

"It's Kitree." The relief in her voice made his chest squeeze.

"How are you? Did you get a nice place to stay?" He wanted to know where she was, but didn't want to come out and ask. She might think it was because he didn't trust who she was with.

"It's okay. The bed has a pretty cover with horses all over it. They have horses, cows, goats, and pigs. Mr. Dahlren was a policeman before he retired."

Hawke nodded. He knew who she was talking about. They'd placed her on a small acreage farm outside of Imbler. Dahlren had been a good detective in his day. But he was in his late seventies. No match for the likes of the men who had been at the lodge.

"You should be safe and happy there. Enjoy all those animals while you can." Knowing she'd never had animals but was good with them, he wanted her to have a good experience.

"I helped feed the goats this morning. Did you know a boy goat is called a billy? I always just though people named their boy goats Billy." She giggled.

The sound of her innocent giggle eased a bit of his worry. "Did you get very close to him?"

"No! He stinks!"

Hawke laughed. "They do have their own strong odor. The girl goats like it."

Kitree laughed. "I'm glad I'm not a girl goat."

"Thanks for calling. I wondered where you were and if you were doing okay. Herb invited me in for breakfast, so I need to go. But you keep calling me, anytime you need to." He hated cutting her off, but he also was realistic that they couldn't continue this type of a conversation all day, every day. She was going to have to become attached to someone else.

"Oh, okay. I'll try not to call you too much."

He heard the disappointment in her voice. "I don't mind. I'm on medical leave now, so you won't disturb my work, but I also don't want whoever is looking for you to find you through me." He mentally slapped himself after the words came out. Now he'd make her scared to call him.

"Can they?" Fear made her voice go up an octave.

"Maybe. Call me if you need to talk. We'll deal with the rest." He hadn't been using his head when he mentioned the call tracing.

"Okay. Bye." The connection went silent.

He hit off on his phone and cursed. His thoughts came out in words. Not a good thing when talking with a child. Another reason, she was better off with the Dahlrens than him.

Hawke sauntered into the main house. No sense

letting food made for him go to waste.

His phone rang. Sergeant Spruel, his superior in Wallowa County.

"Hawke."

"Heard you had a run-in with a bullet." He liked his sergeant because he was a man of few words.

"Yes, I'm on medical leave." Hawke knew what the man was going to say.

"You still need to come by and write up your report and contacts."

"I planned to do that as soon as I eat breakfast." He had a lot to report. There were two agencies that wanted to get their hands on his report.

"Good. I heard you had a visit from the FBI."

"Which time?" He went on to tell about the two who landed a helicopter at the Moss Spring Trailhead and then showed up at his place during the night.

Sergeant Spruel cleared his throat. When he spoke, his voice was quiet. "We always cooperate with other agencies, but from what Titus says, these two are more interested in something they believe the girl has than the girl." His voice became louder. "Get in here and make your report and don't leave out a thing."

The line went quiet. He grinned. This wasn't the first time Spruel had his back. He was sure as long as he worked under the man, it wouldn't be the last.

"You coming in?" Herb called from the back door of the Trembley home.

"I'm coming. I have to check something." While talking to Sergeant Spruel it dawned on him that the items he'd packed off the mountain with Kitree were in the back seat of Herb's pickup.

He walked over to where the pickup, still hooked

Paty Jager

to the horse trailer, was parked. He opened the back door and found nothing. Had the FBI snatched it?

Long strides took him to the house and inside. Herb and Darlene sat at the table, their plates empty except for a few crumbs and swirls of egg yolk.

He took his seat as Darlene rose and returned with the coffee pot.

"We thought you'd decided not to eat here," Herb said.

"Kitree called, then my sergeant." Hawke studied his landlord. "Did the FBI get in your truck last night?"

"I think so. Didn't think there was anything in there that would get us in trouble or tell them where the girl was." Herb stirred a spoon in his coffee. It was a habit the man did when he was thinking even though he drank his coffee black.

"Her pack and belongings were still in the back. We didn't leave them at headquarters with her." Hawke studied his landlord.

"We didn't leave them. No sir," Herb raised his cup and sipped. The twinkle in his eyes, told Hawke the man had hid the girl's belongings.

"What did you do with them?"

"Put them in the cellar last night after dinner. Didn't seem right if the child was being hidden away that her belongings shouldn't be, too." Herb glanced at his wife and smiled.

"After breakfast, I'd like you to bring them all in here. The FBI are looking for something other than the girl."

Herb nodded. "I'll get them now, while you eat."

Hawke dug into the food and thanked Darlene for inviting him to another meal.

"I figure with your arm in a sling, you're going to have trouble making meals and dealing with things." She picked up his empty dishes as Herb entered with the backpack.

Hawke placed all of the girl's things on the table and one by one studied everything about them. He checked the braces of the backpack for any items hidden in the aluminum tubing. The padding in the straps on the back felt even and the same material, but he undid the seam with his pocket knife and checked. Just foam. Nothing in the water bottle lids. The rain coat didn't have any hidden areas. He couldn't find anything that the FBI or the killer could be looking for.

"Thank you for saving this. As far as I can tell, there isn't anything here anyone would want. If the FBI come back, let them have it. I'm headed to Winslow to write up my report."

Chapter Fifteen

Hawke walked into the Fish and Wildlife and Oregon State Police Office in Winslow and braced himself. The employees and officers were a large dysfunctional family and loved to rib one another.

"Hey, Hawke, heard you were lost in the mountains and needed Search and Rescue to come find you," one of the ODFW employees said, as he walked through their part of the building to get to the State Troopers side. He wasn't officially working, which meant he'd driven his own pickup and parked in the public parking lot instead of the State Police lot behind the building. If he'd parked behind the building, he would have had access straight into the State Police side of the building.

He let the comment go and shoved through the door into the troopers' side.

"Hawke, heard you took a bullet," Ward Dillon, another game warden, said.

"Yeah," He raised his arm in the sling and wished he hadn't. Pain shot through his shoulder and down his back on the left side.

Sergeant Spruel stepped out of his office. "Feeling up to writing out those reports?"

"It may take me a while one-handed, but yeah." He walked over to his superior. "Any chance I can get you to check on the female victim's employment background?"

His sergeant stared at him before saying, "You're on medical leave."

"It's my own curiosity." He was curious about Mrs. Poulson's job before her death and the one that had caused the family to be put under witness protection.

"You can ask the FBI. A McKinney and Dolan are coming in to question you at eleven." The sergeant glanced at the clock. "I suggest you get busy."

Hawke swung his gaze to the clock. Ten.

If he'd have been a teenager, Hawke would have rolled his eyes. Instead, he twisted his neck to relieve the tension and walked over to his desk and computer along the wall with the other troopers' desks.

It appeared Sullens and Ullman were out looking for game violators and Dillon was getting ready to head out. It would just be him and the sergeant in the office when the agents arrived. At least there would be someone here who was on his side while they questioned him. He was glad Sergeant Spruel hadn't asked him about Kitree.

His computer screen lit up, and he typed in his security code. He began inputting his long overdue list of contacts. It wasn't the information everyone was interested in. But it was easier to type in names and what he'd talked to them about one-handed, than to type up the events from the moment he received the radio call about the missing family to his return and aggravating the FBI.

At exactly 11 am on his computer screen, in walked the two agents who had rousted him out of bed the night before. They looked as if they hadn't slept since. That was a bonus with their questioning him.

"Trooper Hawke, I believe your sergeant has offered us the conference room to question you." McKinney didn't waste time. He walked to the largest room on this side of the building while Dolan herded Hawke away from his computer.

Spruel stepped out of his office. "Care if I sit in?" he asked McKinney.

The agent flicked a glance at the other agent, but said, "Only if you don't interfere."

Hawke was grateful there would be a witness to the conversation. Especially so, when they started, and the agents didn't start any recording device. It was apparent this conversation was off the record. And why would that be?

"Trooper Hawke, you have yet to record your report on the incident that happened at Minam Lake," McKinney started.

"I was working on it when you pulled me away from my computer." He motioned to his arm in a sling. "It's hard to type with one hand."

"He hadn't started the report. He was logging in his contacts," Dolan said.

"Warming up my hand," Hawke replied and wiggled the fingers on his right hand. He caught a glimpse of a smirk on Spruel's face.

"Tell us how you came upon the Poulson camp?" McKinney asked.

Hawke told them about the radio call, his log book having noted the family planned to camp at Mirror Lake. His finding someone in that area who said they'd seen the family at Minam Lake. He continued with a play by play of how he'd discovered the bodies and subsequently realized the girl was running.

"Did you believe she was running because she'd killed her parents?" the agent asked.

Hawke looked the man square in the eyes. "All of the evidence pointed to a cold-blooded killer, not a little girl. And from the items she took with her when she ran, she hadn't planned that either. She'd left behind several items that if she had planned the whole thing, she would have had in her backpack." There would have been more food, her own clothes, and a flashlight had she planned to hide from officials.

"Why did you go after the girl, if you believed her innocent?" McKinney asked.

"She was headed into the wilderness and away from the trails. She could have been lost or killed by a predator. And I believed she was running because she saw something."

Aha, that was what they wanted to know, given the brief glance between the two agents.

"Why did it take you so long to catch her? We were led to understand you are a master tracker." The smug look on the man's face didn't make Hawke's response any easier to say.

"Because she covered her trail. I didn't expect that from a child. The first time, I realized what she'd done,

I was surprised. The second time, I realized she knew I was following her, and the third time, she'd shown me how smart she was. But it was after it had rained that I caught up to her. She'd hunkered down earlier in the day and that made it easier to overtake her." The memory of sending Dog to bring her down didn't bother him. He'd needed to catch her to keep her safe.

"And when you had her in custody—"

Hawke stopped him. "She was never in custody. She was never a suspect. She was a witness who needed protecting." He glared at the agent, daring him to say otherwise.

"When you caught her, why didn't you radio your location and get her to authorities immediately."

"I tried. But discovered we were being followed by an ex-special ops person."

McKinney leaned forward. "How did you know this?"

"Dog brought us his knife. It's in my pack at Charlie's Hunting Lodge." He glanced at his sergeant, who shook his head slightly. Not sure what that meant, he didn't ask now.

"That knife could have been dropped by anyone hiking in the mountains," Dolan said.

Hawke shook his head. "No. It was clean, a little sticky like he'd used it to cut an apple or piece of fruit."

"What did you do after receiving the knife?"

"I took off Jack's reins, headed him down the trail with Horse following. I took Kitree up the mountainside. My plan was to take her to the nearest guard station."

"Why didn't you radio for help?" McKinney asked.

He stared at the man. "Because it had to be by

radio that the man following us caught up so quickly. I'd radioed my location in that morning. And that night, we had the man following. I didn't trust the radio." He remembered wishing he'd used it to warn Dani and the others. His conscience had banged at him after he'd witnessed the bruises on Dani, Tuck, and Tyson.

"Why did you go to the hunting lodge?" McKinney asked.

Hawke wondered how the man knew so much about his movements when he hadn't filed his report yet. "Because I couldn't live with the thought I'd sent the killer to the lodge by having him follow the horses. I put Kitree in a safe place with Dog. I went to the lodge to make sure everyone was okay." He shook his head. "They weren't. Four men were there and a helicopter." Hawke set his gaze on Spruel. "I tied up two of the men when they were outside the lodge. I overheard the other two saying they were going to set the lodge on fire with the owner, employees, and two guests in it. I managed to get all but Ms. Singer's cousin free and told the owner to fly them all out of there.

"But as I was getting the last person, the two men realized something was wrong. I sent Tyson out the window to get Kitree and take her to the authorities. When I confronted the two men, I was shot. But I saw both men's faces. I plan to look through the database on special operations personnel when I finished my report."

Again, the exchange of glances between the agents.

"It appears instead of hiding the girl, you should be in hiding if you believe these people will kill her." McKinney studied him.

"For all they know, I'm lying dead up at the lodge." The two men knew they hadn't killed him. Not when the one had made the shot go wide of where it had been aimed. But he wouldn't let the agent know that he hoped the man did come after him. He had more than one score to settle with the killer.

"Why didn't you meet the helicopter that came to pick you up on the peak?" McKinney asked.

"Because Ms. Singer said she would pick up Kitree. It wasn't her helicopter. For all I knew it was the person out to kill the girl." He stared at the agent. Only someone stupid would have shown himself to a helicopter he didn't know with a man out to kill them.

"Why did you drive off with the girl when we attempted to get her at the trailhead?"

"Because for all I know you are impersonating an FBI agent to get the girl." Hawke shifted his attention to Sergeant Spruel. "Did Lt. Titus do a check on these two?"

"He did. They are FBI agents. McKinney has been with the bureau for fifteen years, and Dolan has been with them for five."

The two nodded.

"Then answer some questions for me. Why were the Poulson's put into Witness Protection?"

"I can't answer that." Now it was the agent's turn to back pedal and try to avoid giving any information.

"Why? They're dead. Would telling us why, tell us who killed them? Is there a reason the Feds don't want us to know?" Hawke had always had a problem with the FBI. They were called in twice at the reservation for two suspicious disappearances. Two young women had disappeared on the same night while walking home from a party. When the local police couldn't come up with anything, the FBI were called in. The Feds immediately said the two women had run away. And who wouldn't, given the circumstances of their lives. In Hawke's estimation, the Feds liked to tie things up in a nice neat bow without digging to find out what really happened.

"It's classified," Dolan said, and McKinney glared at her.

"Classified, as in, Mrs. Poulson worked for the government?" Hawke wasn't going to let this go.

To his surprise, Agent McKinney placed six photos on the table in front of him. Hawke scanned the photos and tapped four of them.

"Those are the men that were at the lodge. And this one..." he said, tapping the photo of the man who shot him. "...is the one who shot me. From his actions and things he said, I'm pretty sure he killed the Poulsons." He studied pages. "If you have pictures and know where these people are, why haven't you arrested them?"

"It's not as easy as you make it sound. These men work for the person that Mrs. Poulson testified against and put in jail. We weren't sure until you pointed them out, if they were the ones sent to kill her family."

"Why weren't you sure? Is there someone else who could have wanted Mrs. Poulson, her husband, and daughter dead?" Hawke didn't like that there was the possibility of more than one person after Kitree.

"Since they were moved into Witness Protection, Mrs. Poulson has been working on another classified project. One that has a few people upset." McKinney didn't look him in the eye.

"What has she been working on?" Hawke glanced over at Sergeant Spruel. He seemed to be as interested in the conversation. Which meant the FBI were keeping information hidden from everyone.

"It's a matter of national security. I can't tell you who or what or any information. However, it makes me happy to know that this group is the one responsible for the deaths and who wanted the girl dead. Now that we know who we are looking for, I can request more agents be brought in."

It was okay with Hawke to have more agents help find the men. But he still wasn't going to tell them where the girl had been placed. He believed they would eventually find the man. However, he wasn't sure the FBI would care about what happened to Kitree. "Looks like you know who you're looking for. I'm going back to my report."

McKinney shook his head. "We need to know where the girl is."

"She's safe." Hawke stood, nodded at his superior, and left the room. He knew the laws. There was nothing they could do to him to make him give up Kitree's location. As far as his superior knew, Hawke didn't have a clue where the girl was staying. He also wasn't the only one who knew. They could contact the social worker. He hoped Lt. Titus had told her it was vital to keep the child's whereabouts as quiet as possible. The FBI could walk in and take any records they wanted, but he hoped the records hadn't been written yet. Kind of like his report.

He'd get a pre-paid phone and give that number to Kitree to call him. Then if they checked his phone records, they wouldn't notice several calls to or from one number.

Hawke sat down at his desk as the two agents exited the conference room followed by Sergeant Spruel. He waited for the agents to leave the area before standing back up and walking to the sergeant's office door.

"Sir, I'm going to go grab some lunch at the Rusty Nail. Then I'll come back and finish the report." He didn't wait for a reply. Hawke headed out the door of the State Police Office, through the ODFW Office, and out to his pickup.

He drove the three blocks to the Rusty Nail and parked in the back. He knew Merrilee, the owner, had a landline phone in the restaurant. He was going to use it to call the cell service store in the county and see if they had a prepaid phone available.

Inside the café there were very few people for a Thursday at noon.

"Where you been hiding, Hawke?" Marilee asked, shuffling along the counter with the coffee pot. Her more than seventy years had caught up to her, hunching her shoulders and causing her to drag her feet. After five years of trying to sell the café, she'd given up and decided to run it until she died. He wouldn't be surprised if the help came in one morning and found her on the floor.

"Up in the mountains," he said, taking his usual spot at the counter.

Merrilee poured him a cup of coffee and stared at his sling. "Looks like you ran into some trouble."

"Yeah, all in a day's work. I'll have a cheeseburger and fries. Can I borrow your phone?"

Merrilee studied him a moment before she nodded

to the phone sitting on the end of the counter. "Knock yourself out."

Hawke walked down to the end of the counter, sat on the last stool, and pulled out his phone. He googled *cell phone store, Alder* and then dialed the number on the café's phone.

"Hello, Updike Phone Store," a man's voice answered.

"Mr. Updike, this is Hawke. Do you have one of those prepaid phones at the store?"

"You're in luck. We have two."

"Could you hold one for Herb or Darlene Trembley to pick up for me?" He knew the man was probably wondering what a State Trooper would want with a prepaid phone, but he wasn't saying anything.

"Sure thing. It will be forty-nine-ninety-nine." The way the man said it was as if he expected Hawke to haggle.

"I'll send Herb or Darlene with fifty bucks." He pushed in the cradle of the phone and dialed Darlene.

"Hello?" she answered on the fourth ring.

"It's Hawke. I ordered a phone from Updike. Could you or Herb pick it up and leave it in my apartment? It's going to cost Fifty—"

She jumped in. "That man knows he's got us over a barrel with the prices he puts on his phones."

He didn't have time to listen to Darlene's argument about how the business owners used their remote location to up their prices. "Darlene, I have to go. Please, don't give him a bad time. I need the phone." Hawke settled the handset into the cradle of the old-style phone as the federal agents stepped through the café door.

He quickly sat down at the counter.

Merrilee came out of the kitchen as the agents sat one on either side of him. He didn't know if they were following him or had come in to eat and decided to sandwich him between them.

The restaurant owner didn't mention his using the phone or the fact he sat in a different spot. She placed his burger and fries in front of him. Her usual curt and cranky self, made the two agent's eyebrows raise as she took their order.

Hoping to eat and leave before the other two received their food, he took a big bite of the burger and stared forward.

No such luck. Dolan spun her stool and faced him. "You know where to find the girl. We need her to put the killer away for good."

Hawke shot a glance at the agent and turned his attention back to his burger. He wasn't going to let her goad him into saying anything.

"What's this woman harassing you for?" Merrilee asked, clattering the agents' plates of food down in front of them.

"He is withholding information." Agent Dolan glared at him and bit into her sandwich.

He was surprised the senior agent was letting Dolan talk so much.

Merrilee scrutinized the woman agent and asked Hawke. "Are these two federal agents?"

"Yes." Hawke smiled at Agent Dolan and picked up his cup of coffee.

One thing he knew for certain, if the residents of Wallowa County knew there were federal agents trying to get information, they would all clam up. It was an independent group of people who lived in this rural area. They didn't take kindly to federal agents or anyone else in any capacity of the government trying to make them do something they didn't want to do. While he didn't want Darlene or Herb to get in trouble for helping him, he had a pretty good idea no one in the county would say a word if they knew the FBI were looking for a young girl. The community would do their best to make sure the feds were given the runaround.

That was one of the things that he knew and enjoyed about this community. They might fight among themselves, but when they had a government entity breathing down their necks, they pulled together.

Chapter Sixteen

Hawke left the Rusty Nail, smiling. Merrilee had the two agents locked in a glare. She wouldn't say a thing about him using the phone and would be sure to let everyone who came to the café know there were federal agents sniffing around.

Back at the office, he opened his document and began typing in the hunt and peck fashion with one hand as he logged in the events as he remembered them. He added in small details that he'd not taken the time to tell the agents.

It was nearing five when he finally finished the report. What would have taken him an hour with two hands, had taken him four. It was a good thing he was on medical leave. Otherwise, he'd always be sitting at his desk trying to write a report if he were on duty.

Because his curiosity got the better of him, he logged into the coroner's report on the bodies. All the information was pretty much what he'd seen and already knew. Except… It appeared different caliber bullets were used. Which could mean more than one shooter. It was unusual for someone to be carrying two different caliber guns. That would mean carrying extra ammunition.

He mentally thumped himself in the head. He'd been so focused on discovering what had happened to the girl, he hadn't paid attention to whether or not there had been more than one visitor to the camp.

Kitree had only seen one person. The man in plaid with long dark hair. The man who'd shot him at the lodge. Had there been someone before him who shot one or the other of the parents, and the man Kitree saw finished off the other one? He needed to speak to Kitree and see how far apart the shots had been, and if the first shooter had been gone before the second one arrived, or if they came together.

The mother hadn't been killed outright. He'd thought that odd given the point-blank shot of the husband. Had they tried to get information out of her before she died?

He called Darlene. "Have you or Herb picked up that phone?"

"Yes, we put it in your apartment like you asked."

"Thank you. I'll be home in an hour. Things been quiet otherwise?" He didn't like to think the feds might be keeping an eye on his landlords.

"All's good."

"Talk to you later." He closed the connection, knowing he should hurry to his place and call Kitree to ask her about the shots. But something else nagged at the back of his mind.

He spent thirty more minutes reading more of the

reports that he could find on the family. He sighed, ignored his throbbing shoulder, and opened the portal to Washington State Department of Motor Vehicles and typed in Ronald Poulson. The address in Walla Walla where they lived came up. No infractions and past history would all be fake, so there was no reason to even go back that far. He typed in Sylvia Poulson. Pretty much the same information. There was no sense thinking about going to Walla Walla and looking around. He was pretty sure the feds would have cleaned up everything by now. But what about Kitree? What did they plan to do with the child?

His cell phone buzzed. He didn't recognize the number.

"Hawke," he answered.

"This is Dani Singer."

His chest tightened as if he'd sucked in air. It was a surprise to have the woman call him. He was pleased and uncomfortable. Not that he minded a woman calling him, but because he knew she wouldn't be happy with having the FBI question her about his whereabouts earlier.

"Hi. You must be down in the valley." Keep it casual and see what she had on her mind.

"Yes. I haven't been back to the lodge yet. No one seems to know if it would be safe."

He heard the exasperation in her voice. She was used to giving orders not waiting around for someone else to make the call.

"My guess is they are down here looking for Kitree." But knowing the men had been seen by everyone who was at the lodge, it might be best for them to all be down here around more people.

"Is she safe?" Dani whispered.

"Yeah."

"I was wondering if you wanted to meet me for dinner at the Firelight?"

After the owner was murdered and his wife sent to prison for his death, the Firelight had a few months where it was closed before someone moved to town and opened it up again.

He glanced at the clock, nearly six. He still needed to go home and call Kitree. "It would have to be late. Like eight." He was used to eating meals at all times of the day and night, but he wasn't sure the regimented ex-military officer would be willing to wait that long.

"I'll see you there at eight." She closed the connection without preamble.

He grinned. That was one of the things he liked about the woman. She got to the point and told you exactly what she thought. No pussy-footing around with her.

A glance at the time on his computer and he turned off his monitor. He headed to the door.

"Did you finish your report?"

The sergeant's voice made him jump. The man had been so quiet all afternoon in his office, Hawke had forgotten he wasn't alone.

"Yes. It's in the system. I'm calling it a night." He put his hat on his head and walked to the door.

"Be careful. Those men could want you dead for seeing them." Sergeant Spruel studied him.

"I'll be careful. Kitree should be safe where Titus put her." He pushed the door open and walked out. He had to keep telling everyone that, so he believed it too. Someone had tipped the killer off about where he and

Kitree were on the mountain.

He walked out to his pickup, started it up, and drove home, watching his rearview mirror for a dark SUV and the feds, or any other vehicle that seemed to be interested in following him. Nothing seemed out of place. He pulled into his spot alongside the barn and stepped out of his pickup.

Dog ran up to him. Hawke scratched the animal's ears, watching his landlord.

Herb climbed down off a tractor. "You're not overdoing things with that shoulder, are you?"

Hawke hadn't thought about his shoulder all afternoon. Now that he did, there was a slight throb. "No. Thanks for getting the phone. I don't want Kitree calling me on my phone in case someone is monitoring my calls in and out." He pulled out his wallet and opened it, using his sore arm to pull out a fifty-dollar bill. "This is for the phone."

Herb pocketed the bill. "No problem. Want Darlene to set another plate for supper?"

"No. I'm going out after I call Kitree." Hawke noticed the man's interest pick up at that comment.

"Alone?"

"No."

Herb grinned. "Who's the lucky lady?"

"I didn't say it was a lady." His friendship with his landlords made them think they needed to know every aspect of his life. Especially, if he was seeing a woman.

"I can tell it is by your actions." Herb twisted away from him and raised his hand. "Have fun."

Hawke shook his head as he climbed the steps to his apartment. A glance at the bed, and he really wanted to settle back on it and forget everything. However, a child's life was at stake and a murderer needed to be caught.

He found the prepaid phone out of the box and charging. He had to admit, he had the best landlords. After reading the directions, he called his friend Justine to make sure it worked and to have her call the number of the prepaid phone to make sure it worked before he called Kitree. Justine worked at the Rusty Nail and had found Dog for him. Even though he'd put her father and sister in jail, she'd remained his friend with no strings attached. He could count on her to help out and not ask questions.

He dialed the number Kitree had called from that morning.

"Hello?" Mrs. Dahlren answered.

"This is Trooper Hawke, Kitree's friend. Could I speak to her?"

"Oh! Just a minute, she's out with the chickens."

Footsteps faded, a woman called, and within minutes running footsteps grew in sound.

"Hawke!" Kitree said, the happiness in her voice made his lips tip into a smile.

"Hi. How are you doing?"

"Okay. I've been playing with the animals." Her voice dropped to a whisper. "The Dahlrens are nice. Kind of like having grandparents, but I miss Momma and Daddy and my friends at school."

"I know you do. Until we catch the man who killed your parents and find out why the FBI is interested in you, we can't get your life back to normal." He understood her sadness. "Get my business card. I want you to write this new phone number down. It's a phone that no one knows I have."

"Okay." The clunk on the line told him she'd put the phone down and her steps faded and returned.

"Ready," she said.

He recited the phone's number. "This is the one you call from now on. Still any time you want to talk."

"Okay. Is that why you called me?"

"That and I also have a question for you. That day, when you were looking for wildflowers and you heard the gun shots... How many shots did you hear, and how much time was between them?" He listened intently, not wanting to miss anything she said.

It was nearly a minute before she said, "I heard two, but I don't know about time. The echo had stopped from the first shot, and a short silence before the second one boomed. Why did you need to know?" Her voice cracked on the last sentence.

A lump stuck in his throat. He didn't want to cause the child anymore pain, but he needed the truth from her if they were going to make her safe. "The report said two different guns killed your parents. That means there were two people there."

She gasped.

He wished he was there, to help her feel safe and to take away the grief she had to be feeling. "You're safe. I promise no one will hurt you."

"Why? Why would anyone want to hurt them?" Her voice was laced with sorrow. She sniffed. He bet tears were trickling down her cheeks.

"I'm trying to figure that out." He hated to ask her more questions, but he had to. She was the only reliable source he had. "Can you remember anything about before you moved to Walla Walla?"

"Momma was gone at work a lot." She made a

155

noise as if wiping her nose. "We went to a Christmas party. There were other kids, but they were from different countries. Some spoke English, but a few didn't. Momma went in a room with a man wearing a white robe." She made a sound almost like a cough. "That night when we got home, Daddy sent me to my room, and I heard them arguing. Daddy said we didn't need the money. I thought maybe that man had offered Momma another job. She was so busy with the one she had, I didn't see how she could do another one."

Hawke pulled the small tablet on his table over and made a note. Her mother either sold out to another country or she had accepted the job to get information for the government. Either way, she'd put herself and her family in jeopardy.

"Where did you live before Walla Walla and what was your last name?" Maybe he could find something in old newspaper files about her mother.

"We lived in Fredrick, Maryland. Daddy taught at the college and Momma drove somewhere. Our last name was Swearen. Daddy hated the new last name." She sniffed. "Even though he didn't like Walla Walla, he said it was better to live there and be safe." Her voice cracked again.

"Thank you. Your answers will help us figure this out." Hawke hated to bring more sadness to the child by asking questions, but she was the only person he could ask besides the FBI, who would never give him information.

To give her hope he said, "They have photos of the men who were at the lodge. It's a matter of time before they find them."

"I'm glad they know who did it." Her voice wasn't

as strong as he'd hoped.

"Do you have grandparents or an aunt or uncle we can let know you're okay?" He had a hard time believing there wasn't any family member who could take the girl. Even on the reservation, there was an extended family member who would step up when a child needed a home.

"The case lady asked me the same thing. I don't remember ever going to see family. And no one came to our house." Kitree's loneliness was evident in her tone.

"I'm on medical leave. I know where you're staying. Let me see what I can do to come see you."

"Really? You'd come visit me?" Her tone perked up.

"I'll give you a call when I figure it out." He shouldn't promise something he wasn't sure would happen, but he wanted to see her as much as she wanted to see him. "I have to go. Dani and I are having dinner together." He wondered at telling the child what he wouldn't tell his longtime landlord.

"Good. I like her, and she likes you."

"How do you know that?" he asked, wondering how the child would know such a thing having only met the woman briefly.

"Because she was worried about you." Her voice had turned to that of an adult.

He laughed. "She was only worried about her lodge."

"Nope. She was worried about you. Have a nice dinner. Come see me soon."

"I will. Bye."

"Bye," she said, soft and sad.

157

The clunk of the phone and buzzing in his ear said she'd hung up first.

He shed his sling, clothing, and bandages and took a quick shower. The bandage he put on his shoulder wasn't as neat looking as the one he'd received at the hospital but it covered the stitches. He slipped his arm into a snap western shirt and put his sling back on. If Kitree thought his meeting Dani for dinner was a good thing, he might as well be presentable.

《》《》《》

He pulled into the Firelight parking lot at 7:45. Not sure if Dani was staying at the Wagon Wheel Motel while remaining away from the lodge or at the place she rented in the winter from a family in Eagle, he had no idea if she'd walked to the restaurant or drove. And if she drove, he had no idea about her vehicle.

The new owner of the restaurant had made the place more family friendly with easier to swallow prices and a menu with comfort food. He walked into the small entrance.

Dani stood up from a bench.

"I was hoping you'd be early. I'm starving," she said, walking over to the hostess.

The woman led them between tables to a small two-person booth. "Will this be okay?"

Hawke scanned the room. There was a four-person booth by the window. "How about that one?"

The woman looked a little put-out, but she led them to the other table. "Your waitress will be with you in a moment."

Dani plopped onto one of the bench seats. "This is roomier."

Hawke eased onto the bench across from her,

making sure he stayed far enough away from the wall to not bang his shoulder. If he'd conceded to the smaller bench, he would have either had his shoulder hitting the wall or hanging out of the booth for people walking by to hit.

"Yes, better for my shoulder." He picked up the menu. He'd only had dinner here once since the new owner took over.

"They don't have the great chocolate cake that the Cusack's had." Disappointment rang in Dani's voice.

"But the prices are better," he said, hoping that would ease her disappointment.

"Price doesn't matter when it is something of quality that you enjoy."

He glanced across the table at the woman. She looked the same as any other time he'd seen her. Short cropped curly hair, showing a bit more gray here and there. Button-up shirt and dress slacks. No make-up. He liked that she was a woman where what you saw was what you got. Nothing hidden.

"You're right." He opened the menu.

Dani leaned across the table and whispered. "How is the girl?"

"She's missing her parents but doing well." Hawke glanced at the door and cringed.

"What's wrong?" Dani twisted her body in the seat to look behind her. "Oh. Them."

Her dislike of the two brought up questions he'd been wanting to ask her. "Are those the two that you told about the ridge?"

She nodded. "They kept telling me it was for your safety for me to tell them."

"What made you tell them?"

From McKinney's hand gestures, he was asking the waitress to seat he and Dolan where they could keep an eye on him.

"They said they knew who killed the husband and wife. That they were hired killers, and you stood a better chance with the FBI helping you than out on your own." She studied his face. "You didn't let them pick you up, did you?"

"When I saw it wasn't your helicopter hovering over the ridge, I grabbed Kitree and we headed off the mountain toward the Grande Ronde Valley. I called Herb, my landlord, to pick us up at Moss Springs Trailhead. Those two landed at the trailhead in the copter and demanded I hand the girl over." He still believed ignoring their demand was the right thing to do.

"Did you? Hand her over?" Dani leaned back as their waitress arrived.

He was happy to see it was one of the women who had waited on him when the restaurant belonged to the previous owner.

"You want separate checks again?" the waitress, Estella, asked.

Hawke groaned. He'd hoped the woman hadn't remembered the only other time he and Dani had eaten in this restaurant together.

"This time I'm paying," Dani said.

Before Hawke could protest, she said, "I owe you for saving us and keeping the lodge from burning down." Her tone was soft, her eyes conveyed she was grateful for his arriving when he had.

"Then I guess she is picking up the tab," he said to the waitress. "I'll have a beer, a steak with baked potato, and a salad, house dressing."

Dani folded her menu. "That sounds good to me, only ranch dressing."

The waitress finished writing, picked up the menus, and strode off toward the kitchen.

"Where were we?" Dani asked, picking up her water glass.

Hawke remembered what she'd asked but pretended like he didn't. "How is everyone? I see the bruises are nearly gone." His gut tightened, knowing the men he'd led to the hunting lodge with his released horses had left bruises and a cut lip on her. He wasn't sure of the damage they'd done to anyone else. Everything had happened so quickly, he'd barely registered the bruises on the others.

She touched her cheek and her eyes darkened. "If I could have gotten to my revolver before they tied us up, I would have killed every one of them."

"Did they hurt your guests? They aren't blaming you, are they?" He remembered the older couple had looked on the frail side for spending a week at a remote hunting lodge.

"Thankfully, they weren't hurt. The men seemed to realize the Bennings didn't have a clue what they were talking about." Her eyes narrowed. "Poor Tyson. He tried to be tough and it got him a couple of punches to the belly. Tuck and Sage knew less about you, but proved to be loyal. Tuck took a couple hits. Thankfully, they didn't knock Sage around. No, me and my hard-assed behavior got me knocked around more than anyone else." She smirked. "But acting like I was the only one who knew anything, kept them from hurting anyone else."

161

He reached across the table and covered her hand. "I'm sorry I let the horses loose. I knew they'd head to the lodge when I sent them on their way. I was thinking, they'd be taken care of. It was afterwards that I'd realized I'd sent trouble to your door."

She squeezed his hand. "We made it through because your conscience came to our aid."

Their drinks arrived. He withdrew his hand and felt the first bit of anxiety over his actions ease.

A glance at the agents and his gut started squeezing again. How had they figured out he was here? Could it be the other agents around the county were keeping tabs on his vehicle instead of looking for the men who wanted him and Kitree dead?

A thought struck him.

He'd check for a transmitter when he arrived home.

Chapter Seventeen

Hawke enjoyed his dinner with Dani. He was glad she'd called. They'd finished their meal and lingered over coffee and dessert, enjoying the fact the agents were getting antsy to leave.

They finally parted about ten.

She drove off in a car she'd purchased to use while in the valley. He was happy to learn she was staying at the place in Eagle where she lived during the winter months. That meant she had people around her who would look out for strangers.

He arrived home close to eleven. Too tired to look for a transmitter when he pulled into his parking spot at the stables, Hawke greeted Dog and the horses before climbing the stairs to his rooms and collapsing.

In the morning, he checked the bed and undercarriage of his vehicle. A small magnetic transmitter was stuck to the undercarriage. The electronic device had to have been placed there by the

FBI. Giving them information about everywhere he
went. He chuckled at their thinking they'd outsmarted
him.

He fed the animals and cleaned out their stall the
best he could with one arm. With two weeks off work,
he wasn't sure what to do with his time other than go
online and see what he could find out about Sylvia
Swearen. Using his work laptop from his work vehicle,
he tried finding information about her on the Maryland
DMV records, but the government had wiped any trace
of her existence clean.

Next, he started googling her past name and finally
found a couple of newspaper articles.

The articles talked about how she'd been a crucial
witness against an arms dealer. That her meticulous
record keeping had discovered a military officer selling
arms to the countries who paid him the most.

He googled the officer and discovered he had ties
with a country known for terrorism. That wasn't good
news. Had he put a hit out on the woman, and they'd
just found her after a year and a half?

It didn't make sense. But not much about the whole
murder made sense. Why kill the father? They could
have killed Mrs. Poulson when the father was at work
and the daughter at school. Why did they pick a time
when the family was camping in a remote area? Had
they used the husband as leverage to get her to talk?
That made sense with the two bullets. One person
would have had a gun pointed at the husband and told
her to talk. She didn't and the husband was killed.

Had she lured them into the tent with a lie about
having information with her? Then they shot her in a
way they could ask her questions and leave her to die a

slow lingering death. Did she answer their questions?

He pushed the computer to the side and stared at the table.

Hawke wished he could get his hands on Mrs. Poulson's laptop but knew it had to be in the hands of the FBI by now.

He pulled his computer back in front of him and began looking up more information in the papers about the situation that put the Swearen family in Witness Protection.

His eyes grew bleary and his stomach grumbled several hours later. He still needed to do something with the transmitter he'd found on his vehicle.

"Come on, Dog. Let's go for a ride and get something to eat." Hawke closed his computer and grabbed his pickup keys.

"Afternoon Hawke. Looks like you're taking your medical leave seriously," Darlene said from where she leaned against the arena railing, watching a young woman ride.

"The shoulder has to heal before I can go back to work and the best way for it to heal is if I rest." Even though his landlords knew about Kitree, he wouldn't tell them anything he'd learned. That way they weren't dragged into the mess so far they could get hurt.

"Sounds good. Where are you headed now?" Her concern was something he'd come to appreciate about the woman.

"Find something to eat and take a drive." He grinned and headed to his pickup.

Dog leaped into the bed of the vehicle, and Hawke closed the tailgate.

The transmitter sat on the dash where he'd put it

after finding the small device. He planned to find a vehicle in town that moved around a lot, like a delivery truck or a mail carrier and put the device on it. That would keep the FBI busy until they figured out he'd found their device.

He headed to Alder.

《》《》《》

Kitree was at the barn currying the small horse Mr. Dahlren called Sweetie. The man had told her if she curried the horse and got all the knots out of her mane and tail, he'd saddle her up and let Kitree ride. She'd been on horses twice in her life, once when she and her parents had been on vacation and riding around with Hawke.

A car drove in the driveway. Kitree unhooked the rope from the halter of the horse and went up into the small loft of the barn. She'd discovered it gave a good view of the house.

Two men got out of the car. Her hands started to shake. The one had hair like she'd seen on the man who'd walked over the rim at the lake.

Her feet were moving before her brain kicked in. She descended the ladder and landed on the hard-packed earth in the barn. There were close neighbors up and down the county road, but Mr. Dahlren had said there was a neighbor behind them a couple of miles. He was like a hermit who lived in the forest. She'd take her chances with him over the two men.

She crouched low to the ground, jogging alongside one of the fences to a small canyon. Once she was in the canyon, she stood up and ran, until she found what she hoped was the fence line of the neighbor's property. She hoped the hermit would ask questions before

166

shooting.

《》《》《》

Hawke drove through the Shake Shack and collected a burger and shake. He planned to take it to the lake and have a quiet picnic with Dog and maybe take the tram up to the top of Mt. Howard. He always did his best thinking when he was in the mountains and that was the easiest way to get there. It would also give him a chance to see if someone was following him, besides the FBI. He'd already tossed the transmitter into a parcel delivery truck that would be headed out of the valley by nightfall.

If someone followed him up the mountain, it would be a person working for the people who wanted Kitree dead.

His phone buzzed as he drove to the lake.

"Hawke."

"Hawke, this is Lieutenant Titus. I read the FBI reports of their visit to the Poulson house in Walla Walla. Someone had ransacked the place. If they didn't find what they were looking for at the house, or with the parents, you know where they are looking next."

"Yeah. Thanks." He hung up on the lieutenant. His gut felt as if someone had punched him with a two hundred pound sledgehammer. What could Kitree have that the people wanted? And did she even know she had something?

She'd been open about everything with him. He had a feeling she didn't know. He'd gone through the backpack she said was her mother's. As he parked alongside the street, sipping his shake, eating his burger, and contemplating what Mrs. Poulson could have had that so many others wanted, his prepaid phone rang.

"Kitree, I was just—"

"Hawke! They came. I ran. I need you." The fear in her voice stalled all his actions.

"Where are you?"

"I ran to the man behind the Dahlrens. He doesn't have a phone. He brought me to the post office in Imbler. They let me use the phone."

"I'll come pick you up. Stay there." Hawke put his pickup in gear and pulled onto the street. He dialed Lt. Titus. "You need someone to check on the Dahlrens. Kitree called. The men showed up there. She's safe. I'm picking her up and taking her where there is no paper trail." He hung up and headed out of Alder at a normal speed. He didn't need anyone watching him to see him speeding. He knew where he would take the girl. The problem was making sure no one followed him.

He was on leave. No reason he couldn't go stay a few days with his mother at the reservation. But he'd have to say he'd dislocated his shoulder. His mom thought his being a game warden kept him safe from killers and lunatics. He couldn't let her know he'd been shot by a person who wanted to kill the girl he was taking to stay with her.

He drove to his place and went in to pack a couple sets of clothes. He also used this time to dial his mom's number.

"Hello?" her voice was still as active as she was at seventy-one.

"Mom, it's Gabriel. I'm on medical leave—"

"Medical leave? What happened?" Worry laced her question.

"I dislocated my shoulder and can't work for a

week. Thought I'd come visit." He didn't mind telling her a white lie to ease her worry.

"You know you can come any time. You don't have to be hurt to come visit." Her worry had turned accusatory.

He didn't visit near as often as he should, but he showed up on her doorstep more than his sister who was ten years younger than him. "I'm bringing someone with me."

"A woman? You finally found one your mother will approve of?" She laughed.

He grinned. Ever since his divorce, his mother had been after him to remarry. She didn't understand he was happy with his life. "Yes, I think you will approve, but she's too young for me to marry."

"I raised you better." There was the accusatory tone.

"She's ten and just lost her parents. She needs a place to stay while we sort things out." That was all he planned to tell her. Best she didn't know more than that. Less chance of anything getting out to the wrong people.

"The poor child. Of course, bring her over. We'll keep her busy while you find her family." She said something that was muffled. "I'll get your sister's room ready for her. When will you be here?"

"My plan is to be there by dinner tonight."

"I'll add more broth to the stew." She closed the connection.

He knew she'd be cleaning his sister's room and worrying she didn't have enough food for the meal. But she often invited the single parents of the children she watched to have dinner with her. There was always enough food cooking on her stove for several people.

Hawke grabbed his bag and headed out the door. Jogging down the steps caused his arm to throb. He slowed his pace as his mind raced. It would be better to use a different vehicle. There was a good chance his was being watched.

"Stay," he told Dog and climbed back into his truck. He'd call the Trembley's later and ask them to feed his animals.

Driving out the lane to the main road, he dialed Justine.

"Hawke, this going to be a longer conversation than the other night?" Justine answered.

"I've been busy."

"So I've heard."

He heard dogs barking in the background. She was home.

"I need to borrow a vehicle for a few days." Involving one more person was adding to his conscience. Kitree's safety came first. Justine was the only person he knew besides the Trembley's, who the FBI were also watching, who would loan him a vehicle, no questions asked.

"I can only spare the car. I need the truck to take a horse to the vet."

He started to open his mouth to say she could use his truck but that would put her in the crosshairs of the people he was trying to avoid. "That will work. I'll be at your place in ten."

Ending the call, he pressed down a bit more on the accelerator. He knew the longer it took him to get to Kitree the more frightened she would be. Luckily, Justine's was only a little out of his way.

Chapter Eighteen

Hawke pulled up to the Imbler Post Office and stepped out of the silver sedan. He didn't like cars. They were too small, but he didn't have a choice at this point. Entering the building, he noted the small section of locked boxes and moved into the area where the post person stood behind a counter. He didn't see Kitree.

"I'm looking for the girl who—"

A door opened and a small body hit him from behind. "You came."

He spun and knelt, hugging the child's shaking body. "I told you I would." He stood. "Thank you for letting her call me and watching her."

"She was so scared. I felt it was right," the woman in her forties said. "If old Sherman hadn't brought her here, I would have been more hesitant. That she conveyed to him her trouble, I knew it had to be something bad."

Hawke didn't like the way the woman was going

on. "If anyone asks, you didn't see her." He studied the woman for several minutes until she nodded.

"Come on." He led Kitree out the door.

"Where's your truck?" she asked.

"I borrowed a friend's car so no one would follow me."

"Good idea."

He opened the passenger door, and she crawled in. Hawke dropped into the driver's seat and the car shook.

"Wow! You shook the whole thing." Kitree giggled.

"I don't like cars. They don't like me." He glanced over at the market. "Are you hungry?"

"Yes."

"Tell me what you like. I'll go in and get some food. But I want you to remain in the car. No sense anyone else around here seeing you."

She rattled off what she liked as he parked the car beside the market. Hawke locked the vehicle and went inside. He came back out with two bags of snack food and drinks.

"It looks like we're going camping with all this food," Kitree said, opening a bag and pulling out the bag of potato chips.

"No camping."

He turned back the way he'd come.

"Are we going where you live?" Kitree asked between munching on chips.

"I'm taking you to stay with my mom at the reservation." He glanced over at her. She didn't have any clothes but the dirty ones she had on. He'd take her to the store in Pendleton and get her a couple sets.

"The reservation? Like with Indians... I mean

Native Americans?" Her cheeks deepened in color.

He nodded. "You can call us American Indians or Natives, either one works. Don't worry, no one will scalp you."

She hit his arm with her fist. "I know that. I've just never been around...other than you."

"We're all the same. Didn't you see my blood was red, just like yours?"

"We are the same that way, but you live or lived differently. I don't want to upset anyone. Daddy always said that when you are among people of other cultures, you should try and copy what they do to not offend them by doing something stupid."

"That's a good thought, but it would make them wonder at your copying them. They could think you were trying to mimic them to make them look funny." He'd had that experience in middle school with a non-Indian classmate. One kid thought it was funny to mimic anything he did, whether it had to do with his culture or not. It wasn't funny.

Kitree was watching him when he glanced over at her. "Did you have a lot of bullying when you were in school?" she asked.

How the conversation shifted to him in school, he wasn't sure. "Yes. Mostly because I came from the reservation and was Indian."

"But you're a big man. Were you small as a child?"

"Any size person can be bullied if the words sting so much they make you paralyzed." He glanced over again. "Do you understand?"

She nodded. "Yes."

"Did your mom ever ask you to keep anything for her?" He needed to find out what the people wanted so

173

badly they were willing to keep killing to get it. Lt. Titus had called him on his way to pick up Kitree. Mr. Dahlren had suffered a fatal blow to the head. Mrs. Dahlren had been taken by ambulance to the Grand Ronde Hospital. Anyone hiding Kitree wouldn't be safe. However, he believed the reservation was the best place to hide her.

"No. Why?" She twisted her body sideways and watched him.

He wasn't sure whether to tell her what he suspected or just tell her the facts. He opted for the facts. "Someone tore up your house in Walla Walla looking for something. And when I found your mom inside the tent, it looked like a hurricane had landed inside. Didn't you notice that?"

She shrugged. "Momma was packing. I didn't really look around except to find water, the map, and things that would keep me warm." Kitree was quiet for nearly a mile before saying, "You think I might have whatever they are looking for?"

"I believe it's what the men who are after you think."

"The only thing I have with me that has always been mine are my two books." She pulled the *My Side of the Mountain* guide book and the wildflower book out of the back pockets of her pants.

"Do you mind if I take a look at them when we get to my mom's house?"

"No. I don't see how they can be what anyone is looking for. They're just books."

He sighed. "There are more witnesses to their cruelty than just you. They don't seem to care the people who were at the lodge saw them. They only seem to want to get their hands on something your mom had. I think it's the same with the FBI. They don't care about your well-being, only whatever it is the others want."

She wrapped her arm closest to him around his upper arm. "You're the only one who cares that I stay alive." A second later she added, "You, Dani, and Sage."

He grinned. "My landlords, Herb and Darlene. The officers I work with. There are lots of people who want to keep you safe. Including my mother and her friends. You won't have anything to worry about at the reservation."

"I believe you."

She untangled their arms and leaned back in the seat.

Hawke picked the less traveled route over Tollgate Pass to come into the north side of the reservation. There was less chance of anyone seeing them. He'd really wanted to stop and stretch his legs. He could drive all day in his pickup, but this small car was cramping all of his muscles. Stopping might wake Kitree, and she needed sleep. It would also make it easier for anyone who happened to find out where he'd gone to inquire about them along the way.

《》《》《》

It was still light out when Hawke pulled into the driveway of his mother's house. But it was late enough all of the children she watched during the week days had been picked up by their parents.

Kitree sat upright, staring out the window.

"Not what you were expecting?" he asked, shutting the car off.

She shook her head and shrugged. "I don't know what I was expecting."

Hawke laughed. "Come on. Mimi is going to like your candidness."

The girl smiled at him and opened her door, walking up the dirt path to the one-story house.

Hawke stood and stretched before grabbing his duffel bag out of the back seat. He'd give his mom money to take Kitree clothes shopping tomorrow.

"Welcome," his mom said, putting a hand on Kitree's head and staring into her eyes. "You are a strong girl. We will get on well." She glanced at him over the child's head and smiled. "I especially like you, because you have brought my son for a visit."

Kitree giggled.

Hawke ushered the two into the house with his full hand. "I was here not that long ago."

"Only for a couple of hours. From the bag you carry, you will be staying a day or more?" she said it as a question, giving him the option to fill her in.

"I will stay two nights. Possibly three. I would like Kitree to stay with you until I come back and get her." He peered into his mother's eyes. "She has no family and isn't safe until we catch the man who took her family from her."

His mom closed her eyes briefly and her lips moved. She glanced down at Kitree and smiled. "We will have good times."

"Mom, this is Kitree." He motioned to the girl. "Kitree, this is my mom. You can call her Mimi. All the people, even the children, on the reservation call her that."

Kitree ducked her head and asked, "Does the word

mean anything?"

"It is my given name," Mom said and grinned.

Kitree giggled.

"Come along. We'll set dinner on the table." His mother took Kitree by the hand and led her into the kitchen.

《》《》《》

Kitree liked Mimi, Hawke's mom. She talked about the food she'd prepared as they set the table and put the dishes on the table.

"Did you help your mother with meals?" Mimi asked.

"No. Momma didn't like to cook." Kitree placed the bowl of green beans that the woman handed her on the table.

"I see. What did your mother do?" The woman asked it in a way that sounded as if she didn't like Momma. She'd never met her, so how could she not like her?

"She worked on the computer, though she wasn't supposed to be working anymore." Kitree thought about all the times her mom was locked in the office and she had to make her own lunch or get a snack. What had she been doing in there?

Mimi smoothed Kitree's brow with her gnarled finger. "Go get Gabriel for dinner."

The name caught her by surprise. "Gabriel? You mean Hawke?"

The older woman nodded. "His name is Gabriel Gray Hawke, but he prefers Hawke. Why he would want to be called a bird that eats rodents, I don't understand."

Kitree giggled at the woman's words and wandered

177

through the kitchen door to the living room. She found Hawke staring at his phone.

"Are you coming in to eat?" she asked from the doorway.

"I'm coming." Hawke slid his finger across the screen of his phone and stood.

She liked Hawke and his mom. This was the first place she'd felt safe. She hoped Hawke and his officer friends found the man, but if she had to stay here for a while, that would be okay, too.

《》《》《》

Hawke walked to the kitchen and inhaled the aroma of stew. He wasn't sure what his mom put in it, but no one else's ever smelled the same. He'd used her recipe on several occasions and it still didn't have the same smell or flavor. He had a feeling she would go to her grave with the secret of her stew.

"Look! Indian fry bread. I've heard of it but never had any." Kitree sat at the side of the table, her eyes wide and bright.

Mom sat at the end nearest the stove. He took the end opposite her. She'd insisted that was his place ever since his drunken stepfather died.

They said a blessing over the food and dug in.

"Mom, you make the best stew," Hawke said, ladling out his second helping.

"It is good." Kitree said, holding her bowl up for more.

His mother smiled and put another spoonful into the girl's bowl. "I'm glad you like it. You said your mother didn't know how to cook. Do you?"

Kitree shook her head. "I wasn't allowed in the kitchen."

"Tsk, tsk. Everyone should learn how to cook food. You can't eat at a restaurant or a friend's house all the time. If you learn to hunt and cook, you will never go hungry." Mom glared at him as if it was his fault the girl didn't know how to cook.

"She knows what plants are edible," he said, to deflect his mother's disapproval.

"I do! I have a book that I use to find the edible plants. I even started a notebook with the plants I've found." Kitree started to rise out of her chair and stopped. Her face sagged with sadness. "My notebook was left in my backpack. I don't know where it is."

"It's at Herb and Darlene's. They are holding the things you came off the mountain with at their house."

"They are!" Her face lit up. "If I'd lost that notebook, I'd have to start all over. It's taken me two years to find the flowers I have in it."

"When it's safe, I'll take you up to the hunting lodge and Sage can help you finish your flower gathering." The look his mom gave him made him realize what he'd just promised the girl. That he'd escort her up the mountain and that a woman he barely knew would help her. Another mental slap. He really needed to get a good night's sleep and rethink his relationship with this child.

Mom said, "Eat."

Hawke knew her command was directed at both of them. But mainly him to keep his mouth busy and not say something stupid again.

Kitree dug into her second helping of stew and told his mother about the plants she'd found up on the mountains.

"Did you know that my great-grandfather hunted in

those mountains?" Mom said, when Kitree had finished.

"No. What did he hunt?"

Hawke grinned as his mother repeated two of the stories she'd told him over and over again as a child. How the land had come to the Nimiipuu, the name the Nez Perce called themselves.

"Wow. I didn't know that. We don't learn very much about Indians in school." Kitree set her fork down.

"It's a shame. The American Indian has a rich history that could teach others how to live better." Mom stood and started stacking the dishes.

"Let me help," Hawke said, carrying his share of the dishes to the sink.

"You go settle Kitree in your sister's room." Mom started the water running in the sink.

He'd offered to buy her a dishwasher several times, but she'd always refused, saying the day she couldn't wash dishes was the day she should be buried in the ground.

"She doesn't have any clothes. Only what she has on. I'll give you money to take her shopping tomorrow."

Kitree dropped her head, peering at the floor. She was ashamed of her state.

"I would love to take her shopping with your money," his mother joked. She faced Kitree. "For tonight, there are several t-shirts Miriam left here. You can use one for a nightgown." She smiled. "And I'm sure we can find you a fun outfit to wear to town."

Kitree smiled at his mom as if she'd just given her a kitten.

"Come on." He waved Kitree ahead of him, out of the kitchen and down the hall to the bedrooms. His sister's was beside his. Mom's and the bathroom were on the other side of the hall.

Hawke wasn't sure the last time his sister had been home to visit. Some of her photos and stuffed animals from her childhood still sat on shelves. The bed spread was the same horse covered one that she'd worked at the Dairy Queen the summer between her seventh and eighth grade to purchase. The room was clean and ready for the guest.

"You can dig around for a t-shirt and take a shower across the hall. Towels are on the shelves," he said.

Kitree studied the room. "Do you think I should look around? It's not my room."

He walked to the closet door. He wasn't sure what was behind the door. It could be all his sister's childhood possessions or it could be empty. He pulled the door open and discovered boxes with labels. It appeared all of his sister's belongings that weren't scattered about the room were in the closet. "Try the dresser for a t-shirt."

"Does your sister come home often?" Kitree asked, staring at a photo sitting on the dresser of Miriam when she was about twelve.

Miriam wore regalia for a powwow dance competition. That seemed like more than one lifetime away.

"No. She lives farther away than I do and only comes home about once every five years." He put a hand on Kitree's shoulder. "You can stay here as long as it takes for us to make sure you're safe."

She nodded. "I bet your mom misses her."

"She does. But trying to talk Miriam into coming home is like trying to talk a bear out of eating berries. They have their minds set on what they think is best for them and don't listen."

"I'm glad you come see your mom. She would be sad otherwise." Tears glimmered in the child's eyes.

"I know. That's why I come as much as I can and call often." He released her shoulder. "And now she has you. You can come see her whenever you want after this is over."

Her eyes lit up. "Really? I can come see her and you?"

He gave her a hug. "We wouldn't have it any other way."

"What is this?" Mom walked into the room and gathered Kitree into her arms. "Tomorrow after we get you some clothes, we will give your parents a proper good-bye. Tonight," she opened the dresser and pulled out a pink t-shirt with horses running across it, "you take a shower, put this on, and I'll have ice cream waiting."

"I'm going out for a walk." Hawke walked out of the room. For the thousandth time in his life, he was thankful for his mother.

He knew most of the people living in the neighborhood. They had all lived here when he was growing up. If not the parents of the kids he played with, it was the children. Few made it off the reservation. Some because they wanted to stay immersed in their culture and make the reservation better and others because they couldn't get out of the booze, drugs, and abuse cycle.

Hawke wasn't surprised to find a schoolmate and

now a tribal policeman inspecting his, or rather, Justine's car.

"Randy. It's been a while." Hawke stuck out his good hand to shake.

Randy Toombs studied him a moment then smiled. "Hawke. Since when did you start driving vehicles registered to women?" He glanced over Hawke's shoulder. "Did you finally bring a woman home to meet Mimi?"

Just what he didn't need, gossip he had a woman getting to his mom's ears. "I borrowed it from a friend." Hawke walked toward the tribal vehicle and further out of range of the house and anyone who might walk out.

Randy followed and leaned against his SUV. "Why are you borrowing a friend's vehicle?" He nodded to the arm in a sling. "Someone after you?"

Hawke shook his head. "Not me. I brought a young girl whose parents were murdered in the Eagle Cap—"

"I heard about that. You're the officer who was taking everyone on a chase?" He grinned.

"Yeah. It was me. I turned the girl over to State Police. Child Services…"

Randy snorted. "I can figure what happened there."

Hawke finished, "Put her up with an ex-state trooper. But the people looking for her must have access to state records. They showed up. Luckily Kitree was in the barn, saw them, and headed to the neighbor in the back. She talked him into driving her to a phone and she called me." He glanced toward his mom's house. "I brought her here. Any chance you can up surveillance in this area?"

The Tribal Policeman nodded. "That's how I spotted this unknown car. We have cameras up around here. There's been increased vandalism. I can also patrol around more often and give the others a head's up."

"Thanks, Randy. That will make me feel better. I'm only staying a couple nights. I'm on medical leave but want to stay up to date on what the Feds and State Police find out."

Randy whistled. "Feds. You got yourself in something big."

"Unfortunately. All I care about is finding the man who killed Kitree's parents and keeping her safe." Hawke pushed away from the Tribal vehicle he'd leaned against. "Here's my number to let me know what you see or hear." He handed the officer his business card and scribbled his throw-away cell phone number on the back. "Use this number."

"Will do. Be careful." He pointed to the sling and opened the vehicle's door.

"You bet." Hawke strode back to the house. Kitree and his mom were talking quietly in the kitchen. He had a pretty good idea they were conversing over chocolate ice cream.

He sat down in the living room and used his phone's hotspot to get online with his computer. Another try to discover more about the Swearen family before they were relocated seemed important. There had to be something that would give him a clue as to what the killer was after. If he knew that, it would be easier to find.

Another thought struck him. I'm only forty-five miles from Walla Walla. I'll go over there tomorrow and look around.

Chapter Nineteen

The short drive to the area where the Swearen/Poulson's lived was pleasant. Hawke hadn't told his mother or Kitree where he was going. Only, out.

As he drove up the street in front of the Poulson home, he had a feeling this wasn't a neighborhood that looked out for one another. All the shades were drawn, the lawns vacant of toys or anything that showed a family lived in the houses all built from the same house plan. Here and there a car sat on the parking area in front of a closed garage door. There were no extra cars along the street, until he drew closer to the Poulson house.

He opted to turn the block before rather than pass by the two vehicles staking out the house. Assuming they were the FBI and the local police, he didn't want to get into a conversation with them if they believed he was interested in the house.

This tract neighborhood had houses backing up to other houses without alleys in between. He judged which house was most likely to be backed up to the Poulson house and parked in front.

Unsure whether to use his badge or come up with a cover, he watched as the door opened. A woman in her fifties, with short blonde hair and dark roots, came out with a small, curly-haired, white dog on a leash. She turned from locking the door and spotted him. Her eyes narrowed, and she came down the sidewalk toward him like a guinea hen running off an intruder.

"You can move on. I don't buy anything that isn't off a store shelf. You door to door salesmen are all a bunch of con-artists." She punched her fisted hands on her ample hips and glared at him.

"I'm not here to sell you anything, Ma'am." To unruffle her imaginary feathers, he pulled out his badge. "I have a few questions about the neighbors who lived behind you."

She sucked in air as her dog sniffed his boots. "Oh, it's just terrible. Those two nice people getting killed and their daughter...I hope she's okay. She was the only one in the family who would visit over the fence." She motioned to the sidewalk. "I need to take Princess for a walk. I can talk to you as we walk."

He nodded and fell into step beside her. "Has anyone else been around asking questions?"

She nodded. "The local police and an FBI man." She wrinkled her nose. "He was kind of snooty. Asked stupid questions I couldn't answer."

This intrigued Hawke. "What kind of questions?"

"Did I know what Mrs. Poulson did all day? Did she spend time in the backyard?" The woman stopped.

"I don't know what she did all day. She was in the house. I know whenever I was out watering my yard or working in my flower beds, the only one outside was the girl. The father barbequed now and then and mowed the lawn, but the little girl tended the flowers."

She nodded. "That's usually what we talked about over the fence. I'd notice she'd have some unusual plant. She'd say it was edible or used for something."

Hawke grinned. It appeared the curious botanist grew the plants in her books. "I see. Do you know if anyone in the neighborhood was friends with the family?"

The fluffy dog squatted on the closest area of cut grass.

They stopped.

"I wouldn't know who went in and out the front door, but like I told the others, I never saw anyone other than family in the backyard." The woman pulled out a small plastic bag and picked up the little logs her dog had left on the lawn.

He liked responsible dog owners.

She tied the bag of dog poo to the middle of the leash and said, "You might talk with Sarah Riddle. She lives across the street and one door down from the Poulson's. She might have seen who went in and out."

"Thank you." He pivoted back the way they'd come and had a thought. Spinning back around, he asked, "Is there a gate between your backyard and the Poulson's?"

She studied him. "If you're a policeman, why don't you walk in the front door?"

The truth was always the best way to go. "Because I'm the only policeman who cares about the safety of the daughter. I'm trying to figure out why the parents were killed and find the person who did it, so she can come out of hiding."

The woman's eyes widened. "You mean whoever killed her parents wants her dead, too?"

"Yes. And if you liked her as you said, it would help her to let me use your backyard to get into the Poulson house." He studied her. Would she do as he asked, or would she call the police to arrest him for trespassing once he entered the home?

"Come on. I wouldn't want to be the one with the death of the whole family on my conscience." The woman spun around and marched down the sidewalk and up to her house. "Come in."

He followed her into the home only a few square feet larger than his mom's home. It was just as neat and tidy, but more updated furniture. He held his hat in his good hand.

The woman unleashed her dog and straightened. She held out a hand. "Dorothy Bergman."

He switched his hat to the other hand and shook. "Hawke."

She raised a dark penciled eyebrow but didn't say anything as she led him to the sliding glass door. Beyond the door was a yard full of color. She had every flower he'd ever seen in gardens overflowing the borders of the lawn and a few circles in the middle.

"You have a way with plants," he said, stepping out onto the small cobblestone patio.

She shrugged and held her hand out. "You'll need this."

He glanced down at the key in her hand. "What's this?"

"The key to the Poulson's back door."

"How do you have it?"

She shrugged. "Neighbors give keys to neighbors in case of a problem. Kitree must have told Mr. Poulson we talked over the fence. He came over one day and gave me the key in case something ever happened."

Hawke studied the woman. There was more to what she was telling him. But he wouldn't have to worry about breaking and entering with the key. After he checked out the house, he'd have a deeper conversation with Mrs. Bergman.

He put his hat on his head, took the key, and walked across the lawn. The scents of all the flowers blending in the warmth of the mid-day sun made his eyes and nose water. Holding his breath, he found the gate, unlatched it from both sides, and walked through. He strode up to the sliding door, exactly like the one in the house on the other side of the fence, and unlocked it.

Quietly, he slid the door open and stepped inside. The stench of garbage replaced the sickening sweet scent of the neighbor's garden. It was dark, with all the curtains and shades pulled. That would keep the people sitting in front of the house from seeing him looking around.

His initial thought, scanning the dining room and kitchen, was how would he notice anything out of place in this mess. Whoever had ransacked the place hadn't cared about others knowing. The items in the kitchen cupboards had been shoved onto the floor. Drawers hung open and empty. Some even added to the debris on the floor.

One look under the sink revealed the person had

even unscrewed the pipes and looked in those. What would fit in a drain pipe? An SD card, flash drive, microchip. What had Mrs. Poulson been involved in?

Even the contents of the refrigerator were on the floor. No one had cleaned it up. It and the garbage dumped beside the waste basket accounted for the disgusting smell.

The glass and fancy dishes that had once been housed in the china hutch were in pieces on the floor in front of it. This hadn't just been someone looking for something, it had been someone angry that they were coming up emptyhanded.

He moved into the living room. Same rage and items flung everywhere. A photo of the family hung sideways on the wall. Hawke straightened it and pulled out his phone. He took a photo of the family portrait. He'd print it out for Kitree. He didn't know what would happen to all the items in the house once the police released the property.

Walking down the hallway, he stepped around notebooks with papers exploding out of them. He crouched and picked up a paper. It appeared to be class syllabuses. Mr. Poulson must have kept them at home rather than at the college. Or was working on them here.

In the office, books had been pulled off the shelves, rifled through and thrown in a corner. The wires for a computer sat on the desk. No computer in sight. It would have been the obvious piece to have the information. He wondered if they'd determined it didn't have the information and came back, or if they'd continued searching anyway?

The drawers to the wooden desk had been pulled

out and smashed. Were they looking for a secret compartment? He felt along the underside of the desk edges. Nothing.

He was still unclear what he or the intruders were looking for. All the photo frames were smashed. He picked up a small photo of the family. It looked like from a trip to get a Christmas tree. He put that in his breast pocket.

This room like the others had been thoroughly tossed.

The master bedroom and bath had also been trashed. The mattress seams slit. Whoever did this had to have been in here for hours. Had they come in as soon as the family left for the camping trip? And when they couldn't find what they were looking for went after the woman?

He stepped into Kitree's room. He nearly doubled over as if punched in the gut. Her belongings had been just as violated as the rest of the house. The stuffing of her mattress and animals had exploded over her belongings. The cover was ripped and mounds of cotton fluff strewn about the room. He wondered if he dared take any of her belongings. Mrs. Bergman would know he had contact with the girl if he walked back to her house with something. Best to leave it be for now. He saw a pile of books on the floor by a small bookcase.

Kneeling in front of the pile, he picked them up one by one. The hardcover books had the pages ripped out of them. One book caught his eye. It was the exact same wild flower book as Kitree had on the trip. Had she inadvertently been given two of the same book?

He didn't see anything that would help him learn more about what he was looking for. He, the FBI, and the suspects were following an elusive trail. The mouse trail.

His next step would be to talk to people at the college.

Hawke left the house, locked it, and hurried across the lawn and into the backyard of Mrs. Bergman.

She met him at her sliding door. "Did you learn anything?"

Her curiosity set his senses on alert. "No. Whoever killed the Poulson's must have ransacked the house."

It was telling that the woman didn't seem surprised.

"I took the liberty of asking Mrs. Riddle over for coffee." Mrs. Bergman studied him. "You can ask her anything you want while I get the coffee."

Mrs. Bergman ducked into the small kitchen. A woman in her sixties sat at the dining room table, her gaze assessing him.

He took off his hat.

"Dorothy said you were interested in the Poulsons." This woman was tall, thin, and sat in the chair as if she had a broomstick for a backbone. Her hair was gray with strands of brunette swirling in the curls.

"What can you tell me about them?" he asked, taking the seat across from her.

"Not much. They stayed to themselves. I don't think the woman cooked. Different restaurants that delivered food would arrive during the week days. The man and the girl would haul bags of groceries into the house on Saturdays."

"Did you ever see the mother go anywhere?" he asked.

"Only as a family. She never left the house during the day alone."

Mrs. Bergman carried in three mugs of coffee. "I'll get sugar and cream." She hurried back into the kitchen and returned, taking a seat to Hawke's right.

When she put a spoon into the sugar, Hawke studied her hand. She wasn't as old as her hair and puffy, sagging body indicated. He was sure the other woman was in her sixties, but he had a feeling Mrs. Bergman was closer to forty than fifty.

"Why were you two watching the Poulsons? Who had the wife pissed off and what did she do for the government that the family was watched over?" He sipped his coffee and watched the two exchange a look.

"I don't know what you're talking about," Mrs. Bergman said, raising her cup to her lips.

Hawke grinned. "Fine. No sense you getting in trouble for telling me secrets." He wiped the grin off his face and stared at both of them. "I intend to find the son-of-a-bitch who killed Kitree's parents and make sure no one ever comes after her again. You can tell that to whoever you work for."

He drained the cup, placed his hat back on his head, and walked out of the house. He'd bet Jack and Horse that the two women were U.S. Marshals sent to keep an eye on the family. They screwed up. He wondered what they were going to do about it.

Chapter Twenty

Hawke parked in the main parking lot of Penrose House at Whitman College. He remembered it as the admissions building from a couple of times, years ago, when he was dating his ex-wife. She'd attended the college when he'd met her.

He walked through the doors. Even though the attendees were diverse, heads swiveled and watched him walk up to the receptionist.

"May I help you?" The woman was close to his age with narrow glasses that sat on the end of her nose and a beaded chain hanging down from either side of her head.

"I was wondering if you could point me in the direction of the math department?" he asked politely and not smiling enough to make her think he was up to something.

"Are you a student or a parent of a student?" she asked.

"No." He didn't want to give away who he was and why he was here, but she had the look of a prosecutor he'd had to face during a trial. Hawke reached into his pocket for his badge and leaned close to the open window the woman sat behind. "I'm here investigating Professor Poulson." He glanced behind him and back at her. "But we don't want to upset any of the students. It is mandatory to check into victim's habits and such in this type of case."

The woman put a hand to her mouth and then stood up, leaning closer to him. "I heard it was murder. He and the Mrs. were shot."

"I can't confirm anything. I'd just like to talk to his co-workers." Hawke kept his voice low. "And I'd appreciate no one, other than your dean and the people I talk to, know I've been here."

She narrowed her eyes. "Do you think it was one of us?"

"No. Of that I'm sure. I just need some information to help the investigation."

His statement seemed to appease her. She nodded and picked up a brochure. "This is Olin Hall. It's where the Math Department is housed. I can call and have Professor Ling meet you at the entrance. It's finals week. They don't like distractions in the buildings."

"That's a good idea. Tell him I'm just asking questions about Poulson's schedule and any family questions they can answer. No one is a suspect." He wanted to make sure he had everyone's cooperation.

"I'll tell her. She'll understand." The receptionist picked up the phone.

He left the building.

After figuring out what direction he needed to go,

he set out across the grassy campus. There were a few students in groups and others milling around, but it didn't seem as crowded as he remembered when he'd come to pick up Bernie.

At Olin Hall, Hawke scanned the three-story brick building. The aesthetics were pleasing. He walked to the entrance and found a woman of small stature in her forties with dark hair and round, flat face waiting to the side.

"Are you the Officer?" she asked in a hushed tone.

"Yes." Hawke took his hat from his head.

"Follow me."

He fell into step alongside the woman. His boot heels hitting the stone floor echoed in the hallway.

"Could you tread quieter?" she whispered.

He tried placing his feet softer and lessened the rebound of the echo. Not far down the hall, she opened a door and motioned him inside.

"This is the teacher's lounge. The others will straggle in as they finish testing." The woman walked over to a cup-at-a-time coffeemaker. "Coffee?"

"Please." He settled into one of the chairs and felt his body drop into the cushions as if it were a bean bag chair from his youth. Placing his hat on his knee, he scanned the room. Comfortable chairs, a couple of desks, and a kitchenette.

"I'm Professor Ada Ling. I teach calculus." She handed him a mug of coffee and took the chair across from him. "I understand you want to know about Professor Poulson?"

"Yes. What his hours were, how the students and faculty liked him. What his hobbies were." Hawke sipped the coffee and watched the woman. Her

196

eyebrows rose when he suggested hobbies.

"I'm sure we can help you with everything but hobbies. Professor Poulson didn't make friends with anyone and as far as I know didn't go fishing or anything like that with any of the faculty."

He set the mug on his empty knee, using it like a table. "Let's start with his hours."

"He taught early morning classes, finishing about two. He'd be in his office for an hour and leave by three. I think he picked his daughter up from school. He requested the early hours for that reason."

"Did you ever meet the daughter and wife?"

"The daughter, yes. He brought her in one evening to get something when I was teaching a night class. She was inquisitive." Professor Ling tapped the side of her face with a pointer finger. "I don't think I ever met his wife."

The door opened and a man as old as his mother walked in. His white hair was cut military short. A round belly held out the mustard yellow polo shirt he wore with brown slacks and shiny brown shoes.

"Professor Raleigh, this is... I missed your name," Professor Ling said.

"State Trooper Hawke." He set his coffee on the table next to his chair and tried to shove to his feet to shake the man's hand. He couldn't get out of the chair with one arm.

"Don't get up. Those chairs have seen better days. I don't sit in them. I have trouble getting out like you are, with the one arm." The man walked over to a straight-backed chair by a desk and took a seat. "Ada, could you get me a cup of coffee, please."

The woman hopped up and went to the

coffeemaker.

"What are you doing sitting in the math instructors' lounge?" The older man asked.

"I'm getting background information on Ronald Poulson." Hawke picked up his cup of coffee. It was good. He might have to look into getting one of those machines.

"Poulson. Damn shame what happened to him and his wife." The older man's eyes bore into him. "What about the daughter?"

"She's safe."

"Good! The bastard didn't get them all." Professor Raleigh took the coffee offered to him from the woman. "Any news on who did it?"

"We're working on it. Can you tell me anything about Poulson? Did he ever confide in you about anything? Tell you something about his wife or daughter?"

"I know he didn't like it here, but he seemed resigned to the fact. I asked him why he was staying if he was so miserable. He said it was a long story, one he couldn't tell." Professor Raleigh raised a bushy white eyebrow. "His past have anything to do with his death?"

"We think so."

"Oh no! We didn't have some criminal teaching here, did we?" Professor Ling asked.

"No. The past in question isn't his. It's his wife's." Hawke studied the man and woman. They didn't seem to have anything to hide or any knowledge of the wife.

"He only talked about her once. Said she was always on the damn computer working when she should be taking care of their daughter." Professor Raleigh nodded his head. "He wasn't happy with his life at all. When I first heard about it, I thought maybe he killed himself, but then he loved that daughter too much. He wouldn't do something that selfish."

Hawke had thought the same at first. That maybe Poulson had killed his wife and then himself, but the coroner ruled that out. Besides Kitree had seen the man and the same person was still trying to harm her.

It appeared he wasn't going to find out anything about the family here. "Thank you for the coffee and the information." He held out the cup to Ling and slid his right hip to the edge of the chair and pushed up with his right arm. With little lightness and grace, he stood.

"You haven't talked to all the staff," Professor Ling said.

"Was one of the other instructors close with Poulson?" Hawke asked.

Raleigh shook his head. "But you might talk with his student assistant, Mica Troves."

"How do I find Mica?" Hawke was pretty sure if the man didn't confide in his fellow instructors he wouldn't to a student, but at this point he didn't want to leave anything unchecked.

"I'll get her." Ling slipped out the door.

"Her? I thought Micah was a boy's name?" Hawke glanced at the smiling older professor.

"These days, you can't tell what's what even by looking at them." He pulled a small flask out from the drawer of the desk he sat in front of and added a splash to his coffee. The old man winked. "It's the only way I can stay awake this late in the day."

Hawke doubted it was to keep the old man awake. He'd spent eight years watching his stepfather drink for every reason he could come up with. It appeared even college professors weren't above the call of alcohol.

The door opened and a man in his forties entered, followed by Ling and a girl with long blonde hair, a short skirt, puffy blouse, and a vest that hung mid-calf. Her plain, diamond shaped face, was outshone by dark brown eyes gleaming with intelligence and curiosity.

"Mica, this policeman would like to talk to you about Professor Poulson," Ling said, motioning to Hawke.

The young woman's gaze took in his sling, his chest, and then his face. "I don't see a badge."

He reached in his pocket and pulled out his badge.

"Oregon State Police?" she said, in a derogatory tone.

"It's where Professor Poulson was murdered." She was being offhand with him, he'd give it to her straight.

She sucked in air and glared at him. "You don't have to be rude."

"You were." He didn't tolerate disrespect. He'd put up with too much of it growing up. He was an adult and a police officer. He had earned his respect.

"Mica, this man is here to get information about Professor Poulson to help find his killer," Raleigh said.

"I don't know who killed him." The young woman was being belligerent.

Hawke had a feeling it was on purpose. "Miss Troves, why don't you walk me back to my vehicle?"

He didn't wait for her answer. He headed for the door and wasn't surprised when she caught up and walked beside him. "That act for the others?" he asked and glanced sideways.

She had a smirk on her face. "They're used to me

being snotty. Keeps them from asking me questions."

"About what?" He enjoyed when he was right about people.

She sighed. "I bet they all told you Ronald didn't tell them anything. He didn't. He was the last hire, and they would have loved to find anything against him to get him out. When the college brought him in, they docked the others pay to be able to give Ronald what he was worth."

Hawke stopped and faced the girl. "How do you know this?"

She smiled. "I help a caterer to make extra money. One of the events we catered, I heard them all talking in a room. Ronald didn't go to any of the functions. Said he didn't want to leave his daughter alone more than he had to." She started walking. "He loved her. I liked that about him."

"What about his wife?" Hawke was beginning to see a dysfunctional family, yet, Kitree hadn't mentioned anything out of the ordinary. Perhaps her mother not being around most of her life seemed natural.

"He told me once, that she was always working. Didn't have time for him or their daughter. I know he was excited about their camping trip. He thought it would help show his wife what she was missing always being cooped up working." She shrugged. "They are both free now."

Hawke stopped beside Justine's car.

Mica's eyes widened and a grin spread across her face. "That doesn't look like much of a police car. Because you're injured you get the crap car?"

"I'm undercover."

"How's that going for you?" she asked and walked away laughing.

While he had had better conversations with criminals, the young woman had given him a little better insight into the family. He lowered himself down into the car and headed to the nearest fast food place. He'd quiet his growling stomach and head back to the reservation. One more night at his mom's and he was going back to the county. He had an idea and had to run it by his superior.

《》《》《》

Kitree liked Mimi and had fun shopping for clothes with her, but she missed her parents and Hawke. She sat on the floor coloring with one of the kids Mimi babysat after school.

"Why aren't you in school?" Marcie asked.

"I don't have a home right now." As she said it, tears filled her eyes.

"It's okay. You have one with Mimi now. She'll take care of you."

Kitree shook her head. "I can't stay here." She knew until Hawke found the man who killed her parents, she put anyone she was with in danger.

"Why not?" Marcie insisted.

"Just because." She stood. "I don't feel like playing anymore." She ran to the bedroom, threw herself on the bed, and cried. Hawke was the only one who could keep her safe, but he'd been shot protecting her and the old people had been hurt. She knew it even though Hawke wouldn't tell her.

Mimi and the kids she watched would be in trouble too. She had to leave. Tears came faster. But she had no where to go and was too scared to try and run down here. On the mountain, it had been an adventure, here she had more things that could kill her than the man who wanted her dead.

Chapter Twenty-one

The house was quiet when Hawke entered. "Mom? Kitree?" he called.

Nothing. It was close to dinner time. Mom always had dinner cooking and ready for whoever happened to be there. Panic squeezed his chest. Had he been too relaxed thinking the murderer wouldn't find Kitree here?

"Mom! Kitree!" He charged through the house, throwing open doors and fearing what he might see.

"Stop hollering, you'll get the neighbors all in a twit." Mom walked through the back door as Hawke entered the kitchen.

"Where's Kitree?" The panic released his rib cage enough to allow him to take a deep breath.

"Outside. She said she felt safer when she was on the mountain, so we are cooking over a fire in the backyard for dinner." Mom opened the refrigerator door, then closed it. "That child was crying her eyes out this afternoon, worrying her being here would bring trouble to me and others." Her filmy brown eyes peered into his. "What kind of trouble did you bring here?"

He sighed. "Kitree's parents were killed. Shot. We have reason to believe that same man is after Kitree."

Mom pursed her lips. "Why did you bring her here?"

"To keep her safe. I told Randy Toombs about her and that this area needs double surveillance. I don't think the man looking for her will figure this out. I didn't tell anyone where I was going. I borrowed a friend's car. One I hope they don't discover." He put up a hand when his mom started to say something. "I'm leaving tomorrow. I've thought of a way to flush this man out. I'm going to have Child Services fill out paperwork stating that Tuck and Sage Kimbal, the employees at Charlie's Hunting Lodge, are going to foster Kitree. Then have Dani Singer, the owner, pretend to fly the girl in. But by the time the murderer gets the information, we'll already have law enforcement set up at the lodge to catch the person when he shows up." He thought it was a good solution.

Mom shook her head. "You aren't going to fool the man if you don't have a child there for him to see. You think someone who has gotten away from the police for this long wouldn't make sure he saw the child before he attacked?"

"I don't want to use Kitree as bait."

The back door screeched. "I want to catch the man. I want to help." Kitree stood inside the door.

"How much did you hear?" Hawke hadn't wanted the child to know about the plan. Because she would do exactly what she was doing right now.

"Enough to know you need me to catch the man who killed my parents." She walked forward. "The fire is ready."

His mom nodded and opened the refrigerator, taking out a package of hot dogs. "You go start the dogs. I'll bring out the buns and ketchup."

"I can't cook them all." Kitree's gaze landed on him.

Hawke picked up the bag of chips sitting on the table and nodded to the door. "Let's cook our dinner."

Kitree smiled and headed out the door.

Hawke glanced over his shoulder at his mom. "Let's keep the conversation on other things."

She nodded. But he could tell she wasn't happy with him for not telling her the truth, or his idea for catching a killer.

《》《》《》

After dinner as they sat around the fire roasting marshmallows, Hawke brought up Kitree's family. He'd felt the young woman, Mica's, version might have been a clearer picture of the family dynamics than the child's. But he wanted to see if the perceptive girl had known how her parents felt about one another.

"I spoke today with the professors your father worked with." He started. "They said he worked the early morning to early afternoon classes to be able to pick you up from school."

Kitree nodded. "He worked the same time before in Fredrick. He said a child shouldn't have to take care of themselves when they came home from school."

"But your mom was there?"

Her shoulders sagged and she said, "Momma said work was important. That I was big enough to get a

206

snack, watch T.V., or do my homework without her help."

"How much did you see your mom?" Hawke could tell the child had thought about her mother's absence in her life.

"In Walla Walla, she would kiss the top of my head in the morning as I ate breakfast before she went into her office. Daddy would peek in at her when we'd come home." She pulled her flaming marshmallow out of the flames and blew on it. "Daddy would make me a snack and go work on his stuff in his office and I'd watch TV and do my homework. Momma would come out of the office about six, answer the ringing doorbell, and carry dinner to the kitchen. She always put the food in bowls as if she'd made it, but Daddy and I both knew she ordered from restaurants."

"What about weekends?" Hawke asked.

"Daddy cooked. Momma would stay in her office most of the day unless Daddy made plans for us to all go somewhere." She held the blackened, saggy sweet to her mouth. "I don't think Momma liked either of us very much."

The gooey mess disappeared into her mouth, leaving a white and black layer on her lips. She licked at the sticky substance and studied him.

It was as if she hoped he'd refute what she'd said. Instead he asked, "Do you think your father resented your mother for making you all move to Walla Walla?"

She nodded without thinking. "They had huge arguments before we moved. He didn't want to move. He loved where he worked, and I loved my school and friends. But when Momma went to trial, Daddy said she'd just killed us all." Her eyes widened. "Do you think the man after me is because of what Momma did before we moved?"

Since meeting the child, he'd never once lied to her. He'd withheld information but not lied. "It's the only thing I can think of. But I don't understand why they let her continue to work on whatever it was that she was put in protection about." Hawke made a mental note to contact Mrs. Bergman to see if she could shine some light or give him the name of someone to contact about what the woman had done before. She was the only person with the U.S. Marshal or FBI who seemed to care about Kitree.

"What was life like before you moved?" he asked, hoping to get her thinking of times that had been better.

"We had a big, pretty house. A woman, her name was Julie, she came in once a week and cleaned. In the summer, when Daddy and I didn't have school, we'd go on picnics the days she came." Her tone grew happier as she talked. She put another marshmallow on her stick. "Daddy and I did a lot of things together because Momma was always working."

"Did she go far to go to work?" Hawke asked, eating his nicely toasted, tan marshmallow.

"I think so. She'd leave early in the morning and sometimes come home after I'd gone to bed. Daddy said she wanted nice things and believed she had to work hard to get them."

The question in the child's voice said she didn't understand her mother's need to work hard.

"She always took our birthdays off and holidays. Momma said growing up she never got to celebrate her birthday, so she wanted to make sure we never missed ours."

"Why didn't she get to celebrate her birthday?" If the FBI hadn't wiped Mrs. Swearen's information clean, he could discover her maiden name and family's origins. And perhaps find a relative to take in Kitree.

"Something about religion and one of the reasons she ran away from home." Kitree pulled her marshmallow out of the flames. "Do you think I have family that doesn't know about me?"

"Could be." But if her mother ran away because of religion, it might not be a good reunion. "Tell me more about holidays."

"Christmas was always fun. Daddy always complained Momma went overboard, but our whole house was covered in decorations and presents piled up under the tree. Momma loved Christmas songs. She played them at home all month long. This last Christmas Daddy was upset that Momma spent so much money buying all new decorations when she didn't come out of her room long enough to enjoy them." She bowed her head. "They fought about that, too."

"Why did she need to buy all new ones?" Hawke asked.

"Because we were only allowed to bring one suitcase of clothes for each of us when we moved. All of our furniture and decorations were left in Maryland. And our house in Walla Walla is a lot smaller and no one comes to clean. Momma had to do the laundry and cook because she didn't have a job, and Daddy's money didn't cover as much as what Momma made before."

Hawke was beginning to wonder if Mrs. Poulson wasn't happy with how her life had ended up after testifying.

"We know she ordered out instead of cooking, but

how did the house get cleaned if your mom didn't want to do that?"

"I didn't tell Daddy, but one day when I was home sick, a lady came in and cleaned the house. Momma told me not to tell Daddy. Momma always said, she didn't like woman's work. She was smarter than that."

"Did you ever get a chance to see what your mother did on the computer?" Hawke knew it was a minimal chance that Kitree would know anything about what her mother did locked in the office.

"I saw it two times when she didn't get the monitor turned off quick enough. It looked like lines of music but instead of dots there were short lines, dots, and tails."

Hawke pulled out his phone and googled Arabic writing. When a document came up on the screen, he showed it to the girl.

"That's what it looked like." She smiled. "Did I help you?"

His head was pounding. Had Mrs. Poulson been working for the government to uncover terrorists in the U.S. and kept a list? He had a feeling he knew where Kitree's maternal family lived. In one of the Arabic countries.

"Yes. That will help me narrow things down." He glanced over at his mom who had been quiet this whole time. "I think it's time for you to get ready for bed."

"I agree. If you need to go back to Wallowa County with Gabriel tomorrow, you need to be rested." Mom stood, holding her hand out to the girl. "But you'll have to come see me. I'll want to hear all about your new life."

The two wandered to the house, chatting in low

voices.

Hawke pulled out the pay-as-you-go phone and slid his finger across the screen. It was after eight and Lieutenant Titus was probably at home enjoying an evening with his family, but Hawke had to tell him what he'd learned.

"Hello?" his superior answered.

"It's Hawke. The girl is safe. I've learned some things that I think need to be looked into. Do whatever you can to get information about what the Poulson woman did before she was relocated. I think she continued to do it here. And I think it has to do with National Security and transcribing Arabic."

"Whoa! Where are you getting all of this? It sounds like terrorism." Lt. Titus's voice lowered on the last sentence.

"I think she was a refugee from an Arabic country who went to work helping the government root out terrorists. And I think after her trial and need to move, she started doing it on her own, or with the help of a few people from her past. Whoever killed the husband and wife were looking for something. Their house was torn apart. I think the killer believes Kitree has whatever he wants, but I can tell you, I went through the stuff she brought with her off the mountain and I didn't find a thing."

"Where are you going with this?" The man's voice already held skepticism. That didn't bode well for what he planned to say.

"I thought we could get together and make a plan." He repeated what he'd already told his mom.

"Are you crazy? We can't put that young girl's life in jeopardy."

"She is a part of this and could cause us trouble if we don't use her. She doesn't want anyone else to get hurt. It will help ease some of her grief to help capture the person responsible for taking away her parents."

"When will you be back here?" Titus asked.

"I was planning on coming back tomorrow. I'll leave the girl where she's safe until we have this all set up." He hoped he could convince Kitree she was safe here and that he would come get her when the plan was ready to set in motion.

If she didn't believe him, it was hard telling what the determined girl would try.

Chapter Twenty-two

"What do you mean you aren't taking me with you?" Kitree asked, studying the top of Hawke's head as he bent to spoon cereal into his mouth. She didn't want to see the man who killed her parents, but she didn't want anyone else to be hurt.

"Not today. I have to go back and get everything set up. Then I'll come get you." He raised his face and stared her straight in the eyes. "Have I lied to you?"

She thought about her first meeting with the policeman and their talks and events since. "No."

"I'm not lying now. I want you to remain here, safe. Where no one knows where you are. It's going to take a bit to get the information we need from your mom's past employer and to talk Child Services into going along with the plan. Not to mention talking with Sage and Dani." He placed his spoon in the bowl and reached over to her hand.

Kitree placed her hand in his large, wide one.

"We don't want to rush this and have anything go wrong. This is to catch the murderer and keep you safe." He squeezed her hand and let go.

Mimi sat down at the table. "It makes sense to get everyone knowing what to do. Many lives could be at risk if the plan doesn't go right." Her gaze landed on her son.

She wished her mother had looked at her the way Mimi looked at Hawke. This was a mother's love. She'd had Daddy's love. But it was her mother's she'd craved. When she'd wanted to stay with Momma and Daddy to protect their bodies from animals, it had been her mother's last wish that she flee. And to show her mother she loved her and wanted her love back, she'd fled through the mountains.

"Okay. But don't take too long. It's already way past forty-eight hours." Kitree narrowed her gaze on Hawke.

"What do you mean?" His eyebrows scrunched together. She'd said something that he didn't understand.

"On the T.V. they say if you don't catch the murderer in forty-eight hours you have less chance of catching them."

Hawke laughed. As usual the girl came up with something he wouldn't have thought someone her age would know. "It's true, working with fresh clues makes it easier to solve the crime. It's been almost two weeks since the murder. But we are getting closer to knowing what we need to know." He picked up his bowl and drank the milk. "I need to get going. I have a stop to make before I head back to the county."

He stood and Kitree rushed out of her chair and

flung her arms around his waist.

"Be careful. Please," she whispered.

"I will." He patted her head and glanced at his mom.

She had the glimmer of tears in her eyes. "You have wasted years. You would have been a good father. Much better than your father or stepfather."

He put his good arm around her shoulders and squeezed. "I'm sorry I disappointed you."

"Never. You have never been a disappointment. I have wished you had a family. You are too lonely."

"I'll be back. Both of you stay out of trouble while I'm gone." He stepped away from the two and hurried into the living room where his bag waited for his departure.

Without looking back or saying a word, he walked out of the house, dropped down into the driver's seat, and drove away. It was hard not knowing if he was leaving them to fend against the murderer or keeping them safe.

He went north to Walla Walla. There were questions he felt Mrs. Bergman could answer. And he doubted the lieutenant would have any answers yet.

《》《》《》

The block was quiet. The vehicles weren't parked outside the Poulson house. He drove around the block, checking out the house Mrs. Riddle lived in. It was dark, the blinds drawn. The quiet neighborhood seemed unreal after having come from the reservation and the activity that was always going on in his mother's neighborhood.

He parked in front of Mrs. Bergman's house and walked up to the door. Three quick raps and he turned to scan the house on the other side of the street. Quiet.

A car pulled up and parked behind him.

"Are you interested in the house?" a man in his thirties, dressed in slacks and a dress shirt asked, getting out of the mid-sized SUV.

"I'm looking for the owner. Mrs. Bergman."

"I don't know the name. That's not who put it up for sale." The young man pulled a For Sale sign out of the back of his vehicle.

"For sale? Who is the owner of record?" Hawke walked up to the man.

"It is owned by a house management firm. They said they wanted to sell to purchase more condos." The man pulled a hammer out of the car and beat the sign into the ground.

"What's the name of the management company?"

The man stopped pounding. "Eagle Management Company. Why?"

"I want to see what other properties they have." Hawke strode to his vehicle, lowered his body down into the seat, and googled the management company. It looked legit, but he had a feeling it was backed by the government.

He started the car and headed out of Walla Walla and over Tollgate Pass.

Lt. Titus called him as he headed down toward Elgin. "I'm banging my head against a wall. No one wants to give me any information about our victim's previous job."

"Has anyone in Wallowa County noticed less FBI in the area?" He had a feeling all the government entities were pulling out. It was fine with him. The county police agency and the State Police worked well together. They didn't need the Feds mucking things up when they set their trap.

"Word is there are only two left who have been visiting your haunts on a daily basis and asking questions no one is answering."

Hawke grinned. Merrilee must have spread the word to not tell the Feds anything. "Good. It will make what we have planned easier with less agencies involved."

"Hawke, I haven't signed off on your plan yet."

"Are you having second thoughts?" He didn't like that Lt. Titus might not let them set up the snare.

"I'm still thinking it over and talking with the D.A. If this goes wrong, we could be up to our armpits in lawsuits."

"It won't go wrong if we are all one hundred percent committed." Hawke couldn't have Kitree kept under lock and key the rest of her life for fear someone might kill her. That wasn't a way to live.

"I want to make sure. Are you coming to headquarters?"

"If you need me to."

"Yes. I want to make sure I have your plan clear and hear why you think this might be linked to terrorism."

"I'm just entering Elgin. I'll see you in twenty." Hawke hung up and eased back on the accelerator. It was close to noon. He'd grab a couple of Subway sandwiches in Elgin and take the lieutenant lunch. Get on his good side to make him understand the plan was the quickest way to draw out the killer. That or contact the FBI and tell them he had what they were looking for… But he didn't and if they didn't catch the killer with that plan the second one may not work.

《》《》《》

He left State Police headquarters in La Grande feeling more optimistic about his plan. After hearing everything, the lieutenant signed off on it as long as the civilians involved signed a waver to not sue if things went wrong and if Child Services would make up the fake adoption papers.

Once he talked this over with Dani, Tuck, and Sage, Lt. Titus would get the paperwork rolling.

Hawke called Justine.

"Hey, when are you bringing my car back?" she asked as soon as she answered the phone.

He smiled. She really didn't care about the car, but was probably wondering what he had needed it for. "In about forty minutes. Are you home or at the café?"

"Home. It's about dinner time. You want me to put another burger on the grill?"

That's what he liked about his friendship with Justine. She didn't dress up or change who she was when they were together. She knew it was a friendship and neither one felt the need to try and impress the other.

"Sounds good. Need me to pick up anything to go with it?"

"I'm good. See you when you get here." She ended the connection.

As he drove out of Elgin, headed to Wallowa County, he dialed the number he had for Dani.

"Hello?" Her voice sounded as if she were deep in thought.

"It's Hawke."

"Hi. What's happening? Can I go back up to the

lodge?"

"Funny you should ask that. I need to visit with you, Tuck, and Sage. If you can get them rounded up in the morning, I'd like to meet someplace that we can't be overheard."

"That sounds ominous." She chuckled. "How about I see if they can meet us here at my place, say oh-nine-hundred for breakfast?"

"That would be good. Text me if they can make it and your address." Hawke was interested in seeing the mother-in-law apartment she rented from an elderly couple in Eagle.

"I will. See you tomorrow." She ended the connection.

His phone made noise as he coasted down Minam Grade. That was quick. He pulled over across from the Minam store and checked the text message.

Tuck and Sage will be here at nine. They are curious too.

His phone dinged again with her address. He texted back. *See you then.*

Pulling back onto the road, he had the dinner with Justine to feel out what the county residents were saying about the Feds and the rest of the night to make sure his plan was foolproof if executed correctly.

《》《》《》

Justine met him at the door. She always knew when someone arrived due to the ruckus of the barking coming from the kennels. "Your truck's unlocked if you want to put your things in it."

"Thanks." He grabbed his bag out of the back of her car and tossed it in the passenger seat of his pickup.

Stepping onto the porch, he said, "You know, I

should be taking you out to dinner for the loan of your car."

She studied him. "You didn't ding it or anything, did you?"

Hawke laughed, drew in a settling breath, and said, "No. I filled it up in Winslow."

"Thanks. That's all I need for the use of it. Friends help friends."

That was what he liked about the woman. She didn't keep tally of how many times she helped anyone. She just did.

"And I appreciate that."

They walked through the house and out to the patio behind. For June it was hotter than usual. The shaded patio was refreshing.

Her horses walked about the corral, fifty yards beyond the backyard fence, swishing their tails. Sun and Shilo, her dogs, were playing in the yard.

Taking a seat at the small table, Hawke slowly relaxed. It was the first time he'd been able to since finding the Poulson bodies. Even when he had dinner with Dani, the two FBI agents had been present, keeping him from completely deflating.

"This is nice. I needed it." He accepted the bottle of beer Justine handed him from a small cooler by the table.

"Let me check the burgers and then you owe me an explanation." Her dark brown eyebrows rose accenting her determined comment.

He nodded.

She pivoted, walking to the grill on the other side of the small patio.

The beer tasted good. He wasn't much of a drinker.

His drunken stepfather had him vowing at an early age to never have more than one drink. However, in the military, he'd imbibed a few more, only because he'd been taunted by some of the other soldiers that Indians couldn't hold their liquor. Now, thirty years later, he saw how he had only played into their bigotry. He no longer had to prove anything to anyone. He knew who he was and didn't give a rat's ass about what others thought. And he'd learned to ignore others ignorance.

"Now," Justine sat down across from him with a plate of sizzling patties of ground beef. "Tell me why you needed my car."

As they plied their hamburger buns with condiments, Hawke told Justine everything except the plan and where Kitree was staying. It was best if only those involved knew about the plan, and only he and the residents of his mother's neighborhood knew about Kitree.

"I can see where it was wise to switch vehicles, but you know, anyone in the county could have told them you were friends with me. They could have driven by and seen your truck parked here." She took a bite of her burger.

"I had faith in Merrilee keeping everyone's lips glued shut." He studied her over his burger.

Justine laughed. "That she did! I think she must have spent all her free time calling people and making sure no one said a word to any outsiders."

"That's what I was hoping for when I told her about the FBI." He was hopeful the Feds had left Herb and Darlene alone. They didn't know anything about his disappearance other than he needed them to take care of his animals.

Dog, Horse, and Jack would be happy to get out of their pen and head up the mountain. It would take a few days to get prepared and the people all in place, but by the time Dani flew Kitree to the lodge, he and half a dozen officers would be settled in around the lodge waiting for the killer to arrive.

Justine told him about events and happenings in the county the two days he'd been gone. With all she talked about, it felt as if he'd been gone a week instead of a couple days.

After the meal, he helped her carry things into the kitchen. "Thank you for the dinner and the use of your car. I need to get home and take over my responsibilities for my animals. And I'm sure Herb and Darlene will want to know where I've been. If I don't get there soon, I'll be up half the night, and I could use a good night's sleep."

Justine put a hand on his arm in the sling. "How is this healing?"

He stared into her eyes. As much as she'd said she only wanted to be friends, he saw a spark of more than concern and friendship in their dark depths.

"Healing. Hoping to be out of the sling in a couple more days." He backed away from her and walked into the living room, picking up his hat from the table where he'd dropped it when he'd arrived.

"Thanks again for the use of your vehicle and the dinner," he said before opening the screen on the front door.

"You're welcome here anytime." She'd followed him to the door.

"Good to know." He stepped onto the porch and kept on moving to his truck. Getting mixed up with any woman wasn't in his sights. He'd have to rely less on Justine in the future. He didn't want her getting stronger thoughts than he'd just witnessed. He wasn't marrying material. His first bad marriage proved that. And he wasn't one to shack up. That was still a commitment and the woman would expect him to be there when he might not be able to.

He started the pickup, waved, and backed out of the driveway. Yep. He would have to curtail his interactions with Justine. Damn! He really needed to find a male friend he could confide in. But he'd never had many male friends. He'd always tended to navigate to female friends. They didn't challenge him physically all the time. His size and quiet demeanor always seemed to make guys think they needed to best him.

The drive to the Trembley's took fifteen minutes. Dog ran out to the truck as soon as he turned down the driveway. A sure sign he'd been missed.

Hawke parked the vehicle and heard Horse braying. It was hard to believe the stubborn animal missed him too.

"Hey Dog, I've missed you." Hawke knelt and rubbed the animal all over. Dog whined and tried to lick him. "Did you keep the horses company?"

"You were missed by everyone." Herb said, walking over to the barn.

"Sorry I couldn't give you any notice about where I went or how long I'd be gone." Hawke shook hands with his landlord.

"We knew a child's life was at stake." Herb studied him. "Can you tell us anything?"

"Not much. She's safe at the moment, but we're planning a way to get the man to show himself." Hawke lowered his voice. "That's for no one else's ears."

Herb nodded. "I won't tell Darlene."

Hawke grinned. "She tries hard, but she can't keep anything a secret."

"True." Herb glanced at the sling. "How's the shoulder?"

"Healing. Getting stronger. I plan to see a doctor tomorrow and see if I can get this thing off and start using the arm."

"Good to hear. I'll let you settle in. I'm sure Darlene will corner you in the morning. She's at a meeting tonight." Herb headed back the way he'd come.

Hawke was tired. He visited the horses first, giving them a little grain and checking to see if he needed to clean the stall in the morning before he went to Dani's for breakfast. It appeared Darlene had cleaned the stall out that day.

"Come on, I'm sure you'll be happy to sleep in your bed as well," he said to Dog as they both climbed the stairs to his rooms.

He'd turned his phone off before dinner with Justine. He glanced down and saw that Lt. Titus had left a message. Before taking a shower, he listened.

"I have the form for the civilians to sign. I sent the document to your email. District Attorney Lange isn't completely on board but he does want to catch the murderer. As soon as you talk to the people involved, let me know and we'll start things in motion."

Hawke set his phone to wake him at six before heading to take a shower. He had several things to deal with before he met Dani and the Kimbals in the morning.

Chapter Twenty-three

Even after feeding his animals and stopping by the State Police Office in Winslow to make copies of the document Dani and the Kimbals would need to sign, Hawke pulled up to the garage underneath Dani's place half an hour early.

He'd left Dog home even though he'd begged to come. Hawke hadn't been sure how receptive Dani's landlords would be to a dog. He stepped out of his pickup and headed to the stairs at the side of the garage.

"Hey, where do you think you're going?" an elderly man asked in a raspy voice. He stood on the porch of the square, two-story, farm house next door.

"Dani invited me to breakfast," Hawke said, going down the three steps he'd climbed and walking over to the man. "I'm Hawke." He held out his hand.

"Funny name." The man didn't offer his hand. Instead, he called into the open door, "Mabel call Dani and ask if she was expecting anyone by the name of

Hawke."

"It's good to know you're so protective of Ms. Singer." Hawke decided to go into his professional mode.

The sound of a door opening drew both their gazes upward to the walkway on the side of the garage.

"Mr. Woodley, I invited Hawke and Mr. and Mrs. Kimbal. They should be showing up soon," Dani said, leaning over the railing and talking loudly.

"Can't be too careful with the riffraff that showed up here when you were interviewing." The old man spun around and disappeared behind a closed door.

Dani laughed and waved her arm. "Come on up. He's a bit contrary."

"A bit?" Hawke walked back up the steps and stopped at the top where Dani still stood. "You don't have to worry about suspicious people with that watch dog looking out for you."

Dani motioned for him to enter the apartment. "He means well. Just a bit abrupt in the way he goes about it." She closed the door. "I like it. Reminds me of my Air Force days."

He studied the photos of planes, helicopters, and scenes from the sky that filled one wall of the living room. Statues and oddities that looked as if they came from all over the world sat on shelves, a book case, and stands.

"Welcome to my home away from the mountain." Dani sniffed. "Have to get the muffins out of the oven. Make yourself comfortable."

Instead of taking a seat, he followed her into a cheery pale blue kitchen. The towels and wall decorations had sunflowers on them.

She set a pan of muffins on top of the stove and turned. "Oh! I didn't see you follow me in."

"Sorry. Didn't feel like sitting in the other room alone." He took a seat at the small table she had set for four.

"Coffee?" she asked, grabbing a large mug with a sunflower picture from a rack hanging on the wall.

"Please."

"What is this mysterious meeting about?" she asked, placing the cup in front of him.

"I'd rather wait for Tuck and Sage. You know. Say it only once." He picked up the cup and sipped. "This is good."

"Thanks. It's my own blend of different beans I discovered while traveling with the Air Force."

"Where all have you been?" He nodded toward the other room. "From the knickknacks, I'd say a lot of places."

"If I were to put pins on a map, I'd have one in most countries. I spent several years flying dignitaries to secret meetings in foreign countries."

"Does that mean you have high clearance?" A thought struck him.

"One of the highest. Why?" She sat down across from him with a cup of coffee.

"Can you get into top secret files?"

She narrowed her eyes. "I know you and the FBI don't see eye to eye, but I'm not doing anything illegal for you."

Knocking on the door stopped the conversation.

Dani rose to let her guests in.

Hawke had a feeling if he worked on her enough, Dani would see if she could get into Sylvia Swearen's files.

Tuck entered the kitchen. "Hawke."

They shook hands as Mrs. Kimbal entered the room behind her husband. "Good to see you and Sage."

"Your wound must have been worse than you let on," Sage said, her gaze on his sling.

"Just a bad place for healing. Have to keep my arm immobile for a while. I'll see the doctor today. I hope he'll tell me I can get rid of this sling." He sipped his coffee and asked the Kimbals what they'd been doing while waiting to go back up the mountain. Dani placed an egg dish from the oven and the muffins on the table.

Everyone filled their plates and then all eyes were on him.

"Why did you need to see us?" Dani asked.

"Is Kitree safe?" Sage asked.

"The man almost got her where Child Services had placed her," Hawke said, to make them realize how important their participation was to make the plan work.

"Oh no!" Sage put a hand over her mouth.

"She got away and called me. I have her some place safe, but she won't ever be safe if we don't catch the man responsible for her parents' deaths and find out what they are after."

All three nodded their heads.

"Good. I'm glad you all feel that way. I have a plan." He went on to explain what he and Lt. Titus had worked out.

When he finished, he glanced around the table and asked, "Are you three willing to help with this? I want you to be aware there is a risk involved. And the D.A. drew up a form you'll have to sign, saying you won't sue the county and all the law enforcement entities involved if you are injured or killed."

Sage sucked in air. "We could be harmed, couldn't we?"

"Yes. That's why you have to volunteer on your own. I can't make you do this."

Dani cleared her throat. "But you can't do this without the three of us. We have to make the lodge look like it's running as usual."

He nodded and turned his gaze on Sage. "We will do our best to keep you and Kitree safe."

The younger woman stared at her husband. "I can do this. That child has lost so much. We need to help her."

Tuck grasped his wife's hand. "You sure? It could be like losing another child?"

Hawke stared at Dani. He witnessed sympathy in her eyes. He'd wondered about the young couple not having children.

"I know that this time we *can* do something to keep her alive." Sage turned her gaze to Hawke. "Where are the papers we need to sign?"

His shoulders drooped and the weight he'd been carrying, worrying these people would not want to take the risk, fell off. "You can sign them when we finish eating. You'll have to go to La Grande and fill out the adoption papers once Lt. Titus gets Child Services to go along."

"Why do they have to go along? Can't we just go in and sign the papers and get Kitree?" Sage asked.

"No. It usually takes months before an adoption goes through. We can't wait months. I can't guarantee where she is now can keep her safe that long."

"Is she happy where she is?" Sage asked.

"As happy as she can be having lost her parents so tragically." Hawke's heart went out to Kitree. She'd had a good life, a father who loved her, and a stable environment. That had all been taken away in a few minutes and her whole life turned upside down. Like when his wife left and sent divorce papers. His happy content life had shattered. It had taken him nearly ten years to become satisfied with his life. And now he'd do anything to keep it from changing. He couldn't see living and working any other way.

"You know you could be in trouble if her family finds out you used her to lure the killer out." Dani picked up her coffee cup and peered at him over the edge.

"As far as can be determined, there is no family. Unless you can dig some up." He raised an eyebrow.

"Is this part of your asking me if I could get into secret files?" Dani's gaze narrowed and Sage gasped.

"It might be." He glanced at the Kimbals. "But we can discuss that later."

"Let me help you with the dishes," Sage said, picking up plates and heading to the sink.

"Hawke and I will be in the other room," Tuck said, standing and walking into the living room.

Unsure what the man wanted to talk to him about, Hawke followed.

Tuck stood looking out a window. "It's taken Sage five years to get over losing our Amber."

Hawke walked over to stand beside the man, to keep their voices low. "If you think this will be too much for Sage, we can put police officers in your places."

The cowboy shook his head. "She's going to want to help. I won't be able to keep her from it." He glanced over at Hawke. "Is there a chance we could adopt the girl for real? All Sage has talked about since meeting Kitree is how she needs a family."

"That's something you'd have to talk over with Child Services once Kitree is safe." He liked the idea of the couple adopting Kitree. That way he'd get to see her grow up. She'd also have access to the mountains all summer long.

"Our Amber would have been Kitree's age this August." Tuck wiped at his eyes. "Her passing took the wind out of both of us. Then the doctors said we couldn't have any more." His hands balled into fists. "I thought I was going to lose Sage too. This might be our chance to have a family again." He shifted and peered into Hawke's eyes. "We'll do whatever we have to do to help Kitree."

The resolve and passion in the man's features and voice told Hawke he was the right man to have at the lodge to keep Kitree safe.

He put a hand on Tuck's shoulder. "I'm happy to have you with me."

Dani and Sage stepped into the room.

Sage walked over to her husband. "Is everything okay?"

Tuck put an arm around his wife and kissed the top of her head. "Yes."

Hawke glanced at Dani. She had a pad and paper in her hand. Which reminded him they had to sign papers. He picked up the folder he'd set on the end table before he'd entered the kitchen earlier. "Here are the forms you need to sign."

They all signed after reading the document.

Dani sat down in a chair and poised her pen over the notepad. "I'll get a list of supplies ready for you to pick up tomorrow and put in the packsaddles." She glanced at Hawke. "Will you be riding up with Tuck and Sage?"

"Yes. I can help carry supplies if that's what you need." He took a seat.

"Our horses and pack animals are up at the lodge," Tuck said. "How are we going to get up there?"

Dani grinned. "I'll radio Tyson."

"Tyson?" Hawke had a feeling the woman had been holding out on something.

"I sent him back up there after it looked like things had simmered down. He's been up there feeding the animals and anyone who wandered by. I'll have him bring the horses and pack animals down the day you want to go up." She tapped her pen on the tablet. "You aren't the only one who thinks ahead."

"Everything, time wise, happens around Child Services. As soon as I get the word from Lt. Titus, I'll call you." Hawke pulled out his phone. "What's your number?" he asked Tuck.

The man recited his phone number and Sage's in case he didn't answer.

"Once you have the papers signed, then we'll load up and head up the mountain." Hawke tucked his phone back in his belt holster.

"What about Kitree? How will she get up there?" Sage asked.

"To make sure she is safe, Dani will fly her helicopter to where Kitree is staying and fly her into the lodge the day after we get there. I want to have everything checked out to make sure no one is hanging around before we bring her in." Hawke had also asked Lt. Titus to send all the Wallowa County Fish and Wildlife Troopers along with all the deputies the county could spare up to the area around the lodge the day he received cooperation from Child Services.

"That's good. I'd hate to have something happen on the way up the mountain." Sage's relief was evident in the way her facial muscles relaxed.

"But if they don't see us taking Kitree up the mountain with us, won't they know this is all a hoax?" Tuck asked.

"The adoption papers will have a release date. The day Dani will fly her up. If my hunch is correct, they are keeping tabs on the girl through the paper trail of Child Services. They'll be watching you to see if you go after her. When Dani brings her in on the helicopter, they'll know she's there." That would be when they would have to all be on high alert and work to catch the man before he hurt anyone.

"You've thought this all out," Dani said.

"It wasn't just me. The lieutenant helped with the logistics, even though he's not completely happy with it. But he understands we can't keep trying to hide Kitree. We have to bring the killer out so we can catch him." Hawke stood. "I'll be in touch."

Dani stood and walked him to the door. "I thought you wanted me to snoop in some files?"

He took the note pad she held and wrote down Sylvia Swearen. "If you can find files on her without getting caught, I'd appreciate it."

"Who is this?" Dani circled the name.

"Kitree's mom. I'll tell you the rest when we're at

the lodge." He peered into her eyes.

She nodded. "I'll let you know if I find anything."

Hawke wanted to thank her for helping but had a feeling she would just make some comment that would irk him. "Thanks."

He descended the stairs happy the three people had agreed to help. On his drive home, he called his mom from the prepaid phone.

"Hello?" she answered.

"Hi Mom. Is everything quiet there?"

"Except for the police going by several times a day." He heard the disapproval in her voice. "You know having them go by so much only draws more attention that something is happening."

"Hopefully, it will only be a couple more days. How is Kitree? Can I talk to her?" He wanted to let her know he hadn't forgotten about her and they were working on a plan.

"She seems down. But I'm sure talking to you will help. She's out back looking at my flowers."

The phone clunked as his mom put the receiver down. Her feet scuffed as she crossed the kitchen to the back door. "Telephone!"

Hawke grinned. His mom had the sense to not call out her name. It was an uncommon one. One that others might repeat.

Running footsteps grew closer.

"Hawke?" Kitree asked out of breath.

"Yes. How are things there?"

"Mimi taught me how to make fry bread, and I've been putting beads on a piece of leather she says I can make into a bag to carry my books."

"Good. I'm glad she's keeping you busy. I talked

with Dani, Tuck, and Sage today. They are willing to help flush out the man who is looking for you. I'm waiting for my boss to give me the go ahead. When everything is set, I'll have Tribal Policeman Randy Toombs, Mimi knows him, pick you up and take you to Dani. She'll be waiting with her helicopter to bring you to the lodge."

"Really! I get to ride in a helicopter!" The excitement in her voice made him wish the flight was for fun and not to keep her safe.

"Yes. You'll come to the lodge. Tuck and Sage will pretend they are adopting you."

"Pretending? Why pretend? Can't they for real?"

The disappointment in her voice put a lump in his throat. He didn't have the right to tell her that the couple would like to adopt her for real. He swallowed the lump and continued, "That's something you can discuss with them when you see them. But the killer is going to think they have. That is how we are getting him to come to the lodge." He reined in his emotions. "But you can't tell any of this to anyone. Not even Mimi. It could put her in danger."

"I won't tell anyone," she whispered.

"Good. It should only be a couple more days. Put Mimi on. I need to let her know about the policeman coming."

"Hawke, I miss you," she whispered.

"I miss you, too. But I'll see you soon. And remember, you're going to get to ride in a helicopter." He wanted to end their conversation on a happy note.

"Thanks. Here's Mimi."

"What did you tell this child that has her tearing up?" Mom asked him as soon as she had the phone.

"Nothing. She just misses her parents." Hawke shoved his feelings for the child away and said, "Mom, when we're ready for Kitree to come back here, I'll send Randy Toombs to pick her up. He'll know where to take her. Don't ask him to tell you. The less you know, the better. Understand?"

"Yes. I know this child's life depends on our secrecy." There was a pause. "I'll miss her. She's been fun."

Hawke had been afraid his mom would get attached. The girl had a way of wiggling into your heart. "I know. She is one in a million. We'll have to see if she can come visit you."

"That would be nice. I better let you go. You have important work to do. Keeping her safe."

The connection went silent.

There were a lot of people depending on him keeping the girl safe. He was at the top of the list.

Chapter Twenty-four

The sound of helicopter blades thumping the air, pulled Hawke out of the cabin and brought everyone together in front of the lodge.

Dani was landing with Kitree.

Since arriving at the lodge the day before, Hawke, Tuck, and Tyson had put away all of the supplies they'd brought up and moved furniture and belongings around. They'd thought about having Kitree and the Kimbals stay in the lodge but then relented, since anyone watching would notice the change of sleeping arrangements and might get suspicious.

Hawke didn't like the idea of Kitree or Sage having to use the outhouse behind the bunkhouse. It was hidden from the view of his cabin and the lodge. He'd radioed Dani to bring in a composting toilet that could be put in the bunkhouse. He and Tuck had made a makeshift area for privacy in the far corner of the building and had hung a wall of blankets between the

main area where the Kimbals slept and the bunk that
would be Kitree's.

When the helicopter landed and the blades stopped
moving, he and Dog walked up to the aircraft.

"Welcome back," he said to Dani as he helped
Kitree out. Dog jumped up, licking her in the face.

The girl giggled. "Dog, I've missed you." She
hugged the animal around the neck.

"She has a duffel bag full of clothes and stuffed
animals." Dani motioned to the back seat. "And the
composting toilet you asked for."

"Thanks." Hawke turned to set Kitree's bag on the
ground.

Sage ran up, hugging the girl. "It's so good to see
you." She released the child. "We have a place for you
in the bunkhouse with us."

Kitree glanced over her shoulder at Hawke. "Is the
bunkhouse safe?"

He understood her hesitation. "Yes. There is only
one door in and out and there will be people watching it
and any other building you are in." He nodded to Dog.
"He'll be sleeping on the porch."

She smiled and took Sage's hand. The two
wandered over to say hi to Tyson and Tuck, Dog
following behind.

"Is everyone else on the mountain?" Dani asked in
a quiet voice.

"Yes. There are even a couple in tree stands. Don't
look up," he said as she started to glance toward the
trees.

"Right. We could be watched by someone other
than our side." She pulled Kitree's other bag out,
handing it to him. "Your mother made quite an

impression on Kitree." Dani studied him. "Do you think it was safe putting this child in your mother's home?"

"No one found her. Strangers stick out on a reservation."

Tyson walked up to them.

"Grab that box and bring it to the bunkhouse." Hawke grasped Kitree's bags. He glanced at the bag with a stuffed rabbit's head sticking out. It was his old gym bag. He grinned walked to the bunkhouse.

A glance over his shoulder showed Dani heading to the lodge. She'd probably want to do an inspection and make sure everything was as it should be. He grinned and knocked on the door.

"Come in," called Sage.

He stepped in and found the three, Tuck, Sage, and Kitree, sitting at the table. Dog sat beside the girl. Kitree and Sage had a cup of hot chocolate and Tuck had coffee.

"Here are Kitree's belongings." He noticed the beaded leather pouch hanging from Kitree's waist. "It looks like you and Mimi finished the pouch."

Kitree smiled and stood up, showing off the accessory. "We barely had it finished when the policeman called. Mimi said to come back when things are settled and she'd have the right kind of belt ready for it." She flipped the ends of rawhide tied at her waist. "This was all we could come up with to hold it on for now."

"You don't have to wear it all the time," Sage said.

Kitree stared at her. "Yes, I do. It was made to hold my book of wildflowers and wilderness guide."

"Oh, I see." Sage picked up her mug.

"Kitree is studying the edible flowers and plants. I

think she's going to be a botanist," Hawke said, to make the woman understand how important the books were to the child. Not to mention they were the only items she had left from her life before her parents were killed.

"Living up here on the mountain would be a great classroom for you," Tuck said.

The girl nodded. "I love it up here. I'm so glad you are adopting me." Her smile wavered as the adults all looked at one another.

Hawke took the only empty chair and sat.

"Hey, your arm isn't in a sling anymore." Kitree said.

"No. I still have to be careful, but at least I can use it some." Hawke motioned for Kitree to sit back in her chair. "I don't want you to get your hopes up or get too attached to anyone here. The adoption was to get you up here on the mountain where we could control keeping an eye on you and catching the man who killed your parents."

Kitree shot a glance at Tuck and Sage before peering at Hawke. "This is all pretend?" She'd been excited when the policeman said it looked like the Kimbals were adopting her and Dani was picking her up to take her to them. She would have a family again. Now, she didn't know if she'd ever have a family.

Sage touched her arm. "It is right now. But if you like us and want to be adopted by us, we'll talk about doing it for real when the man is caught."

They were making sure she was still alive before they went through the motions. Her stomach felt like throwing up the hot chocolate she'd just drank.

The door banged open.

Dog barked and the hair down the back of his neck stood up. She knew with him around no one would hurt her.

Tyson, the young man who'd chased her down the mountain the last time she was here, walked in carrying a large box.

"Where do you want this?" He dropped the box.

Hawke shot out of the chair. "Don't drop that."

The adults all gathered around the box, forgetting about her.

Kitree walked out of the bunkhouse. Dog trotted beside her as they crossed to the lodge. She needed time to think and would have liked to go for a hike in the trees but knew better than to walk into the man who wanted her dead.

《》《》《》

The composting toilet was unboxed and sitting in the area Hawke and Tuck had made for privacy.

Hawke walked into the main room and panic squeezed his chest. "Where's Kitree?"

"Oh!" Sage started for the door.

"Don't go running out there calling her name." Hawke strode to the door. "Tuck look in the barn. Tyson, check the corrals. I'll check the house."

The words came out of his mouth as he stepped off the porch and headed across the open area to the lodge.

He stepped in the log structure and heard voices down the hall. A peek in the office, and he found the child. She and Dani were looking at photos in a book.

"That was me right after I'd flown my first helicopter," Dani said.

"Wow! You look so happy."

"I'd be happy if you had told us you were leaving

241

the bunkhouse," Hawke said.

They both jumped.

Irritation wrinkled Dani's brow.

Kitree's cheeks darkened in color. "Sorry. You were busy and I wanted to…get away."

"I'll let the others know I found you." He studied the girl, flicked a glance at Dani, and left the room. If the Kimbal's adopted Kitree, it was good to know she and Dani would get along.

He needed the others to keep an eye on her while he made contact with the handful of people watching the area. He knew Sullens was up at Hawke's perch. He would be the easiest to contact.

Hawke walked to the barn. Tuck and Tyson stood by the door. "I found her. She's in with Dani. Keep an eye on her. I'm going to visit with Sullens up at my perch."

Tyson nodded. He knew the place. Hawke had sent him up there to get Kitree. Had it only been over a week ago? This whole ordeal from finding the Poulsons to now felt as if it had been going on for months not weeks.

In the barn, Hawke grabbed Jack's halter and lead rope. He caught the horse and within minutes was saddled and ready to ride out.

Dog ran up to him. "Stay. Guard Kitree."

As if the animal knew exactly what he'd said, Dog ran over to the house and disappeared.

Shaking his head at his thought the animal had understood, Hawke headed out of the lodge area on the trail Sullens could see from the perch. Once he was a mile from the lodge, he turned the horse, taking off through the trees. If someone followed him, he'd know.

After fifteen or twenty minutes of traveling alongside the mountain, he circled down and came upon his own tracks. No one was following. He had a good idea whoever wanted the girl, was waiting for nightfall. Reining Jack uphill, Hawke made straight for his perch.

The other Fish and Wildlife Trooper wasn't in sight when Hawke rode up. He dismounted and pulled a water bottle out of his saddlebag. Jack was winded from the straight uphill trajectory Hawke had taken him, but recovered quickly. The horse was used to carrying him all over these mountains.

"I had a feeling you'd be showing up after the helicopter arrived." The trooper didn't show himself.

It made sense in case he'd missed the fact someone had followed him.

"Just checking in to say the girl and the Kimbals will be in the bunkhouse at night. Wouldn't be a bad idea if a few of you could move in closer to have eyes all around. I can't see them waiting more than a day or two before they go after her."

"Are you keeping her in one building? Her running around outside makes her an easy target." Sullens said.

"She'll move around as she wishes. We'll all keep an eye on her. I believe they want her alive. At least until they get whatever it is they were looking for at the house." The only explanation for the people to still want her had to be they didn't find what Mrs. Poulson hid.

"What are they looking for?" The trooper's voice rang with skepticism.

"It has to be small. I'm thinking a microchip with damaging information. But for who, I don't know. I think the Feds want whatever it is as well." He'd had a feeling Dolan had wanted to push harder than her superior let her.

"That why we're keeping this hush-hush?"

"Yes. I figure the only law around here who doesn't have something at stake in finding the information is State Police and the county." Hawke put the lid back on his bottle. "I'm going to head back down. Be sure to let the others know to move in closer at dark but stay hidden."

"We're on a special frequency. No one will know we're here."

Hawke hoped the man was correct. But he had an eerie feeling he was being watched. Which meant he either had someone stealthy follow him here, or they knew the trooper was here.

He mounted and headed Jack back down the hill. They had no idea who or what they were up against. And everyone at the lodge were sitting ducks.

《》《》《》

Kitree poked the last sticky bite of the jam sandwich in her mouth, chewed, and licked the stickiness from her finger. "Can I sit on the porch?" She liked the lodge, but it felt like a cave. Dark and small.

"As long as you stay on the porch and don't wander off," Sage said. The woman picked up the jam jar. "Or you could help me make dinner."

"Maybe tomorrow. I don't feel like being inside." Kitree slid off the chair and walked out to the porch. She sat on a chair close to the lodge door and scanned the area. Tyson was pulling weeds in what Sage said was a garden. Tuck was rubbing something on a saddle just outside the barn doors.

Dog lay down at her feet. She patted his head. "I wish I had a dog just like you."

His big brown eyes looked at her. She was pretty sure he smiled.

She sighed and opened her pouch, pulling out her wildflower book. All the work she and her parents had gone through to make her wildflower notebook for a class project had been for nothing. She didn't know what school she'd be at next and if they even had a science project competition.

The scent of the pine trees floated by on a warm breeze. She smiled. If Tuck and Sage adopted her, she'd have quite a few of the wild plants around her when she lived up here. She'd get her notebook from Hawke's friend and start a section just from the mountain. Tears burned her eyes. "It could have been book number three." She'd started book one when they lived in Fredrick and wasn't allowed to bring it with her. She missed her friends, their housekeeper, and her teachers.

Dog sat up. He pointed his nose toward the trees.

Kitree watched as Hawke rode out of the forest. He was her hero, but she had a pretty good idea he wouldn't want to hear it. He was what her daddy called stoic. He helped people without thinking about it and didn't like anyone calling attention to it.

She stood up as he walked his horse over to the barn. Dog beat her off the porch, running over to Hawke and touching noses with Jack.

"Did you see anything?" Tuck asked as she walked up.

"Only those I wanted to see." Hawke handed her the reins. "Why don't you lead Jack in the barn and you can feed him some grain while I take the saddle off."

He probably didn't want her to hear what he had to say. She shrugged and took the reins, leading the horse into the barn.

The inside was dark.

Something moved in the corner.

Chapter Twenty-five

"Eeek!" Kitree screeched.

The doors flew open wider and Hawke charged into the barn. Dog rushed to the corner where she'd seen movement.

The most awful sound she'd ever heard, shrieked. Kitree clapped her hands over her ears.

"Dog! Down!" Hawke shouted.

Tuck appeared at her side, putting a hand on her shoulder. "What the—?"

Tyson ran into the barn. "Hey! Leave Rambo alone!" He hurried over to where Hawke was leaned over.

"You can't keep a fawn in the barn. Where's the mother?" Hawke asked.

"The mother died. I found the fawn half dead, lying next to the doe. I brought it back here and have been feeding it." Tyson scooped up the fawn in his arms.

Hawke shook his head. "It's not legal."

"It wouldn't have been humane to leave it out there to die or be eaten."

Kitree dropped Jack's reins and hurried up to Tyson. "May I pet it?"

"Sure." He knelt, holding the fawn while she ran a hand over the animal's head.

"It's so soft. And cute." She'd never seen anything so fragile and beautiful.

Hawke watched the two young people fawning over the fawn and shook his head. Now he knew where the word came from. He wandered over to Jack, trying to figure out how to break the reality of the situation to them. "I'm going to have to report the animal to the proper people," he said, loosening the cinch.

"You can't take him away. He thinks I'm his mother," Tyson said, his tone imparting the first conviction he'd heard from the young man.

"We'll see." Hawke hated to be the bad guy in this, but it was part of his job to make sure civilians didn't take in wild animals. There were organizations and people who specialized in rehabilitating injured and orphaned animals.

He put the saddle over the stall and hung up the bridle. "Are you going to give Jack his grain?" Hawke asked Kitree.

She reluctantly left the fawn and held the grain pan for the horse.

"Should be dinner time when we finish here." He glanced at the girl.

She held the grain pan, but her gaze was on the animal in Tyson's arm. Hawke knew where the girl would be spending most of her time.

He put Jack back in the corral and ordered both

Tyson and Kitree out of the barn. There was no sense in making the fawn too tame. Even if Tyson were allowed to keep it, eventually a hunter would come across the curious animal unafraid of humans and Rambo would end up on a dinner table. The animal had a better chance of survival if it went to a less hands-on environment.

Dinner was good. Sage was an excellent cook. Kitree told her how much she liked the food more than once. Hawke had to admit, it was a treat to have foods he remembered as a kid. Hot dogs, chips, macaroni and cheese, and pudding for dessert. The meal had been made to make Kitree feel at home. He didn't have the heart to tell Sage, anything home cooked wasn't going to make her feel at home since most of her dinners came from restaurants.

Sage and Dani cleaned up the table and started on the dishes.

Hawke led the way to the great room. "Pick a game," he told Kitree.

She stood in front of the bookshelf staring at the games.

"I'll play if you get a game that more than two people can play," Tyson said.

"Grab cards and we all can play," Tuck added.

Kitree walked over to the coffee table where Tuck and Tyson had sat down. She placed two decks of cards on the table. "I don't know very many card games. Mainly solitaire."

Hawke studied the girl. She didn't say it in a "poor me" whine. She just stated the fact. She didn't realize how much she'd missed out on. "It's been a while since I played any games. The only one I can remember is

Spoons." He glanced at the other two.

"I know that one," Tyson said.

Tuck nodded and stood. He walked over to a shelf and brought back four cardboard coasters from various bars. "We'll use these in place of spoons."

Tyson began explaining the game to Kitree. She caught on quickly and giggled at the teasing Tuck and Tyson shot back and forth.

"What's going on in here?" Dani asked as she and Sage entered the room.

Kitree was in a fit of giggles. She drew in a breath and said, "Tyson forgot to use his coaster and I beat him."

Caught up in the girl's happiness, Hawke's cheeks hurt he'd been grinning so much.

"I see. I've never heard of a card game called "Coasters." Dani winked at him and his heart lodged in his chest.

It had been years since he'd exchanged a secret or conspiratorial glance with a woman. He didn't know what to say or do. Standing, he moved away from the couch as Dani and Sage sat down.

"Aren't you playing?" Kitree asked.

"I'm going to go out and look around. You all go ahead." He opened the lodge door, stepped out, and closed it.

Scratching and whining on the other side pulled him from his thoughts. He opened the door and Dog launched out, stopping and staring at him.

"Yeah. I'm a dunderhead." He sat on one of the chairs on the porch and scratched Dog's head. The sun had dropped behind the mountain an hour earlier. Only the open space between buildings and the air strip were lit by the last rays of sunlight.

He stared into the darkness of the forest, wondering when the killer would make his move and if he would be alone. His gut was as curdled as it had been after he'd sent Jack and Horse down here, leading the killer to the lodge. The people inside playing cards as if there wasn't any evil hunkered down out in the trees believed he'd keep them safe.

This was more than keeping civilians safe. Kitree had wound herself around his heart and the feelings Dani brought to the surface in him…he had a lot at stake if this went wrong. Not only personally, but his job. If this went sour, his butt would be strung up and he'd get tossed out of the troopers.

The door opened and Tuck stepped out. "There you are." He dropped onto a chair next to him. "See anything?"

"No. But that doesn't mean they aren't out there." Hawke wanted to make sure the man stayed alert.

"I know. Just thought maybe you'd seen something was why you hadn't come back in." Tuck settled himself even deeper into the chair, but his finger tapping on the arm, showed he wasn't near as relaxed as his posture suggested.

"When you take Sage and Kitree to the bunkhouse, make sure you lock and board the door." He didn't want anyone getting in before help arrived.

"I will. I'll keep my shotgun next to the bed. We've got Kitree tucked into the far corner. They'll have to get by me and Sage." He turned his head toward Hawke. "Sage has a shotgun on her side of the bed, too. They aren't getting by us."

He'd heard the same conviction in a man's voice

before. From a victim who'd refused police protection and ended up dead.

"Don't get trigger happy. If Tyson comes barging in for some reason you don't want to blow his head off." Hawke didn't need Dani up his ass because something happened to her nephew.

"I told him. He knows he'll get shot if he doesn't let us know." Tuck leaned forward, his arms on his thighs. "Sage and I will do everything we can to save Kitree. She's as good as ours. We won't lose her, too."

Hawke was curious. "If you don't mind my asking. How did you lose your child before?"

"Cancer. Took her when she was four. We did everything the doctors said to do, but it didn't work. While we were dealing with the cancer, Sage was so stressed out, she couldn't get pregnant. Then after we lost Amber, Sage didn't want to get pregnant. She was afraid we'd have another sick child and she didn't want to lose another one." He glanced over. "Ever since you brought Kitree here, that's all Sage has talked about. How wonderful it would be to have a child like her. She doesn't want to start with a baby, she wants a child." He sighed. "That child. The one in there beating the daylights out of everyone at Spoons."

Hawke laughed. "Maybe we should go back in and suggest another game." He stood. Kitree and the Kimbals needed one another. It would be a good match when all the dust settled.

He pushed the door open and found Kitree walking along the bookshelf, looking at books.

She turned from the shelf. "Why do you have two of this book?"

"Because it is a popular book and sometimes more

than one person at a time wants to read it," Dani answered.

Two of the same book clanged in his head. "Kitree, why did you have two wildflower books?" He'd thought it strange that there had been the same wildflower book in her room.

"I don't have two. I only have this one." She pulled the wildflower book out of her pouch.

"I went through your house when you were with Mimi. There was one just like it in your bedroom." He studied her.

She shook her head. "I only have one. There couldn't have been."

He walked over to her. "May I see the book?"

She handed it over. "I don't understand." Kitree wandered over to the couch and sat down. She jumped back up. "When we were getting ready to leave, I'd forgotten my coat. The books were in the pocket. Momma said she'd get it. Daddy and I waited what seemed like a long time for her to just walk back in and pick up my coat. Daddy made a comment, Momma must have stopped for lunch." She gave a half laugh before her eyes watered.

Sage pulled her into a hug.

Hawke held the book in his hand. There had to be a reason Mrs. Poulson had the second book. "I'm going to take a look at this in my cabin." He walked over to Kitree. "If I have to take it apart, is that okay? I'll get you a new one."

"Do you think what the people want is in my book?"

He should have known her bright mind would jump to the same conclusion he had. "It could be."

"Find it so we all don't have to be scared anymore."

He nodded and spoke to Tyson and Tuck. "When the rest of you go to bed, someone come let me know. I'm taking first watch."

"Will do," Tuck said.

Hawke shoved the book under his shirt and walked out the door, striding to his cabin with Dog at his heels. It was the closest one to the lodge and bunkhouse. At first, he'd thought about staying in the lodge. The big windows would make it too easy for someone outside to see he was watching. The cabin had smaller windows and a better line of sight to three sides of the bunkhouse.

At the cabin, Dog rushed through the opened door and landed on the bed. "Is that where you think you're sleeping tonight?" Hawke asked as he lit the kerosene lantern.

The dog could sleep there until their watch. Then Dog would be on the bunkhouse porch. He'd let everyone know if someone approached.

Hawke sat down on the end of the bed nearest the lantern and began methodically studying, and feeling, the book cover. There was no way to hide anything in the pages. It had to be in the cover.

Slipping the blade of his knife under the paper glued to the inside of the front cover, he peeled it off the cardboard.

Nothing.

He did the same to the inside back.

Nothing.

Then he peeled the whole printed cover off.

Nothing.

Had he ruined this book for no reason?

He picked it up by the cardboard cover and noticed a gap between the pages and the cardboard spine. Breaking the spine, he discovered a SD disk. The size that fit in his work computer. He walked over to the saddlebags he'd yet to unpack and dug into the side that carried all his things related to work. Normally he wouldn't have his computer up on the mountain. Knowing he might run across something electronic in his hunt for what Mrs. Poulson had hidden, he'd brought it along.

He started up his computer and slid the disk in the slot. While he waited, he pulled out his notepad and pen.

The screen came to life. He clicked open the disk. It was a spread sheet. Names in the first column, occupation in the second, address in the third, and... Hawke stared at the fourth column. Country of origin and the fifth column. Terrorist organization.

It was a list of American citizens who had ties to terrorist organizations. How the woman had gotten her hands on it, he'd never know, but it opened up a whole lot of possibilities as to who wanted it.

He did a quick scan of occupations and noted a judge, several D.A.s, and law enforcement. FBI caught his eye. He backtracked and there staring him in the eyes was the name Jennifer Dolan. That could have been why the FBI had known his movements. Dolan had contacted the killer.

He popped the disk out of his computer and thought. Where could he put the SD card that it would get off the mountain and be safe from anyone searching the lodge and buildings? Dog shifted on the bed.

They'd have to kill him to get close to him. Would the authorities take his body and look at his collar? He doubted it.

"I just need to hide it for tonight and then get it to Sullens in the morning." Hawke cut the stitches holding his knife sheath to the inside of his boot. Using a narrow splinter of wood from kindling next to the woodstove, he shoved the disk as far down as he could get it before putting his knife back in the sheath.

He hated to burn Kitree's book, but he didn't want someone to see he'd torn it apart and suspect he had knowledge of the disk or what was on it before he could get the information to authorities.

Tossing the book into the stove, he added kindling and a log. He lit the pages and watched the flames until the log caught fire.

A soft knock on the door had him turning off the lantern.

"Hawke? It's me, Tyson. We're all turning in."

The whispered words set Hawke in motion.

He opened the door. "I'm ready. Go get some sleep. I'll wake you when I need relieved."

Tyson's dark shadow moved to the lodge. He slept in the small room off the kitchen now that Tuck and Sage had moved into the bunkhouse.

Hawke grabbed his shotgun and Dog. They slipped over to the bunkhouse. "Stay," Hawke whispered and put his hand on Dog's head.

When the animal sat down, Hawke moved into the shadow of the corner of the lodge. He stepped over the porch railing and took a seat on a chair at the very end closest to the bunkhouse. Anyone going to the bunkhouse or the front of the lodge could be seen.

Mouse Trail Ends

From the position of the moon, he'd guess it to be about ten. He cradled the gun in his arms and waited.

Chapter Twenty-six

Dog's low growl caught Hawke's attention. He didn't think he'd dozed off, but the angle of the quarter moon said differently.

He squinted in the inky darkness the crescent moon couldn't illuminate.

Dog's growl grew louder. Someone approached the bunkhouse unconcerned the dog was there. Hawke didn't like that. It meant the person was ready to kill the dog.

He slipped off the porch and crouched by the cabin. The faint moonlight revealed a dark shadow of a person creeping between the last cabin and the bunkhouse. Hawke moved along in front of his cabin and the next one before cutting across as the person reached the bunkhouse porch.

Dog started barking.

The door to the bunkhouse creaked.

"Come!" Hawke called to Dog. The person on the

porch started to run.

The bunkhouse door opened and Tuck stepped out.

"Halt!" Hawke shouted running after the person. When he didn't stop, Hawke gave the command. "Leap!"

Dog flew through the darkness, hitting the person in the back.

Hawke dropped, straddling the person, and grabbing at the arms. He immediately knew it wasn't the killer. The body was too small.

But whoever it was wasn't giving up. He raised up smacking Hawke in the face with the back of their stocking clad head.

His nose throbbed and tears welled in his eyes. The sting and surprise had Hawke riding a bucking body as the person used all of their might to try and dislodge him.

"Need help?" Tuck called from not far behind him.

"Get back to the bunkhouse!" Hawke shouted. This wasn't the killer. Could it have been a distraction for the killer to get to Kitree?

He finally grabbed one wrist. Placed the cuff on and pulled the other arm back and cuffed it. Dragging the person to his feet, Hawke's shoulder started throbbing. It appeared it was a good thing he was still on medical leave. He bit his bottom lip to stave off the pain and tasted blood. The suspect had split his lip as well as smashed his nose.

Not wanting to bother Dani, he shoved the person to his cabin. Dog followed on their heels. The suspect fought him all the way to the small building.

"Dog, Stay," he said, opening the cabin door.

Once inside, Hawke grabbed his flashlight sitting

on the table by the bed rather than release the suspect to try and light the lantern.

He shown the beam in the suspects face.

Dolan!

"What the hell are you doing trying to sneak into the bunkhouse?" He knew but didn't want her to know. "All you would have had to say out there was your name and I wouldn't have treated you like a killer."

Her eyes had blazed with hatred when the light shone in them. Her eyelids drooped, and she looked at him from under the lashes. She was hiding her true feelings, thinking of a way to make this work to her advantage.

What she didn't know was he had her number.

"I wanted to get the girl to the FBI. We need to question her about her parents." She raised her handcuffed hands behind her back. "Now that you know it's me, how about taking these off?"

He shook his head. "I don't like your answer." A soft push and she sat on the bed. "Where is your boss? Did he tell you to do this?"

She dropped her gaze to the floor. "He didn't say do it, but he didn't say don't either."

"You came up here alone to take the girl?" He shook his head. "I don't believe that. Someone had to come with you. How were you getting out of here once you had the girl? How did you get here?"

Her head came up. She glared at him. "You don't think I could have done this alone?"

"If you did, it didn't work, did it?"

Her lips curled up in a sneer.

Dog started barking.

The real killer this time. He was sure Dolan had

been a distraction. Using cording from his saddlebag, he quickly trussed her feet and hands together like a calf and tucked a clean bandana in her mouth.

Slipping out of the cabin, he spotted someone pouring something on the backside of the cabin. They were going to torch the building!

He raised his shotgun, found the man in his sights, and pulled the trigger.

The person screamed, tossed the can in the air, and took off running through the trees. The distance between him and the suspect wouldn't have made the shot fatal. He would, however, have gotten a good peppering of shot.

Hawke hoped one of the people stationed in the forest caught up to him and took him into custody.

Hawke hurried to the bunkhouse door and knocked. "It's Hawke. You need to get out of there."

The door opened. Tuck peered at him. "Was that you who shot?"

"Yeah. There was someone pouring what smells like kerosene on the back of the bunkhouse. He took off through the trees, but someone else could come along and set it on fire." Hawke opened the door and stood in the opening watching the area between the bunkhouse and lodge. "Gather Sage and Kitree. We'll go to the lodge."

He wasn't sure if any of the troopers or deputies watching the place would come in to see what happened. They had to be careful to make sure anyone they saw was planning to do harm and not an officer coming to their aide.

"Got them." Tuck said behind him.

"Kitree, Sage, get behind me and stay close. I'm

going to run toward the lodge. Tuck, you follow close behind."

"Are you hurt?" Kitree asked.

He turned back to the group. "Why?"

"You sound different."

It had to be his smashed nose and thickening lips. "Come on." They'd all see him soon enough if anyone turned on a lantern at the lodge.

As if on cue, a light shone in the lodge.

"Shit!" he said under his breath.

"What's wrong?" Sage asked.

"I don't know if the light in the lodge is from Dani or someone is in there waiting for us to show up." Dog sat at his feet. He and Dog could go check things out but that left the three back in the bunkhouse that could be set on fire.

He glanced at his cabin. Did he dare take them in there with Dolan?

A shadow by the side of the lodge caught his attention. Dog stood and growled low in his throat.

"I see it," he whispered.

"Hawke? Hawke?" Tyson whispered.

"Fetch," Hawke whispered to Dog.

The animal shot out from under the bunkhouse porch and straight to Tyson.

"Hey boy, what are you doing?"

The dog must have grabbed his hand. Within minutes the dog and young man were in front of Hawke.

"What's going on?" Tyson whispered. "Dani heard shots and sent me out here."

"Is she the one who lit the lamp?"

"Yeah."

Without any preamble, Hawke said, "Let's get to the lodge." He took off across the opening, listening to the feet padding along behind him.

As soon as he hit the porch the door opened. Dani herded them inside, giving Kitree a hug. "What happened?"

"Dog heard something. I went out and spotted someone pouring something on the back of the bunkhouse. Smelled like kerosene. I shot and sent him bolting through the trees. I went to get these three to bring them here but saw the light go on and wasn't sure it was safe." He moved them all into the dining room as he spoke.

"Tyson, you sit by a front window and watch for any movement out there." Hawke instructed the young man. "And grab a rifle from the case."

Tyson left the room.

"Tuck, keep an eye out the window in here in case someone tries to come in the back way."

The wrangler pulled a chair over to the only window in the room.

"Ladies, if you think you can sleep, use the beds in here." He scanned the three faces. Dani had determination and defiance on her oval shaped face. Sage's pixie face was wrinkled in worry.

Kitree's small brow was furrowed. Her gaze remained locked on his face. "You are hurt," she said.

Dani moved toward the kitchen. "I'll get water and a rag."

"It's nothing—"

"Mimi asked me how you really hurt your shoulder," Kitree said, leading him over to a chair and pulling him down to sit. "You really shouldn't tell her

263

your job isn't dangerous."

He was supposed to keep this girl alive and here she was chastising him for telling his mother white lies. "She was the one who said my being a game warden wouldn't be as worrisome for her."

Both Sage and Kitree gave him the look. The one women give when a man has said something stupid. That was something he hadn't missed from not having a woman in his life.

"You should have told her different." Kitree sat down on the chair next to him as Dani returned with the water and rag.

"What happened to you?" Dani asked, dipping the rag in the water and wringing it out.

"These two are accusing me—"

"Not now. What caused your nose to bleed and your lip to split?" Dani glanced from him to Sage and Kitree. "Then tell me why these two are upset."

If ever there was a time when Hawke wished he were somewhere else, it was now. "The person I caught—"

"You caught someone? I thought he ran off when you shot the gun?" Dani held the cloth soaking in his blood away from his face and stared at him.

"Before the person trying to torch the bunkhouse, I caught someone trying to sneak in." He licked his lip and wished he hadn't. The salty saliva made his lip sting. "She's tied up in my cabin."

"She?" All three females said at the same time.

Hawke started to stand. He should be helping keep an eye on things.

Dani shoved him back down in the chair with her hand on his sore shoulder.

"Ow!"

Kitree pointed a finger at him. "He told his mother his job wasn't dangerous."

Another scolding look from Dani and he'd had enough.

Hawke stood, making Dani move backwards or be bumped by him. "I have work to do. This is why I don't have a wife. You all worry too much."

He stalked out of the dining room and stopped by Tyson. "You see anything out there?"

"No. You think they are going to try again tonight?"

Hawke glanced at the old clock on the mantle. Four in the morning. "I doubt it. It'll be getting light soon."

"Damn! I was hoping tonight would be it. Now it will be another night without sleep and worrying." Tyson rubbed a hand over his face.

"Go on to your room and get a few hours of sleep. I'll take over here." Hawke waited for the young man to walk into the other room before he dropped onto the chair. He was getting too old for this shit. He stood back up, turned the chair around, straddled the seat, and put his good arm across the back of the chair, settling his chin on top.

The shadows faded as the clock ticked the seconds and the sun rose from the east. Hawke dozed a couple of times.

Dog whined. Hawke shook his head and glanced down. The dog had his nose pointed to the door.

"Need to find a tree, do you?" Hawke rose off the chair and groaned as his stiff muscles complained about the movement.

He opened the door and stepped out onto the porch.

The birds were singing. The faint scent of kerosene mingled with pine in the dewy morning air. He wasn't sure how to take the kerosene off the old wood of the bunkhouse. Or how long it would make the building flammable.

Scratching his healing shoulder with the butt of the shotgun, he glanced at the first cabin. The door was open. Damn! He jogged over and found the rope and handcuffs on the floor. His belongings had been looked through and strung all over.

One more person to be on the lookout for. She'd had balls last night thinking she could get into the bunkhouse on her own. No, he was pretty sure she had been a diversion all along. But now, she was a threat.

He bent over to pick up his things and a shadow fell across his hand. He grabbed the shotgun and whirled.

State Trooper Dillion stood in the doorway a fraction of a second before ducking inside. "What was the shot last night?"

Hawke lowered the gun, sat on the bed, and told him the details of the night before. All but finding the disk. That was better left to very few knowing that bit of information. "Didn't someone catch the guy? He took off running through the trees howling. He had to have taken some buckshot."

Dillion shook his head. "I was in the opposite direction. But no one radioed anything about that. Sullens told me to come see what happened since I was the closest."

"Why didn't you come last night?" He'd planned this for backup should the killer turn up.

"When I asked if I should check it out, someone

said to hold my position."

"Could you tell who said it?"

"It didn't sound familiar. I thought maybe it was a deputy." Dillion pulled out his radio and messed with the dials.

"Damn! They have your radio frequency. They know we're on to them." Hawke stood up and kicked his saddlebag. "They aren't going to wait around. They're going to be here tonight and get the job done." He handed the trooper a tablet. "Here's what you're going to do."

Chapter Twenty-seven

After Dillion disappeared, Hawke returned to the lodge. Tuck was sleeping on the couch in the great room. Sage and Kitree were cooking breakfast. Dani was in her office.

He and Dog entered Dani's office and closed the door.

Her eyebrows shot up at the closed door, but she spun her desk chair to face him. "What's up?"

"I'm sure they will be back tonight. The one I had tied up in the cabin is gone. Someone let her loose." He raised a hand when she opened her mouth. "We'll all stay in the lodge. In the great room. As soon as it's dark, the other officers on this detail will move into the other buildings. I told them to get in close. I'm sure they are going to come for the girl. They can't afford to have her in our hands much longer for fear we discover whatever it is they are after." He wasn't telling anyone he'd discovered what they were after.

268

Dani studied him. "You know what it is."

He shook his head.

"Sorry. I've dealt with a lot of slackers and I can tell when someone lies. But I'll not pry. What do I need to do tonight?"

"Before we go to bed, you need to keep Kitree away from the windows and doors. Anywhere that it would be easy for someone or several to surprise us and swoop in and grab her."

Dani looked around the office. "I'd say this is the best spot. No windows, a door I can lock, and even push the desk up against if need be." She pulled out a drawer. A Beretta M9 lay on top of papers. "I have my sidearm within reach."

He nodded and grasped the door knob to leave.

"Why did you lie to your mother?"

He released a huge lung full of air. "I didn't lie. White lies when it comes to family, in this business, help relieve the stress for them and for us. With her thinking I wasn't in as much danger as a Fish and Wildlife officer as I was when being a full-time trooper, it eased my mind she wasn't worrying as much." He shrugged. "I just wanted to give her peace of mind."

"That's nice, but she is a big girl. Women are stronger than you men give us credit for. And I'm pretty sure she knows you're a good cop. Good cops get hurt less in the line of duty than a sloppy one." She smiled.

It wasn't the first time he'd noticed how when she genuinely smiled her face had a softer, almost sexy quality to it.

Mental slap. He didn't need to go there. Not that long ago he was telling the females at this lodge why he didn't want or need a woman in his life.

"Thanks," he pushed out of his clogged throat and strode into the great room.

"I was looking for you." Kitree launched herself at him, wrapping her arms around his waist.

What was wrong with the females here? He pried her arms off his waist. "Why?" His irritation came through.

Her eyes narrowed and her lips puckered into a sour expression. "You don't have to be so mean."

"Sorry. You took me by surprise." He wasn't going to tell her, he didn't like being undercut by the opposite sex.

"We made pizza. All the way from the crust to the cheese on top."

The amazement in her voice drew his attention. It was apparent she didn't know how pizza was made. Had only eaten it.

"Are you enjoying helping Sage in the kitchen?" he asked.

"Yes." She spun around and walked over to the fireplace. "I like this place. I hope everything works."

He liked seeing her here. Even though Dani had worked hard to make this more than a hunting lodge, the child's presence would give the place more of a resort feel.

"It will. But tonight, you have to do everything Dani asks you to do." He crouched in front of her. "Kitree, I'm pretty sure the man who killed your parents will come for you tonight. You don't need to worry, but you need to do as you're told."

She nodded. "You'll arrest him?"

"That's the plan."

"Good."

《》《》《》

Dinner was over. Hawke, Tuck, and Tyson were all keeping their eyes on the doors and windows of the lodge. The birds had stopped singing about thirty minutes after they'd taken their spots. It was either the deputies and troopers moving in or the person after Kitree.

Hawke sat in front of the big window, looking out at the other buildings. Tuck was in one of the bedrooms keeping watch out a window and Tyson was in the dining room watching the smaller out buildings. Dani, Sage, and Kitree had all disappeared into Dani's office shortly after dinner. Once they had all left, Hawk turned down the lanterns in the great room to see outside better and so no one outside could see in. He didn't want them completely off, if someone entered and they needed light, it would be easy to turn the lanterns up.

He believed the law enforcement officers that were on their side had stationed themselves in all of the outbuildings. Now they just had to wait and see how Dolan and the killer approached the lodge.

The clock on the mantle ticked the seconds in a slow monotonous tone. He would have rather been sitting outside, listening to the forest sounds of the night. They had their own cadence. There was nothing monotonous about the sounds.

A shadow moved over by the helicopter. Hawke hoped someone was keeping an eye on the aircraft. He didn't want Dani to go out and find her plane and helicopter had been vandalized.

He kept an eye on the shadow as it crept towards the barn. The person slipped through the barn door. He hoped whoever was waiting in the barn captured the intruder and kept them silent.

Hawke stood and walked to another window for a different view of the area. He saw two more people walk out of the trees from a different direction.

One headed to the bunkhouse and one to the cabins. Maybe these were the deputies and troopers heading to the buildings. But he'd thought they had entered the buildings earlier.

Unsavory thoughts banged around inside his head. What if the first people he'd seen were actually the suspects and not the law enforcement officers? If that were the case the deputies and state troopers' lives were in peril.

Pacing back and forth, glancing out the window every other step, he chastised himself for getting so many people involved in a scheme that was highly irregular. He'd been confident it would work, but hadn't counted on the FBI having an informant in their midst who wanted the disk at any cost. Who were they working against? A group of terrorists or their own government?

If this didn't work, Kitree could lose her life, they all could be dead by morning. And if he lived, he would never work in law enforcement again.

A noise on the porch caught his attention. He slipped up to the side of the window and peered out.

Dolan.

The FBI agent had something that looked like a tear gas launcher in her hands.

Damn!

He hadn't expected them to try to flush them out with tear gas. There wasn't a window in the office for

the three hiding there to get out or to get fresh air.
Maybe…just maybe...

Hawke hurried down the hallway and knocked
quietly on the door. "Dani. Cover all the cracks around
the door and put the desk up against it. They may be
using tear gas to get in. Stay there until I tell you to
come out."

Hawke didn't wait to see if she'd heard. There was
only one way to stop the FBI agent before she could
shoot the canister into the house. He hurried back into
the great room and threw the front door open, startling
the agent. He grasped the tear gas launcher out of her
hands at the same time he landed a kick to her stomach,
knocking her backwards.

He tossed the gun into the lodge and grasped the
women by the arm, dragging her in before slamming
the door shut with his foot.

"Tuck! Tuck, get out here!" Hawke grappled with
the fighting woman. She knew about his injury. Her fist
or head connected with his sore shoulder as much as
she could, but he refused to let her go.

The wrangler burst out of the back bedroom.
"What's going on?" His gaze landed on Hawke and the
struggling woman. He raised his rifle. "Stop moving or
I'll put a bullet in your leg." His voice sounded more
menacing than Hawke had ever heard him.

Dolan stopped fighting. Hawke grasped both her
hands behind her back. "She was going to shoot tear
gas in here."

Hawke nodded to the launcher on the floor. "Over
there. Grab it and get it away from the window."
Hawke was glad he'd picked up the handcuffs the agent
had left behind when she got loose in the cabin. He

pulled them out of his pocket and quickly had her cuffed and immobile, sitting in a chair.

"Find something I can tie her feet with."

Tuck arrived at his side with cording from the blinds. Both ends had been cut. Hawke cursed in his head. Dani would get him for this.

He tied the agent's feet to the legs of the chair she sat in.

"You think you're so smart. All you had to do was turn over the girl and you wouldn't have had to go through all of this," Dolan said.

"Why do you want the little girl so bad? She knows nothing."

Dolan sneered. "She knows everything."

Hawke shook his head. "I don't know who you've been talking to. She knows nothing. She's innocent. Whoever you're working for is a monster to kill her parents and now to kill her. He knows more than you even know."

She laughed. "You don't know who I'm working for."

Hawke decided it was time to give her a piece of his knowledge. "You belong to the Taliban."

Her jaw dropped down, and her eyes widened as she stared at him.

"Yes. I've seen what you're looking for."

He knew he'd just made himself the new target. But he might have given Kitree a chance to stay alive.

"What are we going to do with her?" Tuck asked.

"Shove something in her mouth, so she can't give us away. Then get ready for all hell to break loose."

Tuck found a box of tissues and pulled out a handful, shoving them in Dolan's mouth.

"Go tell Tyson to keep an eye out. I have a feeling even though the tear gas didn't work, they'll still storm the place.

Tuck nodded and walked into the dining room.

Hawke decided to try a little interrogation with the woman. "Were your people in the out buildings before the law enforcement showed up?"

She couldn't answer with the gag in her mouth.

Words could be held back, but physical reactions were harder to control.

Her eyes narrowed. He was pretty sure that meant she hadn't known there were lawmen in the buildings. This was a relief. It meant there were probably only the killer and a couple others to try the lodge. That gave them a better chance.

Tuck returned. "Tyson said he saw a shadow moving between the outhouse and shower house."

Hawke nodded. "They're probably getting ready to get the girl."

He didn't take his gaze off Dolan. She looked pretty smug. Which didn't set well in his gut. What did she know that he didn't?

Tear gas hadn't worked. What did they have for plan B?

"Do you want me to go back in the bedroom?" Tuck asked.

"No, just open the doors. That way we'll know if someone comes through a window." Hawke noticed the women's eyebrow raise a tad at the mention of the back windows.

"Why don't you set a chair over there along the wall and whoever walks through those doors, blast them."

Tuck grinned. He opened the doors and positioned a chair in the corner by the fireplace and took a seat. "This will be like shooting coyotes."

Chapter Twenty-eight

Hawke noticed the stone fireplace pretty much hid Tuck where he sat in the corner watching the bedroom doors. What if he made it look like there was no one in the great room but Dolan all trussed up?

"Stay tucked in that corner," he said to the wrangler and walked over to turn the lantern light up brighter. "If she tries anything, shoot her," Hawke added and ducked into the shadow of the hallway. He'd catch anyone who came through the back door or the front door.

Hawke leaned his back against the hall wall and listened. Tyson was moving around in the dining room. He hoped the young man hadn't decided to make a sandwich and left his post.

The thought had barely died from his mind and the door to the dining room burst open. Tyson struggled with an arm that was around his throat and the large body behind him making him move forward.

Paty Jager

One look and Hawke froze in the shadowed hall. It was the man who'd shot him, and they were pretty sure had killed the Poulsons.

The man pushed Tyson into the great room. "Where's the girl?" he asked in a heavily accented voice.

"I don't know what you're talking about," Tuck said from the corner of the room. His voice was hard and not a waver in it. The man had to be tough to have ridden broncs, but standing up to a terrorist took a whole different set of balls.

When he figured the intruder had to be far enough into the room he could come up behind him, Hawke crept up the hall and peeked around the corner.

The man was just reaching out with his gun hand to take the tissue from Dolan's mouth.

Hawke rushed in, smashing the butt of his shotgun down on the man's head. The intruder crumpled at Hawke's feet and Tyson fell forward onto Dolan.

Hawke grabbed Tyson. "Go get some handcuffs from one of the other officers outside." He glanced at Tuck. "Get me more cording." He didn't care if he had to buy Dani all new drapes, this man was going to be trussed up like a tom turkey on Thanksgiving.

Tyson ran out the front door.

Tuck arrived with cording and his rifle aimed at the man's back. Hawke pulled the hands behind the man and quickly tied them tight. Then he pulled the man's legs together and tied them tight. He didn't want this person getting loose.

Tyson and Sullens burst through the door. Sullens handed his handcuffs to Hawke. He also put those on the unconscious man not taking off the cording.

"What did you do to him?" Sullens asked.

"Hit him with the butt of my shotgun. Did you get the others?" Hawke stood and glanced at the door.

"We caught everyone who tried to hide in buildings and caught one syphoning fuel from the helicopter." Sullens glanced around. "Where are the women and the girl?"

"I'll get them if you're sure we have them all."

"I believe we do, I can't be sure, since we don't know who all was involved." Sullens' gaze landed on Dolan. "Isn't that the FBI—"

"She's a terrorist who infiltrated the FBI." Hawke smiled as the woman glared at him.

"Does that other agent, McKinney, know about her?"

"I doubt it. Let's radio that we have suspects to transport out of here." Hawke glanced at Tuck. "Keep that gun on him. When he comes to, he's going to be one angry son-of-a-bitch."

"If he tries to cause trouble, I'll put a bullet in him, one limb at a time." Tuck grinned.

"Where do you get your help?" Sullens asked as Hawke led him down the hallway to the office.

"Rural America." Hawke knocked on the door. "Dani, it's Hawke. All's clear. We need to use the radio."

Scraping noises on the other side of the door and some feminine grunts ensued. Several minutes later the door opened.

Sage looked shell-shocked but Dani and Kitree's eyes questioned him.

"We think we have them all. No one but the bad guys were hurt," he said, to Sage.

279

She released a huge sigh.

"We need to radio for a copter to take at least the two ringleaders out of here. The rest can be trailed down on horseback." Hawke stepped aside, to allow the two women and the girl to step out of the room.

"Should we go into the living room?" Dani asked.

"Why don't you three hang out in the dining room until we get the two that are in the great room moved out of the lodge." Hawke didn't want the man or Kitree to see one another. He wasn't sure what the man would do and didn't want the child scared.

Dani nodded and put an arm around Kitree. He watched as they turned at the end of the hall, going straight into the dining room.

Hawke entered the office to contact dispatch. "How many did you capture outside?"

"Four."

He nodded. "Dispatch, patch me through to State Police, Lt. Titus."

The radio crackled and after a minute the lieutenant came on. "Titus."

"This is Hawke. We have six suspects to transport. Two should be helicoptered out of here. You'll want to question them right away and keep a close eye on them."

"Is one the killer?"

"I believe so. If not, he *is* the one who shot me." They could get the man for assaulting an officer.

"Hold them overnight. I'll send a copter there first thing in the morning for the two. Have the officers up there bring the other four out on horseback."

"Copy." Hawke signed off and turned to Sullens. "I think the best thing to do would be to put them all in the barn with guards for the night."

"I agree." Sullens stepped out into the hall. "I'll help you move the two in the lodge."

They walked into the great room and found the man had regained consciousness. As Hawke had figured, his dark eyes spit hatred and his face was screwed in an angry scowl.

"We're moving them to the barn with the others," Hawke said and drew his knife out of his boot to cut the cording holding Dolan to the chair. Her eyes glowed with as much wrath as the man.

Tuck and Sullens stepped to either side of the man. Hawke reached down to cut the man's legs so he could walk and had second thoughts. If he were an ex-special ops soldier he would be deadly with just his feet.

"Grab him under the arms and drag him. I don't trust him to not try something if I untie his feet."

Tuck and the trooper grabbed the suspect and dragged him out of the lodge. The man's dark eyes narrowed on Hawke.

Dolan stood. Hawke grabbed her handcuffed hands behind her and moved her out of the building ahead of him. They may have caught this group of people looking for the disk in his boot, but until he got it into the government's hands, he would be the target of who knew how many other groups who had spies on the list. The woman pushing against him knew he had seen the list and knew he probably had it.

At the barn, he found all the captured suspects sitting on the floor along a wall. He shoved Dolan over to a pole and sat her down with her back to the others. He didn't need her giving any kind of eye blinking morse code to the deadliest man of the group.

Sullens was talking to a deputy.

Hawke walked over. "Keep them gagged. We don't need them talking to one another."

The others nodded.

"And keep the woman away from the men, don't take her gag out, and don't let her make eye contact." He peered into Sullens, and then, the deputy's eyes.

"I'll talk to whoever comes for them in the morning." Hawke walked out of the barn.

The door closed behind him.

Tuck stood by the corral, petting a horse that stood next to the railing.

"You did a good job in there," Hawke said, stopping by the man.

"It seemed like a joke until that man burst out of the dining room with his arm around Tyson. That boy's face was turning blue. That man…" Tuck swallowed loudly. "He would have killed us all given the chance."

"He's a paid killer. Nothing will keep him from getting what he is paid to get or who he is paid to kill." Hawke slapped him on the back. "Let's go. Hold Sage tight tonight. You never know when that could be taken away from you."

"No shit." Tuck fell in step beside him.

In the lodge the women had made hot chocolate and set out cookies. It seemed tame to sip cocoa and nibble on cookies after what they'd gone through. He would have preferred a shot of whiskey. He doubted Dani kept liquor in the lodge. Booze and hunters or families with children didn't mix well.

"Is Kitree safe now?" Sage asked.

The child's gaze landed on him. Hope sparked in her blue eyes.

"I'd like to say yes, but until the right people get their hands on what these people were after, I have to say I don't know." Hawke put a hand on Kitree's shoulder. "You should be safe in the next couple of days. Until then, we'll have to keep smothering you."

She stood and hugged him around the neck. "I'm glad you aren't hurt."

He wasn't going to tell her his shoulder throbbed from the beating Dolan had given it. He'd pushed that aside to make sure they caught the biggest threat. "I'm glad no one from the lodge was seriously hurt." He glanced across the table at Tyson. Bruising had started to appear on the young wrangler's neck.

"How did that guy get in?" Hawke asked.

Tyson's face turned a deep crimson. "I got hungry and went in the kitchen to get something to eat. I came back out and saw him coming through the window. Before I could get to my rifle by the window, he had me in a headlock."

Hawke had a feeling the young man was having second thoughts about becoming a game warden from the way he rubbed his neck.

"I suggest we all sleep in the lodge tonight. Safer in numbers." A glance around the table proved no one objected to this.

"Kitree can sleep with me so you have a bed," Dani said.

Hawke shook his head. "I'll be on the couch in the great room." He smiled at Kitree. "I'm not taking any chances that we missed someone."

"Then I insist you nail the window to the sill in her bedroom. That way if anyone tries to enter, you'll hear breaking glass," Dani said, rising and heading into the kitchen.

Hawke stared after the woman. "I think she doesn't trust that we rounded up everyone."

Kitree giggled. "She said a lot of things while we were in the office listening."

"She did? What kind of things?" He grinned at the child as if they had a secret.

Dani walked back in, and Kitree put a finger to her lips.

"Here is a hammer and nails." Dani handed the tool over to him.

Hawke scooted his chair back. Tuck followed him into the bedroom closest to the hallway.

"How do you put up with her bossy nature?" Hawke asked.

"Just like I've learned over the years. Say 'yes, Ma'am',' no Ma'am' and do what you're told." Tuck grinned and Hawke laughed.

"That is true." He put two nails through the window frame and into the side of the window casing. It was a good idea and one he probably would have come up with about daylight. Speaking of which.

"Have Sage get Kitree to bed. We only have a few more hours and it will be daylight and the helicopter should be landing to take the two away."

Tuck hurried out of the room.

Hawke sauntered through the great room and on into the kitchen when he didn't find Dani in the dining room. She was washing out the mugs they'd had their hot chocolate in.

"Sorry I brought more problems to your lodge," he said, picking up a towel to dry the dishes.

"I'm not. Kitree needs someone. Sage and Tuck are

good people." She turned from the pan of sudsy water. "You're good people."

He stared into her eyes, trying to figure out if she was making a pass at him. "I have my good and my bad days." Dropping his gaze, he picked up another cup. This woman did things to his brain and body that hadn't happened in years. However, now wasn't the time to forget he was guarding a child.

His job was his life.

Chapter Twenty-nine

Hawke rose from the couch. While it looked comfortable, it had a lot of uncomfortable to it. He walked into the kitchen, added kindling to the woodstove, and added coffee to the pot of water Dani had placed on the back burner before they'd left the kitchen.

The thumping of helicopter blades broke the stillness.

He walked out to the front porch and stared toward the landing strip. Dog joined him. It wasn't the helicopter the State Patrol kept on retainer. The glow of sunlight bouncing off the sides made it hard to tell what the aircraft looked like.

The person who stepped out of the helicopter was familiar. What in hell was he doing here?

Hawke grabbed his shotgun that he'd leaned up against the wall by the door when he went in the kitchen and headed across the ground between the lodge and the landing strip. Dog trotted beside him.

"Trooper Hawke, I'm here to take the prisoners," FBI Agent McKinney said.

Hawke glanced at the helicopter. He'd flown the aircraft himself. "Where are the guards?"

"You have them handcuffed, don't you?"

"Who? Who do you think we have handcuffed?" Hawke studied the man.

"The people I've come to pick up."

"How did you find out about them?" Hawke wasn't letting this man anywhere near the people tied up in the barn. He had to be part of the group. Hawke had only read a small portion of the names on the list. McKinney had to be there as well.

"Lt. Titus. He said you had prisoners that needed picked up this morning. I offered to come get them."

"How many did he say needed picked up?" Hawke cradled his shotgun in his arms. He heard footsteps approaching him from behind.

McKinney's gaze flit over Hawke's shoulder then back to him. "Five suspects needed transported."

Sullens stopped beside him. "Morning, Agent McKinney. What brings you to Charlie's Hunting Lodge?"

"I'm here to collect the suspects." The man's tone was losing its bravado.

Sullens shook his head. "We don't have orders to hand anyone over to you." He glanced at Hawke. "Do we, Hawke?"

"That's what I was trying to tell him." Hawke pointed the shotgun at the federal agent. "And I believe when the 'real' FBI agents get their hands on the list Mrs. Poulson was making, your name is going to be on it."

McKinney spun around and sprinted toward the helicopter.

"Dog! Leap!" Dog sprang from his side, tore across the space between them and the agent, and launched off his haunches, landing in the middle of the man's back, taking him to the ground face first.

Hawke and Sullens raced over. Sullens jabbed his knee in the agent's back and pulled his hands behind him, using his own handcuffs to detain the man.

"When the helicopter gets here, looks like we'll be able to transport all of the suspects by helicopter, thanks to McKinney bringing us an extra one." Hawke jabbed the agent in the back with his shotgun. "Stand!"

He walked the agent over to the porch.

Tuck stepped out on the porch. "What the—"

"Wanna grab me more cording. I'm going to owe Dani new drapes in every room before this is over." Hawke pushed the agent's back up to a porch post.

Tuck returned with the cording.

"Tie him to the pole," Hawke said.

"Coffee's on inside," Tuck offered when he had the agent tied. "If you want to get a cup of coffee, I'll keep an eye on this fella."

Hawke handed the shotgun over. "Same as last night."

"Got it. One limb at a time."

McKinney's eyes widened.

Hawke walked into the lodge laughing. He had a pretty good notion they'd just caught the ring leader.

"Did I hear the helicopter?" Dani asked, pouring him a cup of coffee and going back to toasting bread on a griddle on the stove while Sage stirred a large pan of scrambled eggs.

"You did. Think you can fly a copter the FBI use?"

She spun toward him. "Why? Did a pilot get hurt?"

Kitree walked into the kitchen. "Did I hear a helicopter?"

"You did, but it wasn't the one coming to take the bad guys away." Hawke took his cup of coffee and sat down with the child. "I want you to stay here with Tuck, Sage, and Tyson. Dani has to fly a helicopter for me. We'll be back tonight." He pushed a lock of the child's hair off her face. "And if all goes well, we'll have good news for you."

"Do you have the man who killed Momma and Daddy?" She peered into his eyes.

He couldn't lie to her to make her feel better. "We have the man who shot me. I believe it is the same person. We aren't going to know until we compare his gun with the bullets."

She nodded. "But he'll go to jail for shooting you?"

"Yes. He will."

"Good. That will give you time to prove he did kill Momma and Daddy."

Sage placed a cup of hot chocolate in front of Kitree.

"Yes, it will." Hawke stood.

"Tell the officers out there to take shifts and come in and get something to eat," Dani said.

He nodded. "When you get a chance, go check out the helicopter sitting on the landing strip. If you can fly it, we'll take part of the suspects to La Grande."

"I'll go check it as soon as the others get something to eat."

Hawke grabbed two slices of bread and headed back out.

McKinney was trying to tell Tuck that Hawke was the bad person and he should let him go.

"I'm an FBI agent. Check my pocket for my I.D."

Tuck glanced at Hawke. "I think you caught a crazy one here."

Hawke laughed. "Keep an eye on him. I'm going to have a talk with Sullens."

He opened the barn door and noticed Dolan wiggling as if working the cording loose. Hurrying over, he made her drop a cuff key. It glistened in the dirt and hay by the pole. Stupid. He hadn't thought about her having a key to unlock the cuffs.

Scooping up the key, he motioned to one of the deputies. "Check all of their pockets and take out anything they have on them."

He'd have Dani go through Dolan's pockets when she came out to check the copter. Hawke walked over to Sullens. "Send half the men in to get breakfast. When they return the other half can get some."

Sullens ordered the deputies to get something to eat in the lodge. He pulled Hawke to the side. "Will Ms. Singer be able to fly the other helicopter?"

"I'm betting she can. She and I will take the big scary one, the woman, and the FBI agent out front." He had a plan.

"But those three are the worst of the lot." Sullens brows knit with indecision.

"There should be room to take the other four in the helicopter that comes for them. Send a couple of deputies or troopers with them and the rest can ride out of here. I'd be obliged if whoever goes out by horseback leads out Jack and Horse. Ms. Singer and I'll need them to get back in here." The thought of spending six hours leisurely horseback riding up the mountain with Dani pleased him more than it should have.

"Will do."

The first batch of officers returned and the last of them, along with Sullens, headed into the kitchen.

Hawke sat on a wooden box watching the man who shot him and the woman. They seemed as if they were just sitting in the barn because they wanted to. The other four, had wide scared eyes that watched every move everyone made. Dolan and the killer were in a league much higher than the men they'd brought with them. After seeing how flustered McKinney had been, he now had a feeling Dolan was the mastermind. She was the one that had to crack.

Dani stuck her head in the door. "Hawke?"

"Coming." He strode to the door and out before Dani got a good look at the people in the barn.

Out in the sunshine, he squinted at the brightness. "Did you check out the helicopter?"

"Yes. It's just like one I flew about ten years ago. It will be a piece of cake. I'll fuel it up and do a flight check."

"Good. Another thing. Is there a way to record conversations where the arrested passengers will be sitting?"

She studied him for several seconds. "Yes. I think I can make that happen. Why?"

"I'm hoping if they think we can't hear them, they'll talk among themselves." He grinned as the thump of helicopter blades grew in volume.

Dani wandered to the helicopter McKinney flew in. He headed to greet the landing helicopter.

《》《》《》

Hawke sat in the cockpit of the helicopter with Dani as it rose up off the ground. He'd made sure the three in the back were far enough apart they couldn't help the one next to them get loose. They were also handcuffed to a piece of the aircraft preventing them from getting into the cockpit and causing trouble.

The aircraft with the other four suspects and one deputy took off twenty minutes before they had. The pilot of the other helicopter was a man Hawke had known for years. He'd said they were to land at the Union County Jail in La Grande. The trip would take less than an hour.

As they moved laterally, Hawke nodded to Dani to turn on the intercom to the back. McKinney didn't have a gag. Hawke had made sure Dolan's tissues were about to fall out of her mouth when he'd finished leaning over her to fasten her to the aircraft. And he'd nudged the gag on the big guy.

"Did you get the disk?" McKinney asked.

"What do you think?" Dolan spat. "Why didn't you bring in help when we didn't return to the helicopter?"

"I figured these backwoods doofuses would hand you over to me. I am the FBI." He said it as if he wanted the woman to believe him.

"You are working for us. And that Hawke is smarter than you give him credit for or you'd be flying us and not that woman." It was quiet for several minutes. "He has the disk or has seen it." Dolan said.

"He made a comment that made me think the same," McKinney said.

"I should have killed him when I had the chance. Him and the girl." The big man didn't disguise his accent. "If not for that imbecile, John, I would have."

"Mahir, no one saw you kill the couple. The girl didn't see anything. She never saw you. There is no need to kill her. But we must get the disk." Dolan's words faded off as Dani slowly descended to the ground.

The square building that housed the Union County Jail came into view.

The other helicopter was sitting on one side of the parking lot. Dani lowered their aircraft skillfully down in the area across the parking lot.

Several county deputies and two men dressed in suits came out of the jail. When the blades stopped spinning, they all converged on the helicopter, taking away, McKinney, Dolan, and Mahir.

Dani unplugged her phone from a cable and grinned. "We got them."

Hawke nodded.

They exited the helicopter and strode up to the jail entrance. One of the men in suits walked toward them. There was something about the man that looked familiar. Hawke put a hand out to stop Dani.

The man walked up and held out his hand. "Happy to see my blowing it with Mahir saved your life, Trooper Hawke."

Hawke grasped his hand as the man raised his glasses. His hair was shorter but it was the man who'd kept Mahir from blowing his head off at the lodge.

"And you are?"

"Special Agent Sean Acton. I was in the group with Mahir hunting for the girl. It was our best bet of getting our hands on the disk before anyone outside the U.S. government did. After all you'd experienced to keep Kitree alive, I couldn't let him blow your head off. You were our only hope of keeping the girl alive and finding the disk."

Hawke glanced over at Dani to see if she believed the man.

She eyed him suspiciously. "Why did you let him beat me and Tyson up?"

The man did have the conscience to blush. "That was something I wish I could have stopped. But to do that would have blown my cover earlier than stopping him from shooting this trooper. If I had stopped him from hitting you, he would have killed this man and possibly all of you."

Dani dipped her chin as if acknowledging what he'd said. "On the way here, the woman mentioned Mahir killed Kitree's parents. It's on my phone." She held it out to the agent.

The man's eyes lit up. "That will put Mahir away for a long time. Along with having assaulted you." He glanced at Hawke and took the phone. "We at the Federal Bureau appreciate your help."

"What about the disk?" Hawke asked, waiting to see what the man said.

Acton sighed. "We've gone through everything in the Poulson house and can't find it. If we can't say we have it and keep the terrorists named on that list at bay, that girl will be hounded and possibly killed."

"Can't you just say you did find it?" Dani asked, her voice sounded strangled.

Hawke knew how much she cared for Kitree. The thought of the child always being a target for something her mother did irked him.

He pried his boot off his foot, pulled his knife out and cut a few more stitches before turning his boot upside down. A couple of hard shakes and the disk fell into the palm of his hand.

"You found it!" That the man didn't make a grab for it gave Hawke the impression he was for real and not another fake FBI agent. "How?"

"Let's just say, my tracking skills were used." He placed the disk in the man's hand. "Any chance you can give us a ride to Wallowa County?"

"We need your statements first. After that, we'll give you a lift anywhere you want to go."

Chapter Thirty

Kitree paced back and forth on the lodge porch. Hawke had promised he'd be there last night. If he hadn't radioed and told Tuck he would be here today, she wouldn't have slept last night.

Sage was cleaning the bunkhouse, making it ready for them to sleep in tonight. She said with Dani coming home and all the trouble gone, they could start living like a family.

But was the trouble gone? They hauled off the people who had been trying to kill her, but did they find whatever the people were after? Would they come for her again? How could she live up here on the mountain without Hawke to watch over her if the bad people came back? That fear had kept her awake long into the night. She'd heard coyotes yip, an owl hoot, and even the digging of something outside her window. That sound had scared her the most. Had someone come back to get her?

Dog walked up and licked her hand. He'd been her protector last night. He'd slept on the bed and gave her comfort when her heart had raced. With Dog here, she knew Hawke would come back.

Sage walked across the area between the bunkhouse and lodge. "The circles are getting darker under your eyes. Are you sure you don't want to take a nap?" She put a hand on Kitree's shoulder.

"I'm fine. I can't sleep until Hawke gets back."

Dog woofed and headed to the trail heading down the mountain.

Kitree stared at the trail, waiting, holding her breath.

Jack's head appeared, then Hawke. Behind him on another horse rode Dani.

She took off at a run toward the horses. "You're back!"

Dog woofed in excitement running around the horses and her.

Hawke reached down, and she put her hand in his. He lifted her up behind him on Jack. "I told you, I'd be back. Didn't Tuck tell you last night I'd be here today?"

She put her arms around Hawke. "He did, but I didn't know if people were still looking for what Momma hid."

They stopped at the hitching rail by the barn. Dani dropped off her horse and headed to the lodge. Hawke eased her around to his lap and holding onto her, he stepped off the horse, placing her on the ground in front of him.

"No one will be looking for you again. I turned the information over to a real FBI agent. They will make sure everyone knows they have it and not you."

"Thank you!" She flung her arms around the man she'd come to think of as her best friend and cried.

Hawke felt the warm wetness and looked down. Tears poured out of Kitree's eyes. "Hey, there's nothing to cry about." He knelt beside her. Kitree's small arms tangled around his neck. "You have nothing to be afraid of. Tuck and Sage will love you and take care of you, and Dani will be here when you want to vent about your parents."

The child leaned back and looked at him with a furrowed brow. "What do you mean 'vent about my parents?'"

"All kids get mad at their parents now and then. I'm sure being first time parents Tuck and Sage will make some rules you don't think are fair…"

"Tuck and Sage. My parents…" Her tears dried and as the words worked their way into her mind her smile grew. "My second parents."

"That's right. Not many kids can say they've had two sets of parents. You'll have the ones that brought you into the world and Tuck and Sage who helped you grow."

"I like that." Kitree put her hands on her hips. "Get Jack unsaddled, Sage made chicken and dumplings for dinner."

Hawke watched her skip off to the lodge. "Now I have another female toying with emotions I've buried."

Dog sat at his feet and yawned.

《》《》《》

Rattlesnake Brother

Gabriel Hawke Novel

Book 3

Chapter One

Two large objects wrapped in brown sacking hung in a pine tree twenty feet off the dirt road. Two bull elk heads leaned against the base of the tree. A lone camper, closed up as if no one were there, sat thirty feet from the tree with a fire pit between the camper and tree. There wasn't a vehicle in sight.

Fish and Wildlife State Trooper Gabriel Hawke stopped his vehicle. He started to type the camper's license plate number into his computer. No signal. His right hand settled on his radio mic at his left shoulder. "Dispatch. This is Hawke. I'm about five miles from Coyote Springs on Forest Service Road forty-eight-sixty. I've come across a lone camper and two elk hanging in a tree. The camper license is Oregon- …" He called in the number and scanned the area waiting for the dispatcher's reply.

"The camper belongs to Duane Sigler of Eagle, Oregon."

Sigler. The man had a penchant for poaching. "Copy."

Hawke turned off his vehicle and stepped out, putting his cap on his head. He tucked his head down in the fur-lined collar of his coat. The first of November in

Wallowa County always had a bite in the air. At this elevation, three inches of snow covered the ground.

No one appeared to be in the camper. There wasn't the hiss of a propane furnace. No sound, no movement. He knocked on the door just in case someone was sleeping.

No answer.

He scanned the area. Two folding chairs leaned up against the camper. Two elk, two people, that was okay. But then why were they out driving around if they'd already filled their tags?

The antlers were a three point and a four-point. Either one would make a nice trophy of the hunt on a wall.

Hawke walked over. There were tags tied to the base of the antlers. Just as required. That was a good sign, considering one of the hunters liked to not play by hunting rules.

He untied the string around one tag and opened it. The month and date hadn't been notched out. Not a good sign. He glanced at the name on the tag. Duane Sigler. That matched the camper license. He tied that tag back on and untied the other one.

Again, the tag wasn't notched out. Benjamin Lange. Hawke stared at the name. The county district attorney wouldn't be hunting with a known poacher, would he? It could be someone with the same name.

A glance at the address and he was pretty sure it was the district attorney. The D.A. lived on the west side of Wallowa Lake and that was the address listed.

Hawke replaced the tag and decided he'd wait for the hunters to return.

《》《》《》

Thirty minutes later as Hawke finished off a cup of coffee, Sigler's pickup slowly drove up the road. There had been two pickups with hunters and a jeep come by while he waited. He'd talked to the people in each vehicle and wrote them down in his log book.

The '90s faded red, Ford pickup crept up to the trailer. Two men stepped out.

Neither one was D.A. Lange.

Hawke slipped out of his vehicle after turning on his recording device.

"Morning. Looks like you've had a good season," he said, motioning toward the elk hanging in the tree.

Sigler walked over to him cautiously. "Yeah. Bagged them yesterday. Season started two days ago. We're legal."

That the man was already on the defensive didn't surprise Hawke. "I didn't say you weren't. Could I see your hunting licenses and tags?"

The other person with Sigler pulled his wallet out of his pocket. Sigler remained still. They'd had their share of run-ins over the years. The man never helped himself by cooperating.

Hawke took the other man's hunting license, opened his log book and wrote down his name and address. Barney Price. His address was Gresham, Oregon.

"Can I see your hunting tag?" Hawke asked, handing the license back. The man headed to the elk with the D.A.'s tag.

Sigler's lips pressed together and his face grew redder with each step the other man took back to them.

"Thank you." Hawke unfolded the tag already knowing what he'd find. "Mr. Price, why didn't you notch out the date you killed this animal?"

The man glanced at Sigler. "I didn't know I was supposed to."

"And why is the name Benjamin Lange on a hunting tag you put on your elk? Your hunting license states you are Barney Price." Hawke held his gaze on the man, but kept Sigler in his peripheral vision.

Price faced Sigler. "You told me this wasn't a problem. That the person who owned the tag sold it to you."

Hawke put up a hand to stop the man's outrage. "Mr. Price, hunting tags can't be bought and sold among hunters. Only the person who puts in for the tag and purchases it can use it to shoot the animal, defined on the tag." He tucked his notebook back in his pocket. "I'm afraid you have violated several hunting regulations. The worst being you used a tag that isn't yours and,,," he glanced at Sigler, "you provided him with the tag."

"Why you!" Price took a step toward Sigler. "I'm not paying any fines or going to jail. You are! And I'll make sure everyone knows what an unethical hunting guide you are."

Hawke stepped between the two men. "Take those elk down. You'll help me put them in the back of my truck," Hawke told both men.

Once the elk, heads and all, were stowed in the back of Hawke's pickup, he cuffed the two men and put them in the back seat of his vehicle.

While they sat in the back glaring at one another, Hawke confiscated their weapons from Sigler's pickup. He checked to see if they were unloaded. Price's still had a cartridge in the chamber. He ejected that shaking his head.

Stowing the rifles in the tool box in the bed of the pickup, he heard the two men arguing inside the vehicle but couldn't make out exactly what was being said.

Hawke locked the pickup and camper, hoping Sigler had the camper key in his pocket or in the pickup.

When he slipped in behind the steering wheel, both men stopped talking.

Hawke peered into the review mirror at Sigler as he started the vehicle. "How did you get a hold of D. A. Lange's hunting tag?"

Sigler peered back at him. "Lange gave it to me. He said I could use his tag."

Hawke chuckled. "The District Attorney knows you can't gift tags."

Sigler glared at him. "He gave it to me."

"You might want to rethink that story on the way to jail," Hawke said, putting the vehicle in gear and heading back to Alder. Looked like there wouldn't be any more time spent out here. By the time he booked these two and dropped the elk off at the local butcher, he'd have just enough time to catch D.A Lange at work and ask him about "gifting" the tag to a known poacher.

《》《》《》

Hawke walked from the county jail next door to the courthouse in Alder, the county seat. He wanted to have a talk with D.A. Lange.

He walked up the concrete steps, admiring the original two-story courthouse built in 1909. The stone for the building had been cut at a quarry on the slope southwest of Alder. The lower level housed the court room and the county offices that took payments. Tax collector. Water Master.

Hawke walked up the narrow staircase to the offices on the second floor. He'd always thought it was interesting that the D.A.'s office looked out over the city park.

The receptionist, a young woman who had grown up in the area and stepped into her grandmother's footsteps, pulled her gaze from the computer monitor on her desk. "May I help you?"

"I wondered if the district attorney would have a moment to speak with me." He held his State Police ball cap in his hands.

"Just a moment, let me see if he has a moment, Trooper…"

"Hawke."

She nodded and picked up the phone, pressing a button.

He'd given testimony at several of the attorney's trials. He couldn't say he disliked the man, but Lange didn't have a personality that rallied people around him. He was a damn good D.A. He nearly always won his cases.

The receptionist replaced the phone. "If you can wait about fifteen minutes, he'll be through with the meeting in his office."

Hawke nodded and took a seat across from her desk. A magazine rack hung on the wall beside the chair. They were a modge-podge of interests. Women's magazines, athletic, food and nutrition, cars, and hunting. It appeared they wanted to keep anyone who had to wait entertained. What he didn't see were the kind that gossiped about celebrities. After noting the types, he scanned the dates. Some were nearly three years old. It appeared they didn't have a subscription to any of the magazines.

He pulled out his phone. He'd downloaded Sigler's recorded account of how he came to have the tag with D.A. Lange's name on it. Hawke had worked enough with the district attorney to know he'd only believe what he heard.

As he was setting the recording to the section where the man named Lange, the assistant D.A., Rachel Wallen, stalked out of the office.

"Terri, I'll be out of the office until tomorrow morning." Without even looking his direction the woman whipped into her small office, grabbed her coat and purse, and left.

Hawke stood. "She didn't look happy."

"She rarely is. The boss and her clash over everything. Not sure why he hired her." Terri, the receptionist, picked up the phone again. "Do you still have time for the State Trooper?"

Her brown hair, piled on her head, bounced as her head did one nod. She replaced the phone and pointed to the office behind her.

Hawke stood and strode into the room.

District Attorney Lange wasn't a big man. The top of his head came to Hawke's shoulder and his frame appeared as if it would break in a strong wind. He did have a deep strong voice that carried well in the courtroom.

Lange stood and reached across his desk with his right hand.

Hawke grasped the fine bones in his and released quickly.

"What brings you to my office, Trooper Hawke?"

The man sat back down in his chair.

Hawke remained standing. "I ran across a poacher today. Duane Sigler."

The D.A. nodded. "I know of him."

"Just know of him?"

The man's eyes narrowed behind his heavy-rimmed glasses. "Is that an accusation?"

"He had a bull elk tag with your name and residence on it and said you gave it to him." Hawke didn't imagine the flare of anger in the man's eyes.

"I don't know what you're talking about." Lange shot to his feet.

Hawke held up his phone and hit the play button.

"Lange gave it to me. He said I could use his tag." Sigler's voice rang loud and clear.

"Even the District Attorney knows you can't gift tags." Hawke's voice.

"He gave it to me." Sigler's voice held conviction.

D.A. Lange's face was red. "I didn't give that man a tag. I didn't even put in for a tag this year. I didn't have time last year so saw no sense in taking a tag from someone who did have the time to hunt."

"I'm going to look into it." Hawke said, pivoting and striding out of the room, down the stairs, and across to the front door. The man's desperation to make him believe he'd not even put in for a tag had Hawke wondering if the man protested too strongly.

《》《》《》

If you liked the first chapter of *Rattle Snake Brother*, ask your local library or book store to order, book 3 in the Gabriel Hawke series for you.

About the Book

Thank you for reading book two of the Gabriel Hawke Novels. If you enjoyed the book, please leave a review. It's the best way to thank an author.

Continue investigating and tracking with Hawke in book 3, *Rattlesnake Brother*.

As I stated in the beginning. I grew up in Wallowa County and have always been amazed by its beauty, history, and ruralness. Many say Alaska is the last frontier but there are so many communities in the western states that are nearly as rural as Alaska. After doing a ride-along with a Fish and Wildlife State Trooper in Wallowa County, I knew this was where I had to set this new series.

Paty

About the Author

Paty Jager is an award-winning author of 37 novels, 10 novellas, and numerous anthologies of murder mystery and western romance. All her work has Western or Native American elements in them along with hints of humor and engaging characters. Paty and her husband raise alfalfa hay in rural eastern Oregon. Riding horses and battling rattlesnakes, she not only writes the western lifestyle, she lives it.

You can follow her at any of these places:
Website: https://www.patyjager.net
Blog: http://writingintothesunset.net
FB Page: https://www.facebook.com/PatyJagerAuthor/
Pinterest: https://www.pinterest.com/patyjag/

Windtree
Press

Thank you for purchasing this Windtree Press publication.
For other books of the heart, please visit our website
at www.windtreepress.com.

For questions or more information contact us
at info@windtreepress.com.

Windtree Press
www.windtreepress.com

Hillsboro, OR 97124